The Janice Project

'There's not a lot to do when you're pounding the pavement together. That's when Dad found out those things about me.

That I didn't really have any friends.

That I was painfully shy and lonely.

That I wasn't terribly crazy about myself.

That except for the time we were running together, I was basically miserable . . .'

Moving to a new school doesn't change anything for Janice . . . until she catches the eye of school running star Eddie McBee.

*For my mother, Jean Naylor Douthat,
who was one of God's finest projects*

The Janice Project

Nancy Rue

A LION PAPERBACK
Oxford · Batavia · Sydney

Copyright © 1989 Nancy N. Rue

First published under the title *The Janis Project* by Crossway Books
A division of Good News Publishers
Westchester, Illinois 60154, USA

First UK edition published by arrangement
with Good News Publishers

All rights reserved

Published by
Lion Publishing plc
Sandy Lane West, Littlemore, Oxford, England
ISBN 0 7459 1817 4
Albatross Books Pty Ltd
PO Box 320, Sutherland, NSW 2232, Australia
ISBN 0 7432 0135 6

British Library Cataloguing in Publication Data

Rue, Nancy
    The Janice Project.
    I. Title
    813'.54[F]
    ISBN 0 7459 1817 4

Printed and bound by
Cox and Wyman, Reading

1

What does a sixteen-year-old girl do when she feels ugly and lonely and unimportant and too stupid to operate a paper clip without the instructions?

Your normal sixteen-year-old would pick up the phone and spill her insides to her best friend, or quietly open her mother's bedroom door and say, 'Mum — are you awake?'

But at sixteen I was not 'normal', and I had neither friends nor a mother.

So I did what I always did that summer — the summer I felt ugly, lonely, unimportant and stupid about 90 per cent of the time. I picked up my pen, and I wrote to Jack.

It was a muggy night — the kind you get in late August in Virginia. Virginia doesn't know it's supposed to be turning fall then. It's still being summer, and the crickets still fiddle all night, and the air hangs around you like a blanket that's been stored in a damp attic. It was so hot I kept all the lights off except the lamp on my desk, and even that was like a bonfire at my elbow.

But I actually shivered as I searched my desk for a piece of paper. It was spooky in that old house when I was there alone.

'This ol' place will be great for the two of us when we get it all fixed up,' my dad had said in the Virginia accent that had grown thick as pudding since we'd left Chicago. 'You can set your room up so cosy.'

Cosy. I glanced around at the boxes I still hadn't unpacked and at the naked walls and the bare windows that stared back at me like big empty eyes. I hadn't a clue to how you picked out curtains — or where you hung pictures — or where you even *got* pictures.

It was definitely not 'cosy'. And on those clingy summer nights when my dad was at the hospital and I was huddled at my desk with a letter, I felt like I was on the set of a Stephen King movie.

But there was no way I was telling Dad that. He'd have had a 'baby-sitter' in there so fast it'd spin your turntable.

'You'll be fine, Janice,' I said to myself out loud. 'Lose your sense of humour and you really will be a mental case.'

Dear Jack, (I wrote)
Okay, okay, I know I just wrote to you this morning, but I needed to talk to you again. Maybe I won't even mail this one. Probably I will.

I could imagine him reading that in his office in Chicago, leaning his bentwood rocker back as far as it would go and looking inside me with his snappy black eyes until I couldn't look back at him any more. He'd wait, and because I hated talking about myself I'd wait — and we'd sit there sometimes for a whole session — waiting at seventy-five dollars an hour.

But just then I'd have given anything to be back there, seeing him cock his head at me and hearing him say, 'So where are you today, Miss Kennedy?'

Things aren't any better here, and let's face it, they probably never will be. I couldn't even fit in in Chicago where I lived practically all my life. How am I going to make it here where everybody else has lived all their lives?
Of course, Dad still says things will pick up as soon as school starts. Right. He still thinks that just because I make straight A's I love school. And no, I haven't told him otherwise. I don't care what you say, Jack. If it makes him happy to think that, why should I blow it? You might be a psychologist (I said

6

you might *be. I still don't believe a twenty-seven-year-old guy who lifts weights and eats Creme Eggs during sessions could be a shrink), but I've been his daughter for sixteen years. That ought to count for something.*

Anyway, we've been here two months (that's sixty letters to you) and I still feel as gross as I did when I first started therapy eight months ago. You told me I'd really made progress, that I might just get over being shy in this lifetime. But moving here has been like taking forty megasteps backwards.

I feel bad about it too, because Dad loves this house. Did you know it's on the Daughters of the American Revolution tour of famous old homes? I hope they don't bring anybody here until I unpack — which may be never at the rate I'm going. Dad's all excited because it's in such a great neighbourhood, close to the hospital, close to the university, close to the high school. He's still making comments about all the 'hunks' I'll be dating from those 'pickings'. As if I could ever let a boy get close enough to ask me out without breaking out in a cold sweat.

That's when it squeaked the first time — the back screen door to the kitchen. I was one flight above and at the front of the house, but there was no mistaking the sound. I waited to hear it on the nights my father was gone so I could tear downstairs and let him in.

But it couldn't be Dad. He always called before he left the hospital, and I always heard his Golf pulling into the garage out front.

I bent furiously over the paper again, but a definite thump on the door brought my head straight up. It was like someone had expected it to open, and it didn't.

Of *course* it didn't. I had it locked with two dead bolts, a chain, and a kitchen stool jammed under the doorknob.

I came up off the chair, the skin on the backs of my legs stripping away from the varnish in two painful peels, and I waited. As if they were waiting with me, the crickets suspended their bows in midstroke, and the house held its breath. I groped for an explanation.

All the phones in the operating room suite had been tied up so Dad couldn't call, that was it. And the Golf had run out of petrol so he'd walked home, and he'd forgotten his key, so he was trying to break into the back door even as we spoke —

'For Pete's sake, Janice!' I said out loud. 'Lighten up!'

The crickets resumed their third movement, and the magnolia trees started sliding their leaves against one another again. There were no more sounds from below. I could almost hear Jack saying, 'Fear makes us dream up all kinds of lies to tell ourselves.' This one had been a whopper.

I clutched my pen and started scribbling like a lunatic.

> *It isn't just the guys, either. Landing a boyfriend is about the least of my worries. I just don't think I can face starting my junior year at a school where I don't even know one girl.*
>
> *This whole town is like a secret society, Jack. I was at the mall this afternoon. It's just a couple of blocks from here. It's like a street they turned into a shopping centre. Anyway, I saw this bunch of girls standing around, all laughing and talking and stuff. And I remembered what you always say, 'Don't freeze. They're only people, just like you. Let them see that you're approachable.' So I walked by them real slow and I smiled. Honest. And no, my face didn't crack.*

There was more squeaking. I'd have bet about five inches of my hair that I'd heard it. But I bent deliberately over the page.

> *Now I'm not exaggerating — or projecting, or whatever it is you call it. As soon as I got within earshot they all stopped talking and took up inspecting*

their fingernails and going through their purses. They made it totally clear that that conversation was by invitation only, especially this one girl who actually — get this — turned her whole body dead away from me. Talk about body language!

When I got past them (uh, needless to say, I didn't stop to ask if I could borrow somebody's lip gloss, you know what I'm saying?), I glanced in the next shop window and there were all five of their reflections, looking straight at me and taking a survey.

They all started talking like ventriloquists — about me, no doubt. No, okay, I couldn't hear them. But I have a feeling they were picking up on all my 'charming' qualities. How straight my hair is. How dishwater blonde it is. How it must get in the way when I sit down. How bony my nose is. Et cetera. Et cetera.

I'd have bet another three inches of hair that when he read that part, Jack'd frown and say to himself what he'd said to me at least one hundred and three times: 'There you go again, ripping yourself apart. You've got that wispy blonde hair. Those pale blue eyes. That straight, classic nose. That big slice-of-watermelon smile — if only you'd use it.

'I knew you for two months before I found out you had a dimple in your right cheek,' he'd say, holding two fingers under my nose. 'Two months!'

I rubbed my palms against my shorts. The backs of my knees were oozing sweat, and some kind of gnat was drilling its way through the flesh in the bend of my arm. I started to stand up in annoyance, when I heard it again. Noise outside.

This time grass was being walked on just below my room. And the cobblestone courtyard was being tiptoed across. And the bark on the live oak in front of my window was being scraped against like someone was steadily climbing it.

And paranoia had nothing to do with it.

I switched off the lamp, snuffing out the only light in

the house. By the time I pulled my hand back into my lap, I was, in a word, inert. My heart didn't pound, I didn't scream, and every terrified butterfly in my stomach rolled over and died.

It was for real. Somebody or something was hauling its body up the side of the live oak. If I hadn't already turned into a plaster cast, I'd have thrown up, the dread was that sickening.

I don't know how long I stood there before the climbing stopped.

In the dark the thing slithered down a few feet and dropped with a thud. I stared at the window and waited.

The pad, pad, pad on the grass faded.

I still couldn't move. My pen was poised over the stationery in mid-word, and I was clutching it so hard it was cutting a valley in my middle finger. I couldn't write, I couldn't reach for the phone, I couldn't even dive under the bed. I just sat there.

You are an idiot, Janice, my insides screeched at me. Do something. Come *on*.

But I couldn't do anything but listen. My ears were straining so hard I could almost feel them stretching away from my head and pointing up at the ends. Still, I jerked when Whoever It Was started tearing the kitchen door off its hinges.

I could feel it happening — like somebody was ripping into me with a crowbar. Then there was a raucous cackling and muffled swearing — and then the phone rang, giving all of us — Them and me — immediate cardiac arrest.

Its first jangle, right next to my foot, wrenched me out of the chair. It rang twice more before I could get my arm to obey my brain and reach for it. I'd pulled it in from the upstairs hall so I could get to it when my dad called, but now I could barely pick it up, and when I did, I didn't even say hello.

'Janice?' Dad said.

I started to talk in chokes.

10

'Darlin', darlin', slow down. What on earth, girl? Janice?'

His last word came out in a panic, and I knew I'd better find some control. 'There's somebody breaking in here, Dad,' I said in someone else's voice. 'They're at the back door.'

He didn't even hesitate. 'You get yourself in that wardrobe darlin', and you *hide*! I'll be there!'

I think he was running down the hospital hall before I even hung up. Matter of fact, I didn't hang up. I dropped the receiver, somehow got to the wardrobe, and buried myself behind a trash bag full of winter clothes. I couldn't hear a thing beyond my own teeth biting into my hair and my heart slamming in leaden beats in my ears. It shut out whatever might have been going on downstairs, but it didn't shut out the terror.

It seemed like an aeon later when feet pounded on the stairs, just outside my bedroom door. My father's voice made its way into the wardrobe like a warm hand.

'Janice? Darlin'?'

I leaped out into his arms. I'd never been so glad to see that salt-and-pepper hair and those squinty little brown eyes. He pushed my face into his chest and held me.

'It's okay, darlin'. Whoever they were, they took off. It's all right now.'

I melted into a blubbering puddle.

'They tried to break in —'

'Tried to take the ever-lovin' door off the hinges. Are you okay, darlin'?'

He took my face in his hands and rubbed my cheekbones with his thumbs. At five foot ten, he wasn't tall for a man, but he was still half a foot taller than me, and he looked down at me now with a face drawn with concern.

'The police are here. They're going to want to ask you a few questions. You up to it?'

I nodded mechanically.

'And then you and I are going to have a little talk.'

The two policemen were nice middle-aged types who

acted like they had hysterical teenage daughters of their own and halfway suspected me of locking a jealous boyfriend out of the house and calling the cops. They obviously didn't know me.

I'd stopped shaking by then and managed to mumble a few answers which they deductively put together and decided our prowler had just been some kid who wouldn't be back.

They didn't convince Dad, however.

Dad was usually one to beat around the proverbial azalea bush, but as soon as they left he went right for the main artery.

'Darlin', I am *not* leaving you here in this house alone at night any more. My mind is made up.'

I swallowed stiffly. 'Don't you think I'm too old for a baby-sitter?' I said. Ten shades of timid was about as asser-tive as I ever got.

'I'm not talking about a baby-sitter, honey. I just want somebody to be here with you when I have to be out, that's all.'

I turned my face to the floor so my hair hid everything. How some little old lady was going to save me when some-body was ripping the back door off was beyond me.

'Maybe a med. student who needs a room,' Dad was say-ing. 'I'll put up a notice in the student lounge. Now, let's get us some iced tea and forget this whole ugly mess.'

And, as usual for us, that was the end of the 'little talk'.

I declined the tea and went to bed mad at him — so mad it made me forget to wait up all night in case They decided to return to the scene of the crime. But Dad didn't know I was mad — and that's the way I wanted it.

Dad was the best person I knew. Matter of fact, at that point in my life he was about the only person I could carry on a half-decent conversation with — and half was saying something in my case.

I couldn't ever remember his having raised his voice at me, and if he ever did have to reprimand me about something, he side-stepped the thing three different ways to avoid hurting my feelings and always ended up practically apologizing. I guess if I'd been the manipulative type I could've got away with murder, but I usually felt so guilty for putting him through so much misery, I apologized too.

But no matter how much it terrified me to be alone in the house at night — especially now that somebody really had tried to break in — I didn't want another nursemaid. It didn't matter if it was a med. student who looked like Tom Cruise; if somebody moved in to watch over me, that would make him a nursemaid as far as I was concerned.

There had been a long line of them since my mother died when I was five. As an anaesthetist, my father was on call a lot of the time, and with people in downtown Chicago constantly slitting each other up in fights and mowing each other down on the expressways, he attended more middle-of-the-night sewing on of arms than he did daytime tonsillectomies. Naturally there had to be someone there to take care of me, but none of them had ever seemed to be what he had in mind. They fed me my Sugar Puffs and tied my trainers, but none of them ever knew Janice.

I guess I had never been an easy kid to get to know. I'd once heard Dad remark that I'd always been quiet, even when my mother was alive. I always did everything the baby-sitters told me to. What else do you do? I was so shy, I made Dumbo look like an extrovert. It was simpler to supply me with peanut butter cookies and park me in front of the cartoons than to get me to talk. 'Hi' and 'bye' were about the most I managed, besides 'When's my daddy coming home?'

When he took the job with the private practice in Virginia, and got a position on the teaching staff at the university med. school in the bargain, he *said* he was doing it because he wanted to get back to his home state. He was a southerner at heart, but he hadn't lived in Virginia since he and my mother had first married and he was a med. student himself. It was time he got back, he said. They'd always intended to.

But from his long conversations over the phone with Jack

that I eavesdropped on without a trace of guilt, I knew he'd made the move mostly because he thought the small-town atmosphere would 'bring me out'. I felt I *had* to make it here, or we were both lost.

For me, the fact that he'd said he didn't think he'd have to hire a live-in in Virginia was about the only thing that had seemed decent about the move. And now even that was falling through.

Marvellous. New place. New school. New faces. Now a new caretaker.

And no Jack.

Make that ugly, unimportant, lonely — and scared stupid.

2

Dear Jack,

Well, this is it. That day we've all been waiting for.

It's going to be awful, Jack, I just know it. The first day of school was bad enough back in Chicago — and that was at least familiar territory. I might as well be going to the moon or something here.

However — because I don't want to disappoint you or especially my dad, I'm going to try. Now quit blinking your eyes and acting like you're about to have a coronary. I mean it — I'm going to try. I'm not going to hide myself in my hair and I'm going to smile at people — and I might even say hi to somebody. I said 'might'. It depends on how friendly they are.

Oh, Jack, I wish you were here. I'm so scared.

Love, Janice

I was folding the letter when my dad called from downstairs.

'Come on, darlin', I'll give you a lift to school.'

Actually, I'd rather have walked. Maybe then some kidnapper might have come along, snatched me away — and I wouldn't have to face the first day at Madison High.

When I got downstairs he gave me the once-over.

'You look pretty, darlin'. Is that what the kids around here wear to school?'

I looked down at my 501s and navy blue sweatshirt and shrugged. 'I don't know. I haven't been there yet.'

'You'd look precious in a trash bag with your pretty little head stickin' out.'

'Dad!'

'You *would*.'

'I can go change into one.'

He just looked at me and pointed to the door.

When we pulled in front of the school, all I could see were kids waving and hugging and acting like it was homecoming weekend. I'd have given anything to stay in the Golf and let my dad make me laugh all day long.

'You want me to walk in with you?' he said.

It was my turn to give him a look, and he grinned.

' "Get on out of here, Dad",' he said in falsetto, ' "before you embarrass me to tears." ' He smiled softly and cupped his hand under my chin. 'It's gonna be all right, darlin'. You'll have 'em all eating out of your hand by fourth period.'

I doubted that would happen by the fourth *month*, but he wanted to believe it so much I didn't argue. If I made one friend the whole year, he'd probably be in ecstasy.

I managed to get to the office and made it to registration without losing my cool entirely. Everybody was so busy giving summaries of their summers to each other in twenty-five words or less, nobody seemed to care if they got to class, so there was no mad rush around the bulletin board. I tried to look casual as I looked for Room 24B, and then went into double-casual as I strolled towards the stairs.

'You act like you're trespassing on somebody else's turf,' Jack had said to me once. 'You have as much right to be here as anyone else!'

'Okay,' I said to him mentally. 'I will be confident — even if everybody here looks like an ad for Christian Dior.' Another floral skirt swept by me on the steps, and I thanked heaven that at least I hadn't opted for the trash bag.

I'd been sitting conspicuously in the classroom for five minutes when the bell rang and everybody else meandered in. Lesson Number One for Madison High: You don't worry about getting to class on time.

I tried to wipe the caked-on saliva off my lips without looking like I was wiping caked-on saliva off my lips and clenched both clammy hands in my lap. The teacher, a golden-skinned black woman, started handing out the class timetables.

'Tess Hargrave.'

A well-manicured hand took that one.

'Tony — new hairdo this year, Ton'?'

We all looked at the kid next to me, who had his tresses slicked back like a parakeet.

'Corie McBee.'

A dimply brunette on my other side took it, gave it a glance and groaned.

'PE first period! Yuk!'

'Juniors always have first PE,' Mrs Garner said. 'Are you Janice?' she said quietly to me.

I only nodded, because rigor mortis had set in on my vocal cords.

She put my timetable on my desk and patted my hand.

'And we have Coach Petruso for PE,' Corie said to the room. 'He'll work us into a lather and then we'll look like we've been dragged through a hedge backwards for the rest of the day.'

'So what's new?' Tony said across me.

She stuck her tongue out at him, and then peered openly at my timetable. 'You have it first hour too, huh?'

I think I said yes.

16

She looked up at me with twinkly brown eyes and gave her cute wedge of hair a toss. Her grin rambled playfully all over her face. 'It won't make any difference to you,' she said. 'I bet you look gorgeous no matter what.'

'Hey, don't be shy, Corie,' Tony said. 'Just come right up to the girl and tell her what you think of her.' He tossed his head the way she had and grinned wide. 'Hi,' he said to me in a high voice, 'want to be best friends?'

There was general guffawing, during which Corie wrinkled her nose at all of them and went back to studying her timetable. It was all I could do not to pick up my notebook and fan myself with it; my face was like a stove burner somebody'd accidentally left on. Fortunately, the intercom crackled attention away from me, and a disgustingly cheerful voice said, 'Good morning, Patriots!' The class groaned in unison.

There was an enthusiastic 'welcome back' that made Mr Rogers sound like a mummy,nd a a list of announcements that only served to confuse me even more. They must have had every club and team imaginable in that school. Everybody tried to talk through it until Mrs Garner gave them the evil eyebrow. Then they sat in boredom — except when cross-country track was mentioned. At that point Tony stood up, straddling his desk, and said, 'Yes, ma'am!' Mrs Garner let that pass.

When the bell rang, I followed everyone down to the gym, trying not to *look* like I was following them, and accidentally walked up the calf of a Wookie look-alike in the process. He turned around to see who was trying to trample him, but fortunately I was too far below for him to see. The guy was a dead ringer for Chewbacca.

When we got there, the gym was insane. Fifty juniors were yammering around a tall guy with bushy eyebrows who was holding his clipboard up so it wouldn't get carried away on a wave of clamouring pupils.

'I'll hold that for you, Spike,' said a red-headed girl.

'Tanya, you know you can't be student assistant in here until you get a timetable change.'

17

'All I have to do is change government to fourth period, drop typing, which is going to be *so* boring since Bob left anyway —'

'Fine, so go do it. And Tanya,' he said as she whirled her massive head of hair around to leave, 'I am Coach Petruso or *Coach* Spike to you, and the typing teacher is *Mr* Carraway — not Bob.'

She narrowed her green eyes the way I've seen women do on soap operas. 'He's gone now anyway,' she said.

'And so will you be if you don't clean up your act.'

'Going!' she said.

She whipped her body around to beat a hasty retreat and ploughed right into me. At close range, with the little chiselled nose and the tight mouth and the aristocrat's chin square in my face, she looked familiar. I lost my head and said, 'Hi.'

She looked at, up and down, and through me. 'Excuse you,' she said.

I immediately went numb. It was the same girl who'd turned her back on me at the mall. No wonder I thought I knew her. Who could miss that body language?

It must have become obvious to her that I was going to stand there like a lemon because she gave an exasperated sigh and flounced around me. Fortunately, I couldn't hear what she muttered as she left.

Coach Spike tooted his whistle and everyone scrambled to a sitting position at his feet. Lesson Number Two: When Coach toots, you fall in. Lesson Number Three: When Tanya parts the waters, you'd best get out of the way. Lesson Number Four: You don't say hi to anybody or you get your head snapped off.

'Okay, folks, tomorrow's the physical fitness test.'

There was a unanimous groan.

'How will I know where to take you —'

'If I don't know where you are!' they finished for him in unison.

He gave a lopsided grin. 'You got it. Bring your gym clothes tomorrow. Shorts —'

The boys all hooted and whistled.

'Do we have mixed locker rooms?' somebody called out.

'— a T-shirt, and a pair of good running shoes. We'll be doing the 880 first.'

There was an abrupt outburst of applause. 'Everybody in this town must love to run,' I thought, until I saw the real object of their cheering. It was a lanky, dark-haired kid with glasses and a ski-slope nose who had just walked in, wearing, bless him, 501s and a Madison High sweatshirt.

He grinned up at Coach, who grinned back. Lesson Number Five: If you were going to smile at Madison High, you'd better have a huge old loose grin: just about everybody else did.

'Got my timetable changed for student assistant, Coach,' the kid said. His voice was warm, thick, and very Virginian.

'What class did you drop?'

'Nothing. They had me down for something, but it was no big deal.'

Coach smiled at him shrewdly. 'What do you think he's trying to hide, gang?' he said to us.

'It was home ec.!' somebody yelled.

'Shorthand!'

'Hand it over, Eddie,' Coach said.

Eddie put the timetable in his hand and hunched his shoulders, his tan face going scarlet. But he was still smiling, like he was really enjoying the whole thing. I'd have died, personally.

A grin spread all the way across Coach's face until the corners of his mouth almost met in the back of his head. He looked up from the timetable like it was an Academy Award announcement. 'Here it is, folks. Eddie was assigned — as a library aide.'

The gym went crazy. I found *myself* laughing — and I didn't even know why. Eddie just stood up there, mouthing a good-natured threat.

Somehow I got through the rest of the day. Corie sat in front of me in biology, and once when she was passing some forms back she said, 'Oh hi, Jackie.' Tess smiled vaguely at me in the hall when we passed, as if she knew me from somewhere but couldn't put her finger on where. Other than that, I was invisible. The Sugar Puffs I'd had for breakfast had turned to a lump in my throat, and it was growing by the minute.

The worst part was lunch. When everyone started pouring into the cafeteria, I panicked. Lesson Number Six in *any* school: You don't sit at a table by yourself and eat lunch alone while people wonder what's wrong with you that nobody wants to be with you. Besides, I didn't want to look like a fool fumbling around trying to find the trays and the salad bar and the plastic forks. I ended up escaping to the library and started leafing through a *Seventeen* magazine.

As if I weren't feeling like a complete misfit already, some woman with brown brogues and the bottom half of a pair of glasses asked me if I had a pass from a teacher. When I shook my head, she shooed me out like I was some irritating housefly. 'It's starting already,' she said to another woman who looked exactly like her. 'They think this library is a lounge.' No wonder that Eddie kid hadn't wanted to work there.

By the time I got home, I was not only very close to tears, but I was starved. I was eating a double-decker peanut butter and banana sandwich, which tasted like cardboard through the almost-sobs, and chasing it with a Diet Coke when Dad popped in the door. I stopped the tears pronto.

'Hey, darlin'! How was your day?'

Lousy, I thought. 'Okay,' I said.

'Listen, what say we go for a run? You can tell me about it on the road. Let me just get changed.'

It was the only thing that had been said to me since I'd got out of the car that morning that couldn't have been said to just any New Kid who happened along. I went for my shorts.

Out on the road, jogging in step and breathing in rhythm, was my favourite time with my father. That was when we really talked. In fact, that was when we'd actually started getting to know each other at all — ever.

When I was about fourteen, Dad noticed one day that he was putting on weight. You could definitely pinch an inch at any point on his midriff. Somebody told him running would firm him up fast, and since he didn't want to leave me alone in the apartment in the evenings and on weekends, he took me with him.

It surprised both of us when I took to running the way I did. Within a couple of months, we were doing five miles a day, five days a week. And when I was fifteen, we started doing a ten-miler every weekend. We both went through Nikes the way other families consume bags of potato crisps.

But I think the other things my father learned about me while we were running surprised him even more. In fact, I think they flat-out flabbergasted him.

It wasn't that he hadn't spent time with me before that. From the time my mother was killed in the car accident, he hardly did anything when he was off work but be with me. We did movies, museums, circuses. He used to read to me until I'm sure he'd had the Berenstain Bears up the nose. Then when I learned to read, I read to him. Not many dads will sit and listen to every word of the Little House on the Prairie series. Mine did.

But we didn't *know* each other. Those weren't activities where we really talked, so I never told my father I was unhappy — and I guess he was so anxious for me to *be* happy, he thought I was. That was Dad for you.

Running, though, isn't like sitting in a blackened cinema sharing popcorn and Polos. There's not a whole lot to do when you're pounding the pavement together *but* talk. That's when Dad found out those things about me.

That I didn't really have any friends.

That I was painfully shy and lonely.

That I wasn't terribly crazy about myself.

That except for the time we were running together, I was basically miserable.

For a while he tried to change things for me. He constantly told me I was wonderful. He tried to get his partner's fourteen-year-old daughter to take me under her wing

— which turned out to be a complete disaster. And he was forever saying, 'Everything's okay, darlin'. There's no need to be afraid.' When that didn't work, he started sending me to Jack, hoping he could 'fix it'. It turned out to be one of the best things that ever happened to me.

I balked at the idea of going to a psychiatrist at first. Nobody could convince me he was just a psychologist, not a shrink with a couch and a collection of books by Freud. Nobody could convince me the next step wasn't the strait-jacket and basket-weaving classes, either. Nobody but Jack, that is.

Even though I would barely talk to him for the first few weekly sessions, I sort of fell in love with him right away. Maybe it was the jet-black hair and eyes and big barrel body and open-necked shirts. More likely it was the fact that nothing I said made him roll his eyes or start examining his fingernails for more interesting subject matter. To him, I was more than a generic teenager with nothing to say, and I started to unfold.

Of course, when Dad told me we were moving, every-thing came to a screeching halt. I'd put the brakes on on my progess so fast, the dirt had piled up in huge ridges on either side of me. Jack said I was almost buried in self-pity when I left Chicago.

'But it's just a temporary setback,' he told me. 'Just talk to those new kids the way you're talking to me and you'll be all right.'

I grunted out loud now.

Dad yanked on my T-shirt sleeve. 'What was that for?' he said, sweat squeezing out of his upper lip.

'Just thinking.'

'About what?'

'Stuff.'

'What stuff?' he said patiently. That session he'd had with Jack before we left Chicago must have taught him all the techniques of boring into my brain. I looked at him sheepishly.

'It's hard here, Dad. Everybody already knows each other. It's like there are no friend slots left.'

'Give yourself a chance, darlin'. I didn't knock 'em dead my first day on the job.'

'No. It was the second day.'

My father is so sociable he could probably make friends with a petrol pump, and people just automatically trusted him. That was probably fortunate, since he might have to tamper with their consciousness on an operating table someday.

'What else?'

Chugging on, I tried to think of something positive to say. 'Everybody talks funny,' I said.

'Funny ha-ha or funny odd?'

'Funny like you — only more so.'

He gave me a spank. 'You little stinker. I don't talk funny — do I?'

'They say "out" and "about" like "oat" like "aboat", and they never put the r's on the ends of words.' I didn't add that they all spoke like 45s being played at 33⅓. I figured I'd made enough dogmeat out of the Virginia accent.

'So tell me "aboat" your classes,' he said.

'My biology teacher's name is Fruff —'

'No kidding! 'Course, they can't all be Kennedys, can they darlin'?'

'At least nobody asked me if I was any relation to You-Know-Who.'

'See — things are looking up.'

'Hey there! Runners!'

We both looked over our shoulders to see a mop of dark hair and a pair of glasses gaining on us from behind. As the hair got closer, I realized it belonged to Eddie. He was grinning, naturally.

'You're looking great!' he said when he caught up with us. He wasn't even breathing hard.

'You don't look bad yourself,' Dad said. 'You on the track team or just running for fun?'

'Little of both. You?'

23

I realized when nobody said anything that he was talking to me. 'Me?' I said. 'No.'

'Neither?'

'Neither what?'

He laughed in a deep, gurgly chuckle that left little bubbles at the corners of his mouth. 'I guess I broke your concentration. You oughta be on the team. She ought to,' he said to my dad.

'I agree.'

'I'm Eddie McBee.'

'Loren Kennedy.'

'Any relation —'

'No!' Dad and I said in unison.

They shook hands without breaking stride.

'Aren't you in first period PE?'

It was a cinch he was talking to me this time. I kept looking straight ahead and nodded.

'I didn't recognize you at first. With your hair up, I mean. That's some pretty stuff.'

My face was slowly transforming into a red pepper, but, feeling my dad's eyes on me, I managed to say, 'Thanks.'

'How far do you folks run?'

Dad launched into a detailed description of our running regimen, which gave me a chance to do an Eddie survey.

His hair was so thick it fell over the top of his blue sweatband and puffed out at the sides of the elastic band that was holding his glasses on. His brown eyes were small, like Dad's, and alive. They never seemed to stop moving — but then neither did the rest of him. In his blue shorts — with MHS printed in white near the hem — I could see the definition in his legs. There was absolutely no fat — it was all sinew and tendon pulling against his taut skin in a rhythm that almost had me hypnotized.

I looked up to find him grinning at me. There's nothing more mortifying than having a guy catch you admiring his legs. But he got even and started gazing at mine.

'You've really got nice form. Been running long?'

'About twenty minutes, I guess.'

He gave that throaty chortle again. 'Listen, I've got to get back to it or Coach'll be in my face. Ya'll have a good run.'

'Nice talking to you, Eddie,' Dad said.

'Same here. We could use you on the team, Janice.'

I didn't have to look at my father. I could feel him beaming, but at least he waited until Eddie was out of earshot to start in.

'I don't know what you're worried about,' he said. 'The kids around here seem real friendly to me.'

I'd have bet the last inch of my hair he'd say that.

3

It became painfully obvious as I stared into my wardrobe the next morning that I'd never bothered to acquire anything but jeans, T-shirts, and sweatshirts. I got a clothing allowance every month, but who'd ever taught me how to spend it? I had enough money hanging around in my savings account to clothe half the female population of Virginia.

At least I had decent running clothes. I thought I wouldn't stand out like a bucktooth in PE anyway. But as I found out in first period, it was going to take more than clothes to make me inconspicuous.

Tanya had evidently had her timetable changed because she was in the locker room patrolling when we arrived. It was like a scene from *Private Benjamin*.

She gave me a locker between Corie and Tess and started to march on. When Corie saluted behind her back, she did a very abrupt about-face. 'You McBees have always got to be the clowns,' she said.

'Didn't you know? We're under contract with Barnum and Bailey,' Corie said.

'Smart —'

'Ah, ah, ah!'

Tanya's green eyes narrowed. They were already fairly close together, so for a minute she looked almost cross-eyed.

'By the way —' She glanced at her clipboard. 'Kennedy.'

Corie stiffened to mock-attention on my behalf.

'If you're going to take the physical fitness test, you'd better do something with that hair.'

No kidding, Sherlock?

'I don't know why you wear it that way anyway,' she said under her breath. 'It looks like 1968.'

How she knew was anybody's guess. I don't think she'd ever really looked me in the face.

'She's always so bitchy,' Corie said when she was gone. 'Personally, I think your hair's beautiful.' She fingered an end as I pulled it all up in a slide. 'How long have you been growing it?'

'I've never cut it.'

'You're kidding.' Tess looked impressed, which I found a little bizarre. She was absolutely the prettiest girl I'd ever seen. Blue eyes. Strawberry blonde hair. Bow-shaped mouth. She didn't need to envy anything *I* had to offer.

'I wish I had a dollar for every hour I've spent in a hairdresser's chair,' Corie was saying.

'You're a short-hair kind of person,' Tess told her.

They weren't really talking to me, but I gathered up my courage anyway.

'Are you Eddie's sister?' I said.

'Nope. Cousins. 'Course, we might as well be brother and sister. My mom's always worked, so I've spent as much time hanging out at his house as I have at mine. We sure fight like sister and brother — but you probably have brothers, so you know what I mean.'

'I'm an only child.'

'Really? I thought all Kennedys came from big families.'

Tess rolled her eyes. 'Corie, you're such a twit! Come on.'

They walked out of the locker room with me trailing behind like a puppy who couldn't quite remember whether she'd been told to stay or heel.

Out on the field, Coach Spike was already giving instructions. 'Eddie's going to take you fellas in groups to run the 880. I'll time the girls. Now remember, this is not a race, folks. I just want to see what you can do.'

I started to follow Corie to the track when the coach caught my arm. 'Little lady, are you Janice?'

'Yes, sir.'

'Kennedy?'

'Yes, sir.'

'Hon, nobody's called me "sir" since I was in the Marines.' He gave me his lopsided smile. 'Let's put you in this first group with Tess and Corie, okay? Tanya, why don't you run with them?'

I could almost see her red hair standing on end as she actually looked at me for the first time. The way her lip was curling, I'd just as soon she'd never laid eyes on me.

'Why?' she said.

Coach gave her a blank look. 'Because I asked you to.'

'All three of *us* are on track, though. We'll run her into the ground.'

I tried to concentrate on the toe of my left Nike. I just love being talked about as if I'm not there.

'Ladies, as you know, the 880 is twice around the track. Take your marks and I'll start you with the whistle.'

I looked up to see that though he'd been saying all of that for my benefit, he was looking hard at Tanya. I hoped to heaven he never looked at me that way.

I watched how Corie and Tess crouched over the line, and I imitated them to the nth degree. I was trying so hard not to look like I was watching them, I almost missed the start. I felt Tanya leap off the line beside me before I even heard the whistle.

I'd never run terribly fast before. Dad and I were mainly interested in what he called 'getting to the finish line before cardiac arrest catches up with you'. So once the four of us were off down the track, I settled into my usual rhythm, swinging my arms up and down and reaching out my legs to put one more block behind me. I could hear the familiar breathing pattern in my own ears — one-huh-two-huh-three-huh.

On the fourth huh, Tanya shot past me like a subway train. So much for 'This is not a race'. She was putting so much distance between us, I had to look down to make sure I was moving at all. She laid her head back and within about five seconds was ahead of me by half the track. I felt myself automatically go into the dig and kick mode I usually reserved for when our driveway was in sight.

By the end of the first lap, Tanya was still way out in front. I'd completely lost Corie and Tess and I felt like I was alone in an episode of 'The Twilight Zone'.

But about a quarter of the way through the second lap, I could see the smear of sweat sticking her T-shirt to her back. By the time I was able to focus in on the Puma logo on the backs of her shoes, it came to me: she was slowing down.

In a couple of strides I was beside her, but she didn't fall into step. She was grabbing air to beat all. I glanced over at her face, and just as fast riveted my gaze back on my lane. The chick was furious.

A shot of panic went through me, and all I wanted to do was steer myself to the infield, fall down in the grass, and forget the whole thing. Some people could intimidate me that much.

I could feel my pace slowing, and with a triumphant smirk Tanya got a few steps ahead of me. Let her, I thought. It isn't worth having her spit in my face the rest of the year.

Her shoulders heaved and her head came back even farther as she dug in to pull away from me. And then she made her fatal error. With the finish only a hundred yards away, she flipped over her shoulder: 'I knew you couldn't run'.

Body, mind and soul went into revenge mode. With the hyper-space spurt I normally reserve for the last three strides of a run, I took Tanya, and then some. Pulling in air and nearly kicking myself in the back of the head, I went for it.

I guess they all screamed when I crossed the line alone. I didn't care about that. All I knew was, it had taken me eight months with Jack to learn that if I would believe there was just one thing I could do well and feel good about, I was worth knowing. Nobody was going to take that away from me, not after eight months of hard work.

And, honey, if there was one thing I knew I could do well — it was run.

Eddie got to me first, howling, 'Mother of Jefferson Davis, what a woman!'

'Look at her,' somebody else yelled, 'she isn't even breathing hard!'

'Where's the sweat?' Tony, the parakeet, ran a finger down my arm. This sure was a touchy-feely bunch of people.

Corie ploughed into me then, gasping for air. 'Did ya'll see that?'

'No, man, we went out for a coffee break,' Eddie said. 'We saw her. She was great!'

'What was her time? Did you get her time?'

Coach Spike stuck his pencil behind his ear and grinned his big old crooked smile down at me. 'One minute and forty-seven seconds,' he said.

Although the significance of that escaped me completely, it thrilled the heck out of Corie and Tess. Corie plastered a clammy arm around my shoulders.

'You got old Valerie Briscoe Hooks over there,' she said, motioning to Tanya, who was headed for the locker room. From the way she was stomping, it was obvious she wasn't going in to freshen up her mascara.

'Janice, you're a good runner,' Coach said.

'Thanks,' was all I could get out.

Tony cocked his birdlike head at me. 'Hey,' he said, 'she talks.'

That day I hovered in the doorway to the cafeteria for a minute in the thin hope that Corie or Eddie or even the parakeet would see me and invite me to sit with them. But one look at the tables where the lines of demarcation had already been made, and I changed my mind.

The Brown Brogue Twins were in evidence in the library, so I just slunk miserably out of an outside door and sat on the steps. I spent twenty minutes praying nobody would

29

come out and inform me that I had once again committed a felony.

I was famished by 2.15 and was hurrying to get home for at least two ham sandwiches before my dad could catch me in mid-bite again — when I heard somebody shouting my name.

It was Eddie in his little blue shorts.

'What — are you in training twenty-four hours a day?' he said when he caught me up.

I shrugged. 'No. I just have to hurry and get home.'

'Where do you live anyway?' He was walking along with me as if I'd invited him to escort me right to my door.

'Around the corner, on Monroe. In that brick house with the courtyard.'

'Oh — the old Williamsburg house. Nice place.'

'Yeah.'

I hated moments like these, when people were trying to talk to me and I didn't have a clue as to what to say next. I had about as much personality as a marshmallow.

Eddie, however, seemed to be into marshmallows. He just danced along by me — and I do mean danced.

'You sure tore up that track today, girl,' he said, pulling several leaves off a maple tree and sticking them comically behind his ears.

'I guess so.'

'What — are you modest? You've got some *talent*. What do you think? Do I look like Mr Spock?'

The points of the maple leaves were poking out from behind his ears, and his leaky grin was at its widest. I couldn't help laughing.

'You think I'm weird,' he said.

'No,' I said. 'Well, okay, yes.'

'Good. You're intelligent. You'll do great on the track team.'

I could feel my face reverting to marshmallow. 'I don't know —'

'Hey — Tanya is our best female runner. I mean, Tess has promise and Corie has heart – but Tanya's our lead. You beat the pom-poms off that child today. We need you.'

30

I wanted to smack myself up the side of the head. I couldn't do anything but shrug.

'What is that? Sign language for "I'll think about it"?'

He still had the leaves tucked behind his ears and in spite of the fact that I was imitating a corpse, he was having a marvellous time.

'I've never been on a track team before,' I heard myself say.

'So? Had you ever sat on a potty before your mother started to toilet train you?'

'What?' I stopped dead on the sidewalk and just guffawed. He did too. I was finding out that nobody enjoyed Eddie's material more than Eddie himself.

'Just wanted to make sure you were listening,' he said.

'I am.'

'Okay. Go and see Coach Spike before school tomorrow. Tell him yes.'

'Maybe.'

He grinned all over. 'Here — ' He took the leaves off his ears, opened one of my hands, and stuck them into my palm. 'For your scrapbook.'

Before I realized it, he was halfway back down the block.

'Hey,' I said. I didn't want him to go thinking I was a complete idiot.

He danced around.

'Who's Valerie Briscoe Hooks?' I said.

'Who? Oh. Three-time Olympic medal winner — runner. Hey, but she's got nothin' on you, girl!'

Then he was gone.

When I told Dad about the track team, he didn't want me to go to Coach Spike's office the next day. He wanted me to call the man at home right then. I didn't, of course, but all through his two trays of Lean Cuisine at the dinner table, he did his best to make sure my decision was going to be to go for it.

The next morning I still wasn't sure. I mean, yes, I loved to run. It was about the only thing I really enjoyed, the only time I actually felt like I belonged somewhere.

But competition was something else. Maybe I'd just got lucky. I hadn't really *beaten* Tanya; she'd just got tired and *lost*.

Besides, Tanya and people like her were the real problem. Did I really want to set myself up for that kind of treatment? I had enough trouble handling it when people were nice to me.

By the time I got to school, I'd about decided not to even go to see Coach at all. But when I got to the door to my classroom, a delegation of people who had taken a sudden interest in my future met me there.

'Eddie says Coach wants to see you,' Corie said, stepping forward as spokesman and propelling me through the locker crowd by the elbow.

'We're taking you,' Tess said from my other side.

'But I don't know —'

'Yes, you do. Every time he asks you a question, just nod. You'll be great.'

I let them half-carry, half-drag me to the gym. It was a far cry from 'Oh, hi, Jackie,' and I sure wasn't going to knock it.

We could see through the big window to his office that Coach Spike was already with somebody — a *babe* of a guy, I might add, a little short, but *built*, with hard blue eyes and brown curly hair that curved over his forehead in front like he'd spent hours at the mirror getting it to do that. But even though the kid looked like he was heavy into the conversation, Corie and Tess burst right in the door, with me between them.

'Where've you been, girl? I've been waiting for you.' Coach disentangled his long legs from the top of his desk. 'Chuck, give Janice that chair, would you?'

Chuck did, reluctantly, and stood with his hands on his snake-slender hips. My, that boy had a body.

'So — don't you juvenile delinquents have someplace to go?' Coach said to the three of them.

'Talk her into it, Coach Spike,' Corie said.

Chuck looked at me for the first time with his cold eyes. 'Talk her into what?'

'We'll check you guys later . . .' Coach nodded towards

the door, from which Corie and Tess had already beaten a hasty retreat.

Chuck took his time getting out and wandering off, but Coach waited. Then he leaned back in the chair, which squeaked under his expanse of hard muscle, and smiled at me lazily.

'How are you liking it here so far, Miss Kennedy?'

I shrugged, of course. 'It's okay, I guess.'

'It won't take you long to get acquainted. These are some great kids.'

I waited and tried to find someplace in the room to hook my eyes. He waited, too, until I finally looked back at him.

'I'd really like to see you join the track team. Not just because you're a heck of a runner, but because I think it'd help you feel comfortable around here. Give you a place to kind of hang your hat, you know?'

I stared at him. None of my junior high or high school teachers in Chicago had ever taken the time to even try to start a conversation with me – though as Jack had said, it was a little tough to talk to a curtain of hair. Now here was this man on the third day of school actually trying to help me fit in. Self-consciously I pulled my hair behind my ears, which were going cranberry-coloured by this time, I knew.

'Well,' I said, looking everywhere but at him, 'I might.'

His hazel eyes softened at me, and all the skin under his tousled eyebrows crinkled.

'That's good enough for the time being,' he said. 'If you decide you want to, come dressed out for practice after school tomorrow. If you don't show, I'll know you decided to wait until spring.'

He smiled, and so did I.

Corie and Tess pounced on me when I slid into the classroom to the sound of 'Good morning, Patriots!'

'What did you tell him?' Corie hissed.

Tess was bobbing her gorgeous hair up and down.

'That I'd think about it.'

Tony pulled the parakeet head out of a copy of *Mad*. 'Think about what?'

'She's coming out for track.'

'No joke? Guy, you ought to —'

'I still don't —'

'Ladies and gentlemen.' Mrs Garner was flicking her ballpoint at us. They all grinned at her. I slid down in the desk.

Out on the front steps at lunch, I did what Jack had taught me to do when it comes to making decisions. The only thing I was ever sure about in making a choice was that I was going to make the wrong one. He'd shown me how to take a piece of paper and make two columns on it, one for pros, one for cons. At first it had felt pretty stupid listing the pros and cons of whether to buy hot lunch or pack a brown bag, but Jack said I had to start somewhere. Besides, it did work. I guess I like things to be concrete. It would've worked in this case too, because the pros far outnumbered the cons. Trouble was, the con was Tanya.

When I got home that afternoon, there was a letter waiting for me from Jack — just as if he'd known I'd need his input right away. I didn't even stop to grab the Marathon bar I'd been hiding in the freezer and drooling about all afternoon. I scrambled upstairs, manoeuvred between the boxes, and sprawled out on my bed with my letter.

Dear Janice,

Well, one thing's for sure, you aren't holding anything back. Every time one of your letters comes through the slot, I can see it smoking before I even pick it up. I have to wear asbestos gloves. You're definitely spilling your guts — and that's good.

But, you know, now that you know how you feel about the place — what are you going to do about it? Are you going to let it stop you from continuing when you were doing so well, or are you going to 'Run with courage the race that is set before you'?

I know, I know, there I go preaching. But think about it.

Now, on to the news. Linda — you remember, my receptionist — ran off with a Norwegian guy last . . .

I folded the letter and put my head down on it. I could just see Jack's face if I opted not to join the track team. He'd purse his lips and squint his eyes at me and say, 'Well then, we'll wait.'

And he would. And so would Coach. Everybody would.

I rolled over on my back and looked around at my bare room with its pink-flowered-wallpaper-that-didn't-look-like-me and its still-packed boxes. The only thing that looked settled in were the two maple leaves stuck in the frame of the mirror. I was so engrossed in them I jerked right off the pillow when somebody tapped on my door.

'Dad?' I said.

'Who else?' He poked his face in a crack. 'You must have been pretty far away. What were you thinking about?'

'Nothin' much.'

He leaned against the door jamb, arms folded, and gave me a warning eyebrow.

'Okay, okay.'

'What?'

'I decided to join the track team.'

Then I grinned like a fool, because seeing the way he was smiling at me so proud made up for a lot of guilt. A *lot* of guilt.

4

I didn't have a Madison High School track outfit yet, so after school the next day I slid into a sleeveless black leotard and a pair of running shorts Dad had brought home. It was too hot, still to wear much of anything else, and besides, I thought I looked okay.

But, of course, as soon as I saw Tanya stroll onto the track,

I felt like a complete slob. She was wearing a peach-coloured sweat-suit with pleats in the pants and a cowl neck on the top. I wondered for a minute if this were track practice or a fashion show.

She was already stripping out of it, to reveal matching shorts and a white tank top with lace trim, when I walked up.

'We do have a locker room, Tanya,' Eddie said. 'You don't have to get undressed out here.'

But she was completely zeroed in on me.

'Is *she* going to run cross-country?' she demanded.

'Looks that way,' said Chuck, who had just descended from the top of the bleachers to stand beside her. Both pairs of eyes bored through me.

'We don't need another girl.'

'We do too, and you know it.' Eddie was at my elbow, levelling his eyes at her from behind his glasses.

'We only need seven. We already have seven.'

'And only the first five count anyway,' Chuck said out of the side of his mouth.

'What'd you say, Slade?' Eddie said.

Tanya pulled her tank top tight over her chest with an adamant yank. 'He said we don't need her.'

'We need depth,' Eddie said.

'We need a *team*.'

We all snapped our heads towards Coach Spike who was standing quietly behind us, clipboard perched on his hip. He had sunglasses on, but I knew his hazel eyes weren't happy.

'Hi, Coach,' Corie said cheerfully.

He just passed a hand over her shoulder as he walked by.

'Janice is our eighth girl on the cross-country team. Glad you decided to join us, hon.'

'She's a sprinter,' Tanya said. Her voice was contemptuous. 'She'll never make it on the long run.'

Somebody snorted.

'Actually,' Coach Spike said, turning to me, 'your stride is too long for sprinting. But you have endurance. That's why I'm putting you on cross-country.' He looked up at Tanya and Chuck. 'If anybody has a problem with that, they can see me in my office later.' He patted me on the back. 'Okay, let's warm up.'

'Warm up' turned out to be the misnomer of the century. The next twenty-five minutes were about the most exhausting I'd ever spent. Dad and I usually stretched for about ten minutes and then got on with the thing. These people jogged four laps, did all kinds of arm swings and trunk bends and leg lifts, not to mention a lot of other contortions called 'hoola hoops' and 'wood choppers' and 'side winders' — and then jogged another two laps.

'All right, are you ready for the workout?' Coach said.

I was ready for the stretcher, for Pete's sake.

'Let's get some mileage in! Eddie, lead the pack. Where's Eddie?'

'He's in the cloakroom.'

'Again?'

'I'm here, Coach!' Eddie belted out of the gym, yanking up his shorts with one hand and wiping water off his grin with the other. Without missing a stride he took his place at the head of the herd. Chuck immediately started scrambling around his heels like a dog chasing a car.

Tony was right behind them with the Wookie, whose name, I'd learned, was actually Lance and who took one step for every three of Tony's. There were four other guys in the middle, with Tess and a girl named Lisa among them. The rest of the girls — Corie, Robin, Amy, and Dixie — were last. All of their names melted together in my mind except Dixie, who I remembered because she was a little chubbier than the rest. I followed, as usual not knowing what on earth was going on.

'Janice.' Coach jogged up beside me. 'Let's you and me trot along with the rear group here and see what you can do on the long haul.'

My heart sank, but of course I didn't protest. Tanya looked over her shoulder, gave me a saccharine sneer, and took off for the lead group.

'Pace yourselves!' Coach called after her. 'Remember — you have a long way to go.'

He ran ahead for a few minutes, checking everyone out.

When we got off the school grounds and the group started to spread, he slowed down and jogged beside me. I was trying to hold back to match Corie, which was hard. Her short legs churned at a pace about half of mine.

'Eddie tells me you and your dad run a pretty good distance every day.'

I nodded.

'Ever go for speed over a long stretch?'

I shook my head.

'About how fast a mile do you run on the average?'

I looked at him stupidly, but he just waited. He was good at that.

'I guess it takes us about thirty-five minutes to run five miles,' I said finally.

He looked over the top of his sunglasses at me. 'Seven-minute miles.'

That rang a bell. 'We start with a couple of eights to get warmed up. Then we pick it up,' I said.

He grinned. 'I guess the heck so. Well, let's try to increase that speed. A cross-country race is only three miles, so you can sustain a faster pace since you're not running as far. But the demands on your body are going to be different, so we need to watch it.'

I nodded again.

'Okay. Go at whatever speed feels comfortable for you, but don't wear yourself out. There's a sprint at the end.'

I moved off a little, but I could still hear him talking. 'Come on, Corie — let's unclench those fists, hon. This isn't boxing. See how Janice has her arms bent at the waist, shoulders relaxed? She just has her hands kind of cupped — atta girl.'

We trailed through town in little bunches of twos and threes. I stayed behind Tony and Tess, mostly so I wouldn't get lost. Coach shuttled back and forth between us and the group behind us for a while, cheering everybody on and giving instructions. 'Keep the old head up — atta girl, Tess.' 'Ton, good reach, buddy — just don't lean forward too much.' 'That's a nice straight line, Janice. I like that stride.'

When we rounded the last turn we were on a straight stretch towards the school, and I could see the rest of the kids in front of us. It was hard, actually, to get a good view around the Wookie, but I could tell Eddie and Chuck were way out in front, side by side, and that Tanya was the first girl. Coach Spike passed me on the left, took a long look at the whole pack, and then tooted his whistle. Everybody kicked into overdrive.

I still don't know why I did it. The smarter part of me — the part that makes straight A's but not waves — said, let her do her thing. But the feisty part of me — the part I'd felt for the first time in my life the day of the fitness test — pushed me from behind like a giant hand.

I planted my eyes on the track gate and reached for it with everything I had. I think Tess and the Wookie got out of my way. At least I didn't run over them, and I don't think I did much to avoid them.

My heart and my breathing were both pounding in my ears, and my legs were lost somewhere under me. The only thing I was really aware of was the mass of red hair I was gaining on.

Eddie and Chuck had already finished and were standing on the track we were headed for. When he saw us, Chuck went straight up in a spasm. Later it seemed funny to have seen Mr Bad-to-the-Bone losing his cool. At the time, I only knew he was screaming something to Tanya, who looked back at me — and then pushed harder.

I was reaching and kicking so hard the track blurred, but I passed the gate just behind the red hair and the peach shorts. Tanya immediately stopped and doubled over — and I rammed right into her.

We rolled onto the gravel in a heap, and for a split second I thought I felt one of her hands close on my arm. But Eddie was there so quickly, peeling me away from her, I wasn't sure I didn't just imagine it.

'Hot-dogger!' She was on her feet, her face magenta. I know mine wasn't too many shades paler. I hugged my arms around myself to keep from shaking. 'What the — if you can't beat me you're gonna mow me down?'

'You stopped, Tanya,' Eddie said. 'You don't stop at the finish line.'

'Shut up, know-it-all —'

'Knock it off!'

'I won't run with her!' Tanya screamed.

'I said knock it off!' Coach was between us, giving her that look I'd seen before. I hung my head down just in case he planned to bestow one on me. She reeled in her fangs.

'You hit the showers,' he said to her, 'unless you've got a broken bone or something.'

She shook her shoulders sulkily. 'No — I'm okay.'

'Then go. Janice?'

I lurched to attention.

'Are you all right?'

I murmured, 'Yes, sir.'

'Okay — all of you — take a walk,' he barked, and turned on his heel.

'Come on,' Eddie said to me. 'This is the cool-down.'

I was still gulping for air, and every inch of my skin was prickling as I followed him down the track.

'Don't let her get to you,' Eddie said.

'Yeah, she's mean!' Corie had joined us and was doing a two-step to keep up.

'Are you sure you're okay?' Eddie said to me.

Actually there was a raw-looking scrape down the side of my left leg, but I was feeling sort of proud of it. It was my first athletic injury. 'I'm all right,' I said.

'Are *you* okay?' Corie said to Eddie. 'I never saw you sweat like that.'

'I'm a stud.'

'In your dreams.'

'Why is she so mean to you?' That came from Tess who was now on the other side of me.

'I figure it's jealousy,' Eddie said.

'What are you, the team guidance counsellor?' Corie jabbed him in the rib.

'I just have inside info.'

'You've been snooping around.'

'Have not. I just remember when Tanya and Chuck and I were sophomores — before you were born, Squirt.'

'I was a freshman then, dum-dum!'

'We all started out to be sprinters, but it was obvious right off that none of us was cut out for the quarter-mile and such. Chuck and I switched to cross-country the next fall, last year, but Tanya wouldn't go for it. She was gonna tear up that track and be —'

'Valerie Briscoe Hooks,' Corie said proudly.

'Is that the only runner you know?' Tess asked her.

'No, there's —'

'So anyway,' Eddie said, slapping his hand over Corie's still-moving mouth, 'she worked out all summer and fall on the sprints — on her own; I mean you do have to hand it to her.'

'No, I don't,' Tess said dryly.

'But she just never got any faster. Her stride's too long and lopey. She's about perfect for long distance if she wouldn't burn herself out so fast, but Coach couldn't convince her. The only way he could get her to switch to cross-country was by telling her she'd probably be the star runner.'

A light-switch flipped on in my head. It went on in Corie's too.

'O-oh,' she said. 'So Janice is a —'

'Threat,' Eddie finished for her.

We were back at the locker room by then, and Eddie leaned over to drain the water fountain.

'I reckon it isn't going to be easy on you, Jan,' he said, wiping his mouth on his shirt.

'Piece of cake! She'll run the socks off her.'

'Don't count on it.' Tanya emerged from the locker room, hair in a ponytail, make-up flawless. It was all I could do not to duck behind Eddie.

He bowed from the waist, missing the piece of sign language she flipped his way.

'Come on, Tanya,' he said in his throaty talk-laugh. 'We're

41

a team. We're not supposed to be competing against each other.'

'Spare me the sermon, okay? Where's Chuck?'

'I don't know,' Corie mumbled. 'I don't have the Chuck-watch today.'

When she was gone, the three of them laughed, and Corie and the rest of the girls kept laughing all through their showers. I knew from out of the envious corner of my eye that they were popping soap at each other and singing in the team shower, but I slowly went for an individual cubicle and pulled the curtain closed. As much as I wanted to get right in there with them, I still didn't want to risk insinuating myself into a situation where people might say to each other, 'What's *she* doing here? Did you invite her? No — I thought you did!'

Still, when I propped myself up in bed that night to start a letter to Jack, I wrote:

> *Maybe the kids here aren't that bad. I mean,*
> *they talk to me and they remember my name from*
> *one minute to the next. I've told you how back in*
> *Chicago, kids would look at my picture in the year-*
> *book and say, 'Who's that? Was she in our class?'*

I set my pen down for a second — and woke up eight hours later.

To my relief, Tanya didn't speak to me in PE the next morning — that is, until Coach Spike walked over to the mat where I was stretching and asked me how I was feeling. Up to that point she'd been prancing from one end of the gym to the other looking important. As soon as she spotted us, she took a sudden interest in the condition of the pile of exercise mats six feet away.

'You're not real tired today?' Coach said to me. 'No aches and pains?'

'No, sir.'

'Are you dying for a package of M & M's?'

How he knew I was *always* dying for a package of M & M's was beyond me.

He grinned. 'Those would be signs that you overdid it yesterday.'

'Oh. No, sir. I guess not.'

When he walked away, Tanya let the whole pile of mats slide on to the floor and in two strides was standing over me. 'Who are you kidding?' she said.

I shrugged, trying to look nonchalant while my insides reorganized themselves.

'You can't become a distance runner on a crash programme,' she said. 'It takes months of preparation. You don't even know basic track manners. You run people off the road all over the place.'

'I know,' I said to her newly-shaved legs.

She lifted a lip in disgust. 'What are you, a deaf-mute or something? Basket case maybe?'

I just shook my head, reinforcing her suspicions.

'Wimp,' she said.

At least she had that right.

After second period private study, when I chewed my hair and nearly died of boredom for the fourth day in a row, I went on to biology with butterflies emerging from cocoons in my stomach. We were doing our first lab. I was great at book work, but I wasn't so sure about test tubes and microscopes. They'd never let us near them in my old high school.

Corie was already at a lab station when I got there and, to my surprise, flagged me down in the doorway. 'Janice. Over here! Be my partner. Nobody else'll work with me.'

'Watch out, Janice,' Mrs Fruff said in her matter-of-fact voice. 'She's been known to render lab partners unconscious with her concoctions.'

Corie was dimpling. 'I'm not that bad. I don't really do that,' she said to me. 'Once I caught the ceiling on fire with a Bunsen burner, but luckily —'

'You can tell her that tale later,' Mrs Fruff said, never once changing the tenor of her voice or raising her eyes from the sheets she was handing out. 'Right now we have work to do.'

I'd sort of liked Mrs Fruff from the first day. Maybe it

was because I figured it took a lot of guts to go into the teaching profession with a name like Fruff. Nobody teased her about it, at least not to her face. Who would? She had to be five-nine if she was an inch. She had iron-grey hair — stylish for somebody forty-five, but out of the question for one of us — and intense blue eyes. I wasn't sure how it was that while she seldom raised them from her notes or the blackboard, she never missed a play in the classroom either.

The very first day, a kid in the back had shot a miniature paper airplane across the room. Without skipping a beat of her lecture, she caught the thing in midair, flicked it expertly into the trash can, and said, 'Poor design. The trajectory was all wrong.'

I don't think anyone had so much as breathed in there since.

Today she handed out the assignment sheet and had us working almost before the bell rang. Corie immediately started to fall apart.

'What's this hoochie for, Janice?' she said in a panic. She was pointing to a knob on the microscope.

'You don't have to touch that,' I whispered. 'You just focus and look.'

She poked her eye against the lens. 'Ugh! What is that?'

I took a peek. 'Fat cells,' I said.

'No wonder they look so familiar.' Corie patted her thighs and giggled. 'So what do we do?'

'Didn't you listen yesterday?'

'Sort of.'

I sighed.

'I see you've found the hitch in being Corie's lab partner,' Mrs Fruff said from her desk. I looked up, and the network of laugh lines around her eyes went to work.

I got both Corie and me through the lab without smashing any slides or toppling any microscopes off any counters. That was the first miracle.

The second came at the end of the period when I went up to Mrs Fruff's desk to hand in my drawings. 'I like the way you handled yourself in this lab today,' she said without looking up from her grade book.

I almost said, 'Who, me?' but the room was empty and I definitely didn't want to look like an idiot in front of this lady.

'Thank you,' I mumbled.

'Pardon me?'

Her eyes were on me now, and I pulled my head up to look at her. It was as if she'd commanded, 'Look at me, child!'

'Thank you,' I said.

'Do you have a second period class?' she said.

'Yes, ma'am.'

'What is it?'

'Private study.'

'Well, then, you don't have a second period class.' Her voice was stern as usual, but her eyes were twinkly.

'Do you need a study period?' she said.

'No, ma'am.'

'I didn't think so.' She put down her pencil and folded her hands. 'I need a lab assistant for my second period general science class. It's freshmen. They're squirrelly, but I think you'd do quite nicely.'

She waited for a reply, which I couldn't find.

'So it's settled then?' she said. 'I'll see you Monday.'

'Yes, ma'am. But how do — what do I — '

She patted my arm. 'Just ask Corie to help you with the timetable change, and I'll sign it for you. If there's one thing she knows how to do, it's manipulate the office people.'

Her face relaxed again. I smiled back.

I flew through track practice that afternoon like old Valerie Briscoe What's-Her-Name herself. I had an unfamiliar feeling, which I've since learned is the feeling attached to the word 'up'. It was a new one on me.

Practice was different that day. Instead of mileage, we did interval training, which boys and girls didn't do together. I was disappointed that I wasn't going to get to see Eddie. I called myself every name in the book for it, but I'd already figured out where his classroom was and discovered he had government second hour — and it wasn't beneath me to plan my route so I could get a glimpse of him.

I gave myself a mental smack now. 'Don't be an idiot, Janice!' I thought. '*You* and a boy that popular? *You* and a boy — period? Dream on.'

Coach Spike nudged me and handed me a hand-written sheet.

'This is your individual work-out schedule, hon,' he said. 'There's a lot on there, but you only have three weeks to train for the first meet at the end of this month. The rest of the team's been at it since the end of July. But —' He squeezed my shoulder, '— I think you're up to it.'

I stared blankly at the squiggles on the paper. Words like 'fartlek' and 'interval' popped out at me, and I could feel the anxiety pumping in my saliva glands.

'Don't worry,' Coach said, 'Eddie'll help you decipher that. He's about the only one who can read my writing.'

Eddie jogged up to me then and kept running in place. 'Don't let him jive you,' he said. 'I wrote it.'

'Where've you been?' Coach said. 'No, don't tell me. The cloakroom.'

Eddie grinned.

'Boy, you pee more than a puppy.'

'Nah. It was the three cartons of milk I drank for lunch.' Eddie grabbed my arm. 'Come on, Jan.'

Instinctively I jerked away.

I don't know why I always did that. It was a knee-jerk reaction, like yanking your hand back when you burn it on a curling iron. 'You put up signs all around you that say, "Don't touch me", "Don't talk to me",' Jack had always said. At that moment, I figured I looked like an entire picket line.

Eddie was gazing at me — and there's no other way to describe it: he had an *interested* look on his face. Without saying anything else he exchanged glances with Coach and led me to the track.

By the time we got there, Eddie seemed to have forgotten that I'd just acted like an escapee from an institution, and for the next hour and a half he was my all-business coach. I kept waiting for him to go on to his own work-out, but he finally told me he and Coach worked out before school and after practice, so he didn't need the time.

'I'm gonna be a coach myself someday,' he said. 'You're my guinea pig.'

I said my usual eloquent, 'Oh.'

There wasn't much time to talk anyway. He had me sprinting a quarter, walking for thirty seconds, and then going for it again, until I got the quarter down to seventy-eight seconds. He barked so many 'go's and 'stop's at me, I felt like a ride at an amusement park.

'Can I rest for a second?' I asked him once.

He gave me a maniacal grin. 'You won't die from running hard,' he said. 'You'll just think you might.'

I'll just wish I would, I thought.

By the time he ran the mile cool-down with me, I was, as my dad would say, 'whupped'. Eddie, on the other hand, loped along beside me like an adolescent dog just released from the kennel. I expected his tongue to loll out any minute. Darn, he was cute.

'You like it here, Jan?' he said.

'Uh-huh. Pretty much.' At least I'd done more than nod.

'You aren't letting Tanya get to you, are you?'

I almost said no, but the way he looked down at me, the word stuck in my throat.

'You are, aren't you?' he said.

'Yeah. I guess.'

'Bananas. If you weren't you'd be Superwoman.'

Bananas? I actually laughed

'What? What's so funny. Huh?' His eyes teased me, and for a minute I thought he was actually going to tickle me. I didn't know what else to do — I didn't want him to think I was a total moron — so I took off at a gallop.

'Hey, girl, this is a cool-down! Jan! Hey — wait!'

But I was gone, and he was after me, hooting and hollering all the way. He trailed me to the locker room, where he stood outside laughing and gasping over the water fountain.

'I'll get you next time, woman,' he called to me through a mouthful.

He could've got me that time if he'd wanted to — but I'm not sure he'd have known what to do with me once he caught me.

That was okay. Everything was okay. I was even okay.

Until I got home and found a strange woman in our kitchen.

5

She was standing with her back to me facing the sink, one long leg propped against the other, flamingo style. A thick mass of blonde hair cascaded in layers of curls, almost touching the collar of her oversized shirt. She looked so casual, peeling a carrot and humming an Amy Grant tune — it was like she belonged there.

I realized immediately that she did. She had to be my dad's latest choice for a nursemaid for me. But it didn't matter who she was — I owed it to myself to hate her guts.

Before I could say anything, she was wiping her hands on the back of her white shorts and flashing me a smile that was just as white. Friendliness rippled out of her.

'Hey! You must be Janice,' she said. I nodded dumbly as I stared at her. I'd always thought *Dad* had a southern accent, and I'd thought Eddie's was the drawl to end all drawls. But this woman — I was convinced after the first slow, thick 'Hey', spoken in eight syllables, that she was putting me on. She wasn't.

'Suzanne St Claire,' she said, extending a hand. I let her pump my arm silently and then backed up against the counter.

Her smile faded a little. 'I get the feeling your dad didn't tell you I was coming today.'

'He didn't tell me you were coming at all.'

'Oh.'

'I knew he was looking for someone to "baby-sit" me, but he didn't let me know he'd found somebody.' I started to move towards the hall. 'He sure didn't tell me they were coming this afternoon.'

'Well, sugar, he really didn't know.'

'So what did you do, break and enter?' I couldn't believe I'd really said that out loud. Normally I only thought stuff like that. But I had an excuse. I was mad.

She tossed her beautiful head back. I'd have sworn she was doing her Scarlett O'Hara-at-the-Barbecue imitation, but she was actually laughing — for real. Her little round shoe-button brown eyes got sparkly, and she put her hands on her hips, such as they were. The vixen — she had a figure like a *Cosmo* model.

'Sugar, you are great! No, honey, listen, I saw his notice on the bulletin board this mornin', I called him, he had a few minutes free, so I scooted right on over to his office — and it just happened. He gave me the room on the spot, he let me in — and here I am.'

Yeah. Here you are. I didn't say what I was thinking this time. I didn't have to. My face evidently did the talking for me.

As I picked up my stuff where I'd dropped it on the counter, I could feel her studying me. When I got ready to stomp out of the kitchen, I stole a glance at her, and her eyes stopped me.

'Frankly I don't blame you if you're not crazy about this idea. You and your dad have your privacy and your routine.'

I didn't say anything.

'I think — and I was only with him for a bit — but I just think he wants the peace of mind — knowin' somebody's here at night. That's all I intend to make of it.' She wrinkled her nose at me in a cute way. 'Between the two of us we could probably yank off a burglar's pants so he couldn't run out into the street with the goods. Other than that, you could do just as well on your own, no doubt. I reckon some things you just have to do 'cause Dad says, huh?'

'I reckon,' I said, and made a dash for the stairs.

'Want some raw veggies?' she called casually after me.

'No. Thank you.'

'What do ya'll eat around here, anyway? All I found in the freezer were ice cubes and a candy bar . . .'

I turned on my heel and was back in the kitchen before she could start describing what pitiful stores she'd found in the refrigerator section. I opened the freezer, grabbed the Marathon, and clutched it to my breast.

Her eyebrows went up. 'That's obviously yours,' she said calmly.

'Yes.'

'Okay. I'll keep my paws off any Marathons I find. 'Course, if you leave M & M's lyin' around, sugar, I can't be responsible. I'm a nutrition major, but I'll take M & M's over a piece of raw cauliflower anytime.'

I suddenly felt very stupid, very childish, and very much as if I wanted to turn *into* an M & M if that's what it took to get out of the ridiculous spot I'd put myself in. But she kept on chattering and peeling carrots.

'The silly things still melt in my hand. Unless I pour them right from the bag into my mouth.' She giggled.

I left the kitchen, still clinging to the Marathon bar. She knew how to let a person save face, but I still didn't have to like her.

About an hour later I was in my room, scrawling out a letter to Jack for all I was worth, when I heard the Golf pull into the garage — just after I'd started smelling the delicious aroma of melting cheese from downstairs and was actually plugging my nose so I wouldn't enjoy something *She* was doing. That's the frame of mind I was in when Dad finally got to my door — after spending at least fifteen minutes, as far as I was concerned, in the kitchen 'chatting' with *Her*. I was trying to plug my ears, too, when he came in.

'Hey, darlin'.'

I'd have sworn his accent had thickened since I talked to him that morning. I just shrugged.

'Bad day?'

I shrugged again.

'Mind if I sit down?'

You guessed it — again.

He lowered himself onto the edge of my bed and talked as if I weren't glowering at my split ends in silence. 'You know, as soon as I met Suzanne I grabbed her right away. I think she's going to be perfect for us, don't you?'

If he knew I was mad, he wasn't admitting it.

'I guess I should have got your approval, darlin', but if I didn't take her right away she was going after another job. She would've been snatched up right away.'

You should have let her be, I thought, and looked away. 'It's okay,' I lied.

'She seems like a super person. We're going to all have dinner together. Suzanne's fixing quiche.'

I skipped asking what in the world that was and said instead, 'Is she going to be eating with us all the time?'

He kept smiling. 'That isn't the plan. I told her she could use the kitchen any time, and she's invited us to share what she's fixin'. It smells great, doesn't it?'

I sniffed — and not to take in the scent of broccoli and cheese, believe me. I wanted to stand up and scream, 'Get Scarlett O'Hara and her raw veggies out of "heah"!' I also wanted him to at least *notice* that I was not writing this memorable date down in my diary. But of course neither happened.

Instead, Dad stood up and rubbed his hands together like a game show host. 'I just thought it would be nice for us to all get to know each other a little this first day, okay?'

It wasn't okay. Nor was the dinner — though I have to admit the two bites of quiche I grudgingly put into my mouth were the most delicious things I'd ever eaten (and only pure stubbornness kept me from devouring half the pan).

Dad and Suzanne talked like they'd known each other since high school — and I refrained from reminding them that when Dad was in high school, Suzanne was in Pampers and had a dummy. I mentally stopped up my ears, eyes, nose and throat and asked to be excused before she brought on the Georgia peaches she'd bottled that summer, topped with whipped cream — which she assured Dad was a diet recipe she'd concocted.

I retreated to my room, stomach growling, mouth watering. I probably would have remained there for the balance of the weekend if I hadn't had a phone call.

I was stunned when Dad yelled up from the kitchen that it was for me. When I picked it up, I almost went into a catatonic state right there in the upstairs hall.

'Hey,' Eddie said, 'what do you mean, runnin' away from me like that?' He chuckled. 'Whatcha doin'?'

My brain was stuttering. 'Nothing much. Writing a letter.'

'To me?'

'You?' It was hard enough talking straight to people. I had to wind up in a conversation with somebody who threw curve balls every other second.

'Me,' he said.

'No. To Jack.'

For a few seconds there was a hesitation, which was unbelievable considering that Eddie always seemed to be able to think of something to say, even if it didn't make any sense.

'Is he your boyfriend back home?' he said.

'No! He's just — a man.'

'Oh, so you go for the older types. Does that mean you won't run six miles with me tomorrow?' The usual tease was in his voice. 'I thought since you need to do a little catch-up training, we could do a 10K. You owe me.'

'Owe you?'

'For beating me today.'

'You let me win,' I said.

'Eddie McBee does not "let" people win — as you will find out. So are you coming?'

I got out an 'okay'.

'I'll be at your place at 10.00. It's the Williamsburg House, right?'

'Oh —'

'Do you get up that early?'

'Um —'

'Don't worry about lunch. My mom'll make us a sand-wich. You like egg salad?'

'Well —'

After we hung up, I wondered if he would have even noticed if I'd said no.

When Eddie drove up in a faded green pick-up truck, Dad was out planting tulip bulbs around the courtyard. It just tickled the heck out of him to have a yard to potter in. I, personally, was pacing the porch, half-afraid Eddie wasn't going to show and half-afraid he was.

He bounded out of the truck almost before it was stopped, grinning his sloppy grin. He and Dad shook hands like old golf cronies.

'Do you mind if I leave this heap here while we run, Dr Kennedy?' Eddie said, tossing his mop of hair towards the truck.

'No problem,' Dad said.

'I can park it down the side street if you want.'

'Why? It's fine here.'

'If I had a house this nice, I wouldn't want that thing in front of it.'

Dad had a companionable arm around Eddie's shoulder. 'Don't worry about it! You two kids go on and have a good time.'

Eddie looked at my slyly. 'Good time? I'm going to run her into the ground!'

'Don't count on it,' Dad said. 'She can really move!'

'I've noticed.'

I ended that embarrassing line of conversation by bending over into a stretch. Eddie fell in beside me. 'You learn fast,' he said. 'Stretch out real good.' He winked at me. 'You're gonna need it.'

I don't know why, but I suddenly thought of Suzanne, and wrinkled my nose at him the way she did. He wrinkled his back.

After Eddie downed the inevitable three glasses of water,

we were on the road and he was all business again. That was good, because I had such a bad case of the shys I couldn't have been sociable anyway.

'Now the idea,' he said as we turned out on to Monroe, 'is to run the same distance you've been running, only do it faster.'

'I don't know if I can.'

'Sure you can. People *think* they're tired before they really are. Besides, women are incredibly strong — a lot stronger than they realize.'

'How do *you* know?' I didn't mean to sound so abrupt, but at the pace he had set for us, it was hard just to talk and run at the same time. Throw in being nice and you were asking a lot.

'I was a girl once myself.'

'You were not! Were you?'

'Gotcha! Come on. Let's pick it up.'

Pick it up? The boy was a sadist.

We hoofed it down the sidewalk through town, trotting past the colonial mansions that disguised the fraternities living inside, in and out of lines of trees that were at least a century older than we were, and straight through the pedestrian mall where, fortunately, nobody was shopping yet — least of all Tanya. That's where I'd first seen her, and where, from the looks of her wardrobe, she spent the better part of her free time.

'The trick is,' Eddie said when he'd settled into a pace, 'to concentrate on something else so you won't think about being tired.'

Good luck, I thought.

'In a race you'll have a strategy so you can set your mind on that.'

'I will?'

'Sure you will.'

'I don't know —'

'Of course you don't. But do you think your coach is going to let you go into a race without one?'

He was grinning at me. 'I guess not,' I said.

'Today we can just think about — oh, stuff.'

Stuff. Wonderful.

'Like the Courthouse.'

What Courthouse?

'What do you think about when you see the Courthouse?'

'What Courthouse?' I said.

For a second he actually broke stride. 'How long have you lived here, girl?'

'Couple months.'

He grinned. 'You been wearin' a bag over your head? Come on. We gonna have a *good* time today!'

He was true to his word. He gave me a tour Charles Kuralt would have envied. It was as if a movie I'd been watching in black and white were slowly being converted to technicolour — right before my eyes.

Eddie ran me past the Courthouse in Court Square, with its immense columns and stern sort of beauty. Eddie said it made him feel proud to be a citizen or something. I just liked the way everything about it was even and orderly and clean.

Then we tore through the campus, where Eddie brought the place alive. I thought some guy in a powdered wig was going to call down to us from the dome to 'step it up'! Eddie kept saying things like, 'Can't you just feel all that knowledge oozing out?' or 'What if every professor in the place *thought* at the same time? Wouldn't that be powerful?' I nodded a lot, but I was focusing more on the pillars and the domes and the silence.

When Eddie wound us off campus and on to a quiet, country-looking road, he said we'd gone three miles and we were lookin' good.

'Three more to go,' he said. 'Tired?'

'No,' I said.

He wiggled his eyebrows. 'You will be.'

Maybe I was as we picked up the pace and half-flew up a tree-lined semi-dirt road. But to tell you the truth I didn't notice. I was thinking how the leaves were jostling each other. How the sun splashed through the branches. How our feet sounded, padding the ground in the same rhythm. And how even the birds seemed to notice how great we looked running together.

And how it was a good thing nobody could read my mind or they'd think I'd lost it.

'You're doing great!' Eddie said. 'Only about a half-mile to go.'

'Where *are* we going?'

'To my house.'

I stopped doing great. My legs kept running, but my heart sank right down into one of my footprints. His house — where there would be people I didn't know who would ask questions while I tripped over my tongue.

He babbled on. 'Nobody's there — miracle of the ages — but don't worry.' He smiled half a smile and pushed me even faster. 'My mom promised there'd be some food for us.'

The last hundred yards before the grey house on the hill we went into a sprint, and to say Eddie didn't let me win would be an understatement. But I didn't come in *all* that far behind him, and he let out a whoop when he looked at his watch.

'You knocked a minute and a half off your time *per mile*, woman! I knew you were hiding it in you someplace.' He shook his thick mop of hair and let the sweat fly.

I was taking in air like a drowning victim, but I smiled. 'That was a great run,' I said.

'That's what I love about runners. After they're *through* running they talk about how terrific the run was, but to look at them while they're doing it, you'd think they were dying!' He put his arm around me for an instant, but almost before I started to turn to stone he ultra-casually let it drop.

'Come on,' he said. 'We'll walk up the hill and cool down.' He led me up a winding driveway to a sprawling grey house that looked like it had been quickly added on to every time the mother left for the hospital to have another baby. There were tubs of chrysanthemums all over the yard, punctuated by bicycles, deckchairs, croquet hoops and a rake or two. Eddie kicked lazily at one of them. 'I was supposed to rake the lawn today, but I told them I had a student to coach and they let me off the hook.'

You're welcome, I thought. And then I said it. He laughed.

We went in through the back door, and I was surprised at how clean things were on the inside. Clean but not neat. There were books, magazines, piles of sheet music, and half-crocheted blankets all over what I guessed was a family room. But out of the midst of the clutter it seemed to say, 'Come in. Sit down. We like you.'

'Sorry about the mess —'

'I like it. It looks like somebody lives here,' I said.

'Somebody does.' Eddie picked up a stack of mail from the table. 'Even people who don't live here, live here. My brother Jeff's been in college in DC for two years, and my brother Bobby's been married a year and has his own place — and their mail still comes here.'

'I wouldn't want to leave this home, either.'

'You would if you had to live with Bernadette and Carla. My sisters. Man, those two can talk longer than you can listen to 'em.'

Eddie straddled a chair and motioned for me to take the couch, but I couldn't sit down. I just wanted to wander around that busy, lumpy-cushioned, lived-in room and absorb it right through my pores.

'You don't have any brothers or sisters, huh?' he said.

'Nope.'

'It's just you and your mom and dad.'

'Just me and Dad. My mother — died.'

'Good, Eddie,' he said, shaking his head.

'You didn't know.'

I went over to the fireplace and studied the pictures on the mantelpiece — there must have been thirty of them. I even recognized one of Corie with no front teeth. There was a big one in the middle, probably of all the McBees. They were laughing and hanging all over each other, and every one of them had that smile that opened up and connected in the back.

57

As I looked I should've predicted my next move, which was to knock somebody's wedding picture on to the floor.

Eddie had it scooped up almost before it hit the rug. 'It's the hunger,' he said. 'You're starving to death. Oops!' He purposely tripped over a footstool and went head-first into the couch. 'See? It's starting to get to me too.'

He put together two of the thickest, sloppiest-looking egg salad sandwiches I'd ever seen, plopped them on to paper plates, and poured apple juice into two tall glasses with pictures of Road Runner on them. He handed those to me, after making me take an oath that I wouldn't drop them on the way out.

Then he led me out the back door and across the yard to a fat shade tree, where he ordered me to park myself and eat that sandwich before I did any more damage.

Over those same sandwiches and at least two more gallons of apple juice, I got Eddie's whole life story — how he'd grown up in the grey house with two big brothers and two little sisters and more cousins than even he could count. How his dad was a preacher and his mother was everybody's mother — so that sometimes he felt like he had to take a number to get her attention — which I didn't believe for a minute because he seemed way too secure ever to have suffered from neglect, as Jack would have pointed out.

He told me all about his years at Madison High, from the first time he met Coach Spike to the day he and Lance (the Wookie, who, it turned out, was his best friend) got caught filling Coach's office with inflated balloons. He even told me about a few old girlfriends, one of whom, it flabbergasted me to discover, had been Tanya.

'It was right when I first found out that girls weren't just soft boys, and I thought I was this ladies' man or something and could sweep any chick off her feet, you know?'

I was sure he probably could.

'I'd known Tanya for ever. The Earlys have lived on their "estate" — that's what Tanya calls it — since old T.J. himself was here, I think.'

'T.J?'

'Thomas Jefferson.'

'Oh.'

'But I didn't notice what a fox she'd turned into until we were sophomores. One day I just looked at her and said "wow". Only trouble was, she was meaner than a snake — or hadn't you picked up on that?'

I just looked at him, and he gave his drunken giggle.

'I decided if anybody could change her, *I* could. I was going to date her and turn her into a little angel. So I started writing her all these romantic notes and sticking little bouquets of flowers on her locker. It's enough to make you throw up, isn't it?'

Only if he were doing it for Tanya. But I nodded.

'I even wrote poems for her. Bad move. She loved them.'

'Are you serious?'

'As a heart attack. For about a week she purred like a kitten. Then she started calling me in the middle of the night to tell me she'd just had a bad dream. Or when I called her she'd make me promise I wouldn't speak a word to another person after I hung up, so hers would be the last voice I heard before I went to sleep.'

'I *am* going to throw up,' I said.

'Hey, that's not all.' He was starting to laugh so hard his words were slurring. 'I had to have my arm around her at all times — I mean at *all* times — which was tough on Fruff's science class.'

'Really.'

'And if I didn't say something "poetic" about her hair or her eyes or her nail polish every ten minutes, she'd pout or give me the old cold shoulder. I felt like I was in the North Pole 90 per cent of the time.'

'Yuk.'

'I'm a little slow, so it took me another two weeks to realize that it wasn't me she liked. It was all the romance and stuff. If I wanted to make out or buy her some mushy card, fine. If not, I was going to suffer.'

'So did you?'

'What, suffer? When I first broke it off with her, you bet. She went at me with her fingernails!'

'She attacked you?'

'Sliced my cheek open. I had to tell my mother our cat did it. Took Mom four days to realize we didn't have a cat, and by then the thing had healed.'

'I can't believe it.'

'Hey, never underestimate Tanya. The chick is vicious. And then she threatened to commit suicide, which I took seriously and was going to call her mother and be the knight in shining armour, until about two hours later when I saw her sharing a meatball sandwich at Poe's with another guy. She was really torn up about it, you know?'

'I can tell.'

Eddie tossed his now-empty paper plate aside and stretched all six foot two of his slender self out on the grass. I nervously plucked two weeds and started braiding them. It was strange how one minute I was so comfortable talking to Eddie, and then the next I'd feel so shy I could have crawled into one of my own ears.

'She's had at least seventeen other boyfriends since then,' he was saying. 'I can always tell when she's just broken up with one of them — they always have a black eye or something!'

'So — now she goes with Chuck.'

'Slade? Eh —' He gave a nonchalant iffy motion with his hand, but the very definite sneer of dislike crossed his lips at the same time, and just as quickly disappeared. 'I guess they can take or leave each other. They sort of hang together until something better comes along. You know, Jan, the thing I don't get about people is, they're afraid *not* to be madly in love with somebody. It's like they think they're nobody unless they're attached.'

He launched into an off-key rendition of 'You're Nobody 'til Somebody Loves You', which I'd heard on one of my dad's old Dean Martin albums. Eddie sounded tipsier than old Dean himself. Then in mid-bar he broke off with, 'I like to date around and stuff, you know, have a good time and get

60

to know a girl, but I just can't get into, you know, *belonging* to somebody so you can't even talk to anybody else without her permission — and you better call her the minute you get home from school or she cries and thinks you don't love her any more. She might as well tie you up and lock you in a dungeon like a prisoner — Ah! Help! No, not the steady girlfriend! Anything but the steady girlfriend!'

He was clutching his throat and pretending he was being dragged down the hill by one leg. I was laughing so hard my jaws ached.

'Janice! Don't let them take me!' He grabbed for my wrist and went limp. 'Oh, thank you, thank you. How can I ever repay you? I owe you my life.'

'I thought you didn't want to belong to anybody.'

'This is different. You saved me.'

He was still hanging on to my hands, and when I noticed it, I slowly drew them away. 'You cruel, cruel woman,' he said, and rolled over to look across the hilltop at the misty view of the Blue Ridge.

'So let me ask you about you,' he said suddenly.

'Why? I'm just — boring.'

'Stop it.'

That's exactly what Jack would have said. I laughed.

'What's funny?'

'Nothing.'

He was giving me his interested look again. 'I'm going to ask you a question, and if you don't want to answer it, you don't have to.'

I already knew I wouldn't want to, but I just chewed my hair and shrugged.

'Why does it bother you for me to — well, no.' He jiggled his leg impatiently. 'Do I make you feel self-conscious or something?'

He was looking me right in the eyes, until I almost couldn't stand it. I guess that was obvious because he said huskily, 'I'm sorry.'

I had to say something. He was trying too hard to be nice for me to just switch him off. 'No,' I said, staring straight at the ground. 'It's — just — I'm not used to talking to people.'

'You sure can't tell. You were doing all right here today.' He leaned back on the grass. 'Now come on,' he said. 'Keep talking.'

But I was saved from revealing anything about my fascinating life by the arrival of a noisy station wagon in the drive. I couldn't tell what made the most racket — the horn, the engine, or the two little girls in the front seat. Both of them were out of the vehicle and headed in our direction before the dust settled.

'Oh oh!' Eddie said, hiding his face in his arms. 'They're back.'

'Your sisters?'

'Godzilla and The Incredible Hulk.'

The little one — who had to be Carla and looked to be around nine, arrived chanting, 'Eddie has a girlfriend, Eddie has a girlfriend.'

Eddie tackled her while Bernadette, the thirteen-year-old, gave an unsolicited rundown of the day's events.

'We went all the way to Richmond and couldn't find coats for either one of us. Nothing fitted Carla and everything I wanted was — too expensive, so —'

'So tomorrow we see what we can find at Goodwill.'

'*Mo*-ther!'

The round lady with the greying hair who'd been at the wheel of the station wagon had joined us, eyes twinkling behind her glasses. Although she was short and roly-poly, she was Eddie all over again in the face.

Eddie got a kamikaze hold on Carla and grinned up at his mother. 'Mama, this is Janice Kennedy. Jan, my mother.'

'Hey, Janice — nice to meet you, honey.'

'How come Eddie gets to be alone with a girl in the house and I can't have a boy in when you aren't home?' Bernadette said, hands planted firmly on negligible hips.

'Because I *trust* Eddie,' Mrs McBee said dryly. 'Ya'll want some ice tea? I've got some in the fridge.' She looked closely at Eddie. 'Honey, how far did you all run today? You look awfully pale, son.'

'Jan ran my feet off. Is there any chocolate cake left? I couldn't find it.'

'Bobby ate it all last night,' Carla said.

'Bobby? Was he here last night?'

They drifted off towards the house, still talking, all three of them at once.

Eddie shook his head as if to check for loose parts.

'Now you see what I have to live with. No wonder I'm looney, uh-looney, uh-looney . . .' He slapped himself to stop the cycle.

I was looking at the receding figures of his family. 'I think they're neat,' I said, as much to myself as to him. 'You're really lucky.'

He grinned the McBee grin. 'This is not lucky. This is the cruel hand of Fate.'

I grinned too, and he cocked his head at me. 'You have a neat smile,' he said. 'You oughta smile more often.'

Looking nowhere in particular, I stood up. 'I have to go,' I said.

'You're not getting off the hook. Someday you're going to tell me about yourself.'

Funny, I thought as I picked the grass off my shorts, this was one hook I didn't think I wanted to get off.

6

Eddie was all set to drive me home when we realized he'd left his truck at my house. So he 'drove' me three and a half miles on his ten-speed bike.

It was incredible that we were neither picked up by the police nor mown down by any of the drivers who passed us doing double-takes: me sitting on the seat and Eddie crouched over the handlebars. Once he even stood up on the pedals and looked at me upside down from between his legs.

When we got to my house, he piled the bike into the back of his pick-up and gulped down the contents of his water bottle. I backed across the courtyard towards our front door.

'Well, thanks,' I mumbled.

'Don't mention it.' He grinned, of course. And then I turned and ran into the house.

I was lying in bed the next morning, thinking about that graceful exit and wondering if Eddie thought I was nuts. The thing was, I really liked him.

He was off-the-wall, that was for sure, but I liked that about him. I'd had guys come on to me in Chicago on a regular basis — although once they discovered I could turn them into a tray of ice cubes with one glance they always backed off. Not one of them ever knew I was just shy, and that was okay with me because as far as I was concerned they were all on ego trips with no destination.

Eddie didn't seem to be putting on an act. He couldn't be. I mean, who would *attempt* to be as silly and crazy as he was? How many guys did I know who would make you a sandwich or ride you through town on their bike or give you an old maple leaf for a present?

'Darlin,' are you awake?' Dad said from the door.

That was a good question, I thought as I rolled over. My life had suddenly taken on a dream-like quality.

'I think so,' I said.

He put his head in, smelling like Old Spice and wearing a white T-shirt and slacks — the way I'd seen him on a hundred Sunday mornings.

'You want to go to church today?' he said.

'You're going?'

'I reckon it's time we got back to it.'

'I'll go,' I said, sighing, and threw off the covers for proof. I'd have to get back to Eddie-type thoughts later.

We hadn't been to services at all since we'd moved to Virginia. We'd got out of the habit, I guess you could say.

In Chicago, it had been a real ritual with us, and I went along with it because I guess it made me feel secure. Rituals do that to you.

There was something about being in a pew beside Dad, smelling his Old Spice and feeling the gabardine of his suit against my cheek, that made the rest of the trash in my life fade into the background for a while. I can't say I'd ever really listened to a sermon, and I wouldn't have been able to recite two consecutive verses from the Bible if my next meal had depended on it. I mean, I believed there was a God, but he was in another league. It was pretty apparent from the way my life had gone that he hadn't really noticed me, either. I was willing to pay tribute to him, though, because that was what you did.

That Sunday, in honour of the occasion, I even put on The Dress — the only one I owned — a sort of peasant-looking thing I'd bought for my ninth-grade graduation, if that tells you anything. I took a brush to my hair — 'that pretty stuff', as Eddie had called it — and decided it was going to be an okay day.

Until I got downstairs and found Suzanne all dolled up to join us — in a pink raw silk suit and pearls, naturally. I wanted to burn the peasant dress, go back to bed, pull the covers over my head, and die.

'Suzanne's going with us — okay?' Dad announced.

What could I say — 'No way, José! Send this broad back to the plantation'? I just shrugged.

'Now you ladies wait on the porch and I'll bring the car around for you. Let's do this in style.'

I moaned inwardly.

As soon as he'd gone out of the side door to the garage, Suzanne looked me square in the eye, which was tough to do since I was staring at the floor.

'I *know* we are gettin' off on the wrong foot here,' she said. 'I told your daddy I thought you two should go on ahead alone this mornin', but he said not to be silly. Listen —' She looked up at the ceiling, and for the first time I realized she was really upset. 'I am not here to interfere with your life and be some mother hen — I swear it. It just keeps seeming to turn out that way. How 'bout if I just stay here?'

'No. It's okay,' was all I said. I could feel a streak of meanness creeping up my back, and I didn't do a thing to stop it.

The church Dad had picked out was like just about everything else in town, steeped in the sweet elegance of the Old South. I was really beginning to have a thing for white columns and magnolia trees, and the church had both.

As soon as we were seated in a long mahogany pew, Dad nudged my elbow and pointed his finger at the church bulletin he'd picked up. 'Look,' he said, 'Eddie's dad must be the preacher.'

There it was, all right. Edward McBee, Sr, Pastor.

And there, several rows ahead of us, was Eddie, Jr. He and his mother and the two little McBee sisters and an older guy who was a clone for Eddie only with a receding hairline and a wife, and Corie and a bunch of little kids in various stages of McBeeism, and Lance and Tony and Tess and Robin and Dixie — they all took up about six of the front pews.

When a very tall, very thin, very bald Pastor McBee started his sermon, my mind, as usual, skittered over everything but the topic. I wondered if Eddie was going to go bald someday, and what it must have been like to grow up with a father who put people to sleep with words instead of anaesthesia, and whether Eddie ever paid attention to the sermon.

The other thing I wondered was whether he'd see me. He did.

Right after the service he was beside me — and he brought the rest of the kids with him.

'Jan!' said Eddie. 'You came to church!'

'Nah, man,' Tony said. 'It's an optical illusion.'

'Shut up, idiot.' That came from Lance who lifted Tony

66

off his feet with the same motion he used to clap a hand over his mouth.

'You should have come to Sunday school before church,' Corie said. 'We have a great class.'

'If you can call it a class.'

'It's really our youth group meeting.'

'You oughta come next time.'

'Eddie's our president.'

'Ha.'

Eddie looked for the source of that comment. 'What do you mean, "Ha"? You fools would be lost without me.'

'We wouldn't be fools without you!'

It was obviously an in-house joke, because everybody laughed a little louder than they needed to for that punch line. I felt stupid laughing with them, but I'd have felt stupider standing there straight-faced. It was a good thing too, because when the laughter died down, they all looked at me, and I could practically see their brains scrambling for something to say.

Eddie turned to Robin and Dixie who flanked him. 'Did you guys work out this weekend, huh?' He put an arm around each of them, at which point something inside me pulled the covers over its head.

'Did they even get out of bed this weekend?' Tony said.

'Janice and I did.'

'What — get out of bed?'

'No, Laser Brain.' Eddie thumped Tony on the arm, but his face had gone scarlet.

'Tell us about it, Eddie,' Dixie said, giggling. 'Is that why the Chapstick's in your pocket?'

'I'll tell you what,' Eddie said, pulling out the stuff and smearing it on his lips. 'You guys better look out. She's gonna flat tear up that track.'

'All right!' somebody said.

Then there was another somebody-say-something silence. Somebody finally did.

'So who's got chemistry homework?'

'Ugh. Give me a break.'

'Hey, did you see Joe Stransky after school yesterday?'

'No. Why?'

'He was so —'

I started to back out of the circle.

'You going?' Corie said to me.

'I have to.'

'Okay.' She almost looked relieved. As I walked away I had the uncanny sensation that they were all feeling as 'new' as I was.

'Where are you off to, girl?'

I felt Eddie's warmth behind me.

'I have to go,' I said. You're so charming, Janice, I thought.

'Well, wait a minute.' He lifted a strand of hair from my shoulder and started toying with it like he'd decided we were going to stand there all day. He was *so* weird.

'I had a good time yesterday,' he said.

'Oh. Good.' More charm.

'I like getting to know you.'

'Oh.' I almost choked. 'Okay.'

'You're sure it's okay?' He put my hair under his nose like a moustache. 'Well, frankly my dear Scarlett . . .'

'Eddie, come on!' It was Carla tugging at his belt. 'Mom's got a roast in the oven.'

'You were saved by the bell this time, girl,' he said as his little sister dragged him away. 'Next time you might not be so lucky.'

Yes, he was definitely weird. Probably even weirder than me.

All day I could barely concentrate on learning the geometry theorems I had for homework. I'd got up that morning feeling, for a change, like it was worth getting up. Now I was developing insides of jelly again.

The trouble was, always before if I started feeling overwhelmed, I could just hide in my hair and nobody seemed to care a whole lot. Boring, but safe. But ever since Jack, and especially since Coach and Mrs Fruff and definitely Eddie, it was getting harder to find doors I could hide behind.

I slapped my maths book shut around 1.30 and started doing stretching exercises on the floor, but my mind didn't stay on my Achilles tendon. Little doors kept popping into my head.

Jack had been a big one for 'concrete images' to explain psychological phenomena which had fourteen-syllable names. He was for ever talking about the doors in my personality that I kept locked, bolted and chained, and he'd pointed out more than once that I also kept my porch light off so that nobody even bothered to knock.

Now either people were ignoring my Do Not Disturb sign, or I'd forgotten to hang it out.

Coach Spike was banging on one door and hollering, 'Come out and run!'

Mrs Fruff was tapping politely on another and requesting the presence of my brain in her second period class.

Eddie was standing upside-down outside another, rapping out a beat on it with his feet, and saying — who knew what. I hadn't figured that one out yet.

And then there was Tanya, crouched by the door that read 'GUTS', waiting for me to try to show some intestinal fortitude so she could tear up my hide.

I went into a hurdler's stretch. What if I let them in? Would I become a track star, a biology whiz, Eddie McBee's Woman, and a gutsy little chick nobody walked on? Or would they discover I had no talent, no brains, no courage, and no personality — and start slamming doors like there was no tomorrow?

I stretched my quadricep muscle. Yes. Jelly inside. For sure.

At that point, Dad tapped on the door and then peeked in.

'What is going on in here, darlin'?' he said.

'I'm working out,' I said.

'You're working your way through the floor and into the livin' room.'

'Sorry — '

'For what? Look at those legs, girl. You're getting some definition in those muscles.'

He went on to describe every tendon with its Latin name, and I went into my look-interested-but-tune-into-another-channel mode. But several sentences into it, he brought me to attention with: 'Well, if you're going to get serious about this, we better get down to the store and get you some shoes that'll give you some decent support for your —'

The rest was Greek, and besides, I was in the car before he finished the sentence.

For the two hours it took us to find *the* perfect pair of Nikes and try them out with a short jog — during which Dad checked the things at least eight times to make sure they weren't rubbing anywhere — I forgot about the condition of my doors.

But when he left, after announcing that he was sure 'Suzy' and I were going to do 'just great' on our first night alone, I was back to chewing my hair. 'Suzy?' Oh, puh-leeze.

I went immediately to my room to establish an incommunicado status, but as soon as it got dark, fear came in to join me. It didn't matter whether Suzanne was there to protect me or not. It wouldn't have mattered if an SAS team had been guarding the place. I just kept thinking about the back door being torn off its hinges and me holing myself up in the wardrobe. To avoid taking leave of my senses completely, I picked up on the letter I'd started to Jack last Friday.

> *Dad ended up getting me a 'baby-sitter' after all. Her name's Suzanne and she's only in her late twenties, but as far as I'm concerned she's still here to 'take care of me' when Dad's gone at night, and I hate it. To make matters worse, she is absolutely gorgeous. I mean it. She is this southern doll with all the manners and stuff to go with it. She can cook, she paints her toenails — she does everything perfect. I feel like a glob of cranberry sauce next to her. Dad just thinks she's the greatest thing since sliced bread, and he keeps inviting her to do things with us — like go to church. She's not pushy, I guess — I don't know — it just bothers me. We don't need her.*

There was something about those last few sentences that made me squirm. If I hadn't known better I'd have sworn Tanya had written them. I was scratching them out when the noise started outside.

A car which seemed to be minus its muffler roared to a stop out front and stayed there, motor grumbling impatiently. It sent a shock like a sparkler up my spine. Even if I hadn't been a nervous wreck, it would have at least made me look up twice. The street was so quiet most of the time, it made your ears ring. You never even heard brakes squealing or horns blowing. It was un-genteel or something.

This driver obviously didn't know that and gave the accelerator a couple of warning taps. With a mouth the consistency of stale bread, I went to the window and stole a look. Even as I sidled up and peered stealthily towards the pane, I felt ridiculous. Why was I sneaking to look *out* of my own window?

The driver couldn't have seen me, but the maniac chose that moment to pull away and disappear around the curve. I gasped, jerked, and banged my head against the wall. The car left me with the smell of burning rubber and the throb of my cranial bones.

The tap on the door that came next didn't help. I lurched again and connected with the wall in the same spot.

'Janice?' she said.

It was Suzanne.

Reluctantly I said, 'Come in.'

She only opened the door a crack.

'Did you hear all that racket?'

'Yes,' I said irritably.

'What in the —'

She looked like she was going to head right through my door to the window, so I interrupted rudely. 'Just fraternity guys,' I lied. 'They do it all the time.'

'Oh.' She gave a relieved smile. 'Animals.'

She waited for me to say something, which of course I didn't. I just stood there rubbing the fast-rising knot on the side of my skull. She tossed her head to one side, almost shyly.

'I've got some tea and toast made,' she said, 'and if I eat it all myself I'll be a blimp. Want to join me?'

Tea and toast. Nursemaid's menu.

But to my own disgust, I nodded. No way could I stay in my room alone now, scaring myself to death.

I gasped when I walked into Suzanne's room, right across the hall from mine. It looked like something out of *Better Homes and Gardens* with Suzanne's abundance of class splashed all over it.

She had white mini-blinds at the windows and a white bedspread with little green flowers on the bed and throw pillows in all shades of green strategically placed everywhere. There was a big oak cedar chest, a rocking chair, and embroidered flowers in oval frames on the wall above the bed. One wall was even papered in dark green and yellow.

'Would you like to sit down?' she said, nodding towards the rocker.

No. I wanted to run and put a padlock on my door so she'd never see the condition my room was in. Thank goodness she'd only seen it through a crack in the door.

'Two pieces of toast to start with?' she was saying as she loaded my plate from a wicker tray on the bedside table. 'We'll get a sugar high and then we'll be up all night.'

The toast was bubbly with butter and cinnamon, and the tea was spiced with orange and something else that sizzled on my tongue. 'Spiked tea,' she called it. 'But relax. It's nothin' stronger than ginger.'

I sat stiffly in the rocker. She lounged, lithe and lovely, on the bed. She was wearing men's boxer shorts and a man's yellow dress shirt with the sleeves rolled up, but she still looked like something off the cover of *Ms*.

'When did you wallpaper?' I said awkwardly.

'Yesterday, when you were off with your boyfriend.'

My heart caught on a snag.

'Eddie isn't my boyfriend,' I said.

'Oh. Is he going to be? He's sure cute as a bug.'

'Probably not.'

'Why? Does he pick his nose or something?'

'No!' I swallowed a guffaw. 'I just don't think I'm his type.'

'Bilge water. As darlin' as you are?'

I stared at my toast.

'Have you known him long?' she said.

What is this, a cross-examination? I thought. But instead I blurted out, 'It's just that everybody likes Eddie. And he *loves* everybody.'

She cupped her hands around her tea mug and surveyed me through the steam. ''Course, even the life of the party may need one special honey.'

I crimped my lips together. Why was I telling her all this?

'Well — I hope it works out if you want it to.' She went on quietly sipping her tea and looking totally at ease. 'Do you like it here?'

'Do you?' I was determined not to be on the answering end of any more questions.

'So far. 'Course, any place would be a relief. I *had* to get out of Georgia. Too many memories. Sometimes a change of scene can give a person a whole new perspective.'

I could feel my eyes widening. Something in her life wasn't perfect?

'And it'll be worth it. A Master's from this university is going to take me places — I hope.'

I hope it does, I thought. Faraway places. My mean streak was widening fast. And then she put her finger right on it.

'I'm scared half out of my mind, of course, but then who isn't when they pick up everything they own and move someplace they've never set eyes on before.'

My eyes popped.

'Your dad's been real sweet, though, and I sure appreciate it. Going to church this mornin' made all the difference. It reminded me what my priorities should be.'

I could feel myself shrivelling down to cockroach size. I stood up abruptly. 'I have to go,' I said.

'You do not. Let's dig into the M & M's. Now mind you,

I don't share these with just anyone. Normally I hoard 'em like a squirrel.'

She was chattering on as if I'd agreed to hang around for at least another two hours. But I shook my head.

'I have more homework.'

'Don't say that word. Classes start for me tomorrow — and then *I'll* be up to my eyes in books 'n' papers.'

She paused. I already had my hand on the doorknob, and she was watching me closely. I opened the door.

'See you,' I said and, feeling like Jerk of the Year, I left.

7

'Your job is to see that no one burns off a digit with a Bunsen burner or decides to do independent study with the hydro-chloric acid.'

Mrs Fruff's eyes were teasing, but her voice was dead seri-ous, and the awesome burden of my responsibility as her lab assistant set itself down right between my shoulder blades.

She put her hand on my arm. 'No matter what they say to you, don't smile. In fact, never smile until at least Christmas.' She winked slyly. 'We have to show them who's boss.'

She turned to the rows of desks where thirty ninth-graders were doing aerobics in their seats. I'd been grading their papers and setting up their lab for a week, but this was the first time I had had to work with the little jackals and I wasn't exactly pawing the ground to get started.

'As soon as you have arrived at your station with your partner,' Mrs Fruff said, 'Miss Kennedy will hand you your assignment sheet.'

Some kid snickered.

'Is there a problem?' Mrs Fruff said.

Dead silence, of course.

'Good. I'm certain you'll give Miss Kennedy the same respect you give me — or I will rip off a few phalanges.'

It was a cinch I wasn't going to be a buddy to the kids, but at least I was protected. What kid was going to test whether she'd *really* tear off someone's fingers?

As they filed into the lab area, Mrs Fruff drilled on. 'Once you have softened the glass tubing and closed one end over the Bunsen burner, have Miss Kennedy or I check it before you proceed.'

'Say, baby,' somebody said to me in a low voice.

I continued to pass out sheets, until I felt a tug on the hem of my jacket.

'Say, baby.'

I looked down into a chocolate-brown face, a pair of huge black eyes, and a mouthful of very white teeth.

'What's happenin'?' he said.

It was a good thing Mrs Fruff had warned me not to smile or I'd have burst out in giggles. The kid couldn't have been more than five feet tall, but I'm sure he thought he was Eddie Murphy.

'Do you have a question?' I said.

'You got any answers?'

'Depends on the question.'

I moved on to pass out the last sheet, but he closed his fingers around the corner of my jacket. 'What we s'posed to be doin'?'

'Reading the sheet and doing what it says.'

He scowled. 'You teachers all alike. Don't nobody want to help nobody.'

'I *am* helping you. I told you — the directions are right there.'

'Hey — you, *Miss* Kennedy,' another kid hissed at me. 'How do you get this thing to light?'

I went over to his table, but my eyes kept floating back to the black kid. He looked at the sheet for a minute, then turned it over on the counter and looked around the room with guarded eyes. He got so jittery I was sure he was going

75

to attempt an escape any minute. As soon as I got the burner lit, I went back to him.

'Don't you have a partner?' I said.

'Don't nobody want to be my partner,' he said.

'How come?'

He grinned broadly. ''Cause I mess around too much.'

'Obviously.'

He just kept grinning up at me, and I was so afraid the twitches at the corners of my mouth were going to leap into a smile, I snatched up the sheet and read the first item out loud.

'So do it,' I said when I was through.

'Is this right, Miss Kennedy?' said a little blonde with glasses. She was so nervous her test tube was shaking.

I checked her work, and when I got back to my protégé he had the burner going and was doing a drumbeat on the counter.

'Good,' I said. 'So do the next step.'

'Read it to me,' he said.

'What am I, the maid?'

He flashed his teeth. 'That'd be a switch!'

Glancing uneasily towards Mrs Fruff's back, I grabbed the sheet again and read number two to him.

The kid watched my lips as I read and then did exactly as I'd told him. His finished test tube was a work of art.

'Say, baby, that is *all* right!' he said. 'Now what I gotta do?'

I thrust the paper into his face. '*You* read it.'

His face clouded over. 'I don't like readin'.'

I waited.

With the enthusiasm of a person about to eat burnt toast, he took the paper from my hand, blew out a big puff of air, and pursed his lips over the first word. It came out like a moan.

'Lincoln.' We both jerked our heads towards Mrs Fruff. 'Are you monopolizing Miss Kennedy?'

His mouth came open like a switchblade snapping out. 'Hey —'

'I'm just checking his work,' I said quickly.

She nodded in approval and turned away. I took the paper from Lincoln and read number three.

For the next half-hour, I did my best to look like I was helping everyone in the area, but I spent most of the time helping Lincoln to read the directions. That's about all I did for him too, but he came out with the frothiest-looking purple liquid of anyone in the class. Fortunately, that was what he was supposed to come out with.

'That's your name — Lincoln?' I said to him at one point.

'You got some kind of problem with that?'

'Why should I? I'm a Kennedy myself.'

'Lincoln my first name, girl,' he said. 'Lincoln Darnell Lewis.'

'Oh. Nice to meet you.'

'You strange,' he said.

When it was time to clean up the lab, Lincoln put his feet on the counter.

'You're supposed to wash out your test tubes now,' I told him.

'I ain't no janitor.'

'I ain't no maid either, but I helped you, didn't I?'

'That's yo job, woman.'

I wanted to smack him, but I pushed his legs off the counter instead. 'It wasn't my job to help you read the whole assignment sheet, but I did it.'

His cocky grin faded. 'You saved my butt from Miz Fruff,' he said almost inaudibly.

'So get it off the chair and get busy,' I said.

When the bell finally rang and they were gone, I breathed a sigh of relief that came from my absolute toenails. As I was getting my books together, Mrs Fruff cleared her throat at me.

'Look at this, Janice,' she said. 'Lincoln Lewis aced this lab.' She looked through me. 'Or did he?'

My jaw went loose at the hinges. 'Yes, ma'am! I just checked off his results!'

'Of course.' She tapped her pencil thoughtfully on the stack of papers. 'It's certainly curious. Lincoln can't seem to do a thing in class except imitate Mr T, and then he goes into the lab and performs like a third-year tech. Why do you suppose that is?'

'He seems to have difficulty reading,' I said, half to the floor and half to her. 'But he did all right with some encouragement. He just needs more confidence — he's a bright kid.'

I glanced at her quickly, and she was nodding.

'I do believe you're right,' she said. 'Good eye, Miss Kennedy.'

I thought about the little shrimp all day — until that afternoon at practice. That was enough to wipe everything else out of my mind.

For the past week, I'd been working with Eddie almost entirely, except for the days we all did mileage together. Then it had been all I could do to concentrate on trying to stay out of Tanya's way. She'd practically flattened me twice passing me on the sprint, and she never went by me without hissing or something. I was getting more tense by the day — but I didn't realize everyone else was, too.

When Tess, Corie and I got to the gym to change, Tanya was standing in our locker area, cleaning the dirt from under her fingernails.

'Are you lost?' Corie said.

'Coach wants everybody changed — double time — and out on the bleachers for a meeting,' Tanya said.

Tess looked up from the lock she was struggling with. 'What for?'

'You'll find out when you get there,' Tanya said, and sailed off.

'She doesn't know either,' Corie said when she was out of earshot.

'She sure loves to pretend she does,' Tess said. 'Hey, Janice, you got some new runnin' shoes!'

'I got them last weekend,' I said to my shoelaces.

'I could sure use a new pair. Look at this!' Corie flopped her loose insole up and down like a tongue.

'How long have you had those, Corie? It takes a *while* for that part to come loose,' Tess said.

''Bout since Noah ran track. Why haven't you been wearing them?' she said to me.

I turned red for no reason at all except that I was Janice Kennedy. 'I've been breaking them in slow at home,' I said.

'You better get them broken in before Saturday,' Tess said, snapping a rubber band around the gorgeous bun she'd just twisted onto the top of her head. 'You've got to win this meet for us.'

'Me?' I said. 'What about Tanya?'

Corie grunted. 'You've never seen Tanya in a meet. She gets so hyped up, she takes off like she's running the Olympics at the start, but about halfway through she's worn out. The only way she ever places is to use psychological warfare on the other teams.'

I didn't even have to ask what that meant.

Coach was getting everybody seated on the bleachers when I got out to the track, and his face was grim.

'Folks, I'm going to get right to the point,' he said. 'The tension in the air this past week has been so thick you can go at it with a chain-saw and still not make a notch. I don't like it, not with our first meet coming up this Saturday.'

He had on sunglasses, so it was hard to tell if his eyes were resting on anybody in particular, but I, naturally, was seething with nameless guilt.

'We are a team. It's nice to be a star, but you're in this outfit to help the team run to victory, not just yourself. We can't afford to have all this competition within the ranks, people. It's going to cost us the meet, I guarantee. Now I want to see you characters pulling together, helping each other — or we forfeit the race.'

He surveyed us all sternly, and most of us took to examining the toes of our running shoes. The silence itself pleaded guilty as charged.

'Starting today, demerits will be given for any unsportsmanlike conduct. Score five and you work for me after track practice. Score ten and you don't run in the next meet.'

'That isn't fair to the team,' Tanya whined. 'What if one of our best runners fouls out?'

'We have depth on the team now,' Coach said calmly. 'Nobody's indispensable.'

'What counts as "unsportsmanlike conduct"?' Chuck said.

Coach put a big hand on one hip. 'If you don't know that by now, you're in big trouble.' He continued to look at us for an eternity, then gave a short toot on his whistle. 'All right, let's take some warm-up laps. Ladies first. Janice, lead the pack.'

I could feel Tanya's eyes drilling right through my back.

I took the warm-up laps lightly, giving my new shoes their final slack before I showed them what they were really going to be put through. The left one seemed a little loose, so I stopped just before we took off and retied it.

'Out already?' Tanya said as she trotted past me.

That's good for a demerit, I thought. But I pressed my lips together and shot out to take the lead. For once, Tanya didn't slide into overdrive and go by me.

I set a pretty fair pace as we rounded the curve, and I looked back to see the guys charging up behind. My shoes were feeling good so far, so I dug in a little. Two strides later a pain seared up my leg, and I thought I'd been shot right through the heel. I took another step, and it was unbearable.

I grabbed for my ankle and went down on the grass beside the sidewalk. I sensed Tanya passing me, but all I could think about was the drill being driven through the bottom of my foot.

I was surrounded by legs right away, and it only took a few seconds for a set of long, cool fingers to close over my shoulder.

'Jan!' Eddie said. 'What happened? What's wrong?'

'My foot,' was all I could say.

'Did you twist your ankle — or what?'

I kicked my left foot and tried to keep the fast-approaching tears from making a real entrance.

'Get her shoe off,' somebody said.

Eddie ripped off my left Nike and my sock. 'Where does it hurt?'

'My heel. Ow —' It felt like he was tearing out a bullet.

Thirteen heads bent over my foot as Eddie examined the heel. I was the only one who didn't gasp, because I was the only one who couldn't see.

Eddie let my foot drop and grabbed for my discarded shoe. We all watched in disbelief as he flipped up the insole — and produced an industrial-sized thumbtack.

'This went through your heel,' Eddie said.

'What's going on?' Coach Spike joined us, and everybody started talking at once. Eddie handed him the tack and my shoe.

'Was this like this when you put your shoe on today?' Coach said, sticking his hand under the loose insole.

'They're brand new shoes!' Corie said.

He smothered my foot with his hand and went over it with squinted eyes. The team looked on like interns at an operation.

'It doesn't look that bad,' Coach said. 'It's a puncture wound, though. When was your last tetanus shot?'

'Ah!' Eddie let out a shriek. 'A shot! Let's get her!' He brought his face down close to mine. 'The syringe they use is only six inches long. You'll never feel a thing!'

I cringed, and he laughed his drunken laugh.

'Can you stand on it?' Coach said.

He and Eddie each took an arm and got me to my feet. When I brought my heel down it was tender, but nothing like before.

'You'll probably be okay, but no more running today, hon. Why don't you go take a shower, and then we'll see that you get home.'

'Come on, Janice.' Eddie scooped me up into his arms, amid a chorus of whoops.

'Put me down,' I said through my teeth.

He grinned at the fans and took off towards the school.

'Mañana!' he called over his shoulder.

'McBee, I want you back out here in five.'

'Si, señor! Five hours.'

'Minutes, McBee!'

'Okay, okay — but on my way back I'm gonna stop at the —'

'I know, I know. You've taken out a mortgage on the john. Five minutes!'

I punched Eddie's arm. 'Put me down,' I said.

'No way. You're an invalid.'

'Put me down!'

But of course he didn't. He was having too much fun jiggling me up and down and offering me to passers-by.

'I give you this girl real cheap, man,' he said to a sophomore going by with a trombone case.

The kid just stared at him.

I gave it up and tried to hang on. I hated to admit it, but his arms felt wonderful around me. Even so, when we got to the girls' locker room, I leaped out of them and on to my good foot.

He just grinned and waited. Naturally my charisma didn't fail me. 'I gotta go shower,' I said.

'Wait when you're done. I'll take you home.'

'You don't have to.'

'Yes, I do. Somebody has to make sure you ask your dad if you've had a tetanus shot.'

While he was still wiggling his eyebrows, I fled to the showers.

When the rest of the girls trailed in later, sweaty and still heaving hard, I was already in my jeans.

'How's your foot?' Corie said.

'Okay. I can put all my weight on it now.'

'Well, limp on over to Coach's office. He wants to talk to you. He still has your shoe, too.'

Coach Spike was all concern when I arrived, and he insisted on checking out my heel one more time. It was getting pretty embarrassing.

'I've been taking a look at your shoe,' he said — after I'd demonstrated with a promenade around the cubicle that I wasn't going to need immediate amputation. There was something about the hard look in his eyes that kicked my heartbeat into high gear.

'When did you get these?'

'Last Sunday.'

'You've worn them before.'

'Some.'

'Did you have them locked up all day?' he said.

'Yes, sir. I put them in my locker this morning before school.'

'Does anybody else know your combination?'

'No, sir.'

'You're sure?'

I nodded heavily. I knew what he was getting at. But I'd already decided while I was taking a shower that what I was thinking was not going to get out from behind the door marked 'GUTS'.

'Was anything else amiss in your locker? Things arranged differently from the way you had them?'

I shook my head.

'Have you seen anyone hanging around your locker who had no reason to be there?'

Oops. My head went down, and my hair fell protectively into two curtains. 'No, sir,' I said.

'Janice.'

I didn't look up.

'If somebody sabotaged your shoe, hon, I have to know about it. We can't have this kind of thing going on here.'

I forced myself to look at him. 'Nobody was there that shouldn't have been,' I said. 'She — everybody had a reason to be there.'

I often wondered if I subconsciously *tried* to put my foot in my mouth several times a day, or whether I was just naturally a clod.

The blunder hadn't been lost on the coach. His eyes were penetrating mine. But all he said was, 'You think about it, and if anything comes to mind — anything at all — you can let me know.' He gave my shoulder a squeeze. 'It'll just be between you and me.'

In my usual poised form, I shrugged.

'Now get out of here, would you?' he said. 'McBee's been pacing outside for the last ten minutes. He's about to wear out the floor out there.'

I looked up at the glass. Eddie was parked there, one hand on his snake-hip, grinning. I could see the happy bubbles of saliva even from where I was.

In spite of the fact that I usually tried to time my showers so I'd step out of the girls' locker room just about the time Eddie was passing, that day I'd rather have crawled through an escape tunnel, shoe under arm, than walk out of that door in Eddie's path with my face beetroot-red. But since Coach didn't offer one, I didn't have many options. Eddie almost jumped into my pocket.

'Get your stuff,' he said. 'I'll take you home.'

'In your truck?' I said.

'Nope. Only got two wheels.'

The image of the two of us trundling down Monroe Street on his bike flashed into view, and I shook my head.

'I'll let you ride in front,' he said.

'No!'

'Okay, fine.' He turned around — and flung me across his back caveman style.

I squealed in his ear. 'Put me down!'

'No. You've insulted me. Now you're going to have to take the consequences. Do you have all your stuff?'

'Stop it!'

But I might as well have been screaming instructions to a deaf-mute. He carried me on his back — all the way to my house. I'm sure half the little old ladies on Main hobbled to their phones and called the police to report an abduction. I quit screaming at the corner of Monroe and started pounding his chest.

'Oh. You want to go faster. What do you think I am, woman?'

But he shifted into a canter and started me shrieking again. I quit when I saw Suzanne crossing our courtyard, but it was too late. She'd already stopped, open-mouthed, to stare. She immediately became hysterical when Eddie dumped me unceremoniously on the grass and dusted off his hands.

'It was a tough job,' he said to her, 'but somebody had to do it.' He stuck out his hand. 'Eddie McBee.'

'Suzanne St Claire,' she said, laughing and meeting him shake for shake.

I headed for the house.

'Are you going to get me some water?' Eddie said.

'No. I'm going to lock myself up.'

I took two more steps and I was off the ground again, this time head down, legs straight up over Eddie's shoulder. Suzanne, I could see from upside down, was doubled over.

'This is the thanks I get,' Eddie said to her.

'Put me down!'

'I lug an injured woman *seven miles*, and this is the thanks I get.'

'Put me down!'

'I'm going to hold her here until I receive proper appreciation.'

'I'll throw up!'

'Or until she throws up.'

He dumped me on the grass again. Suzanne was helpless.

'Has she had a tetanus shot?' he said to her.

'*I* don't know!'

'Find out, would you?'

He looked down where I was lying on the grass. There was no point getting up. He'd have had me back down again, anyway.

'You sure you're okay?' he said, planting his foot gently on my stomach.

'I will be when you back off!'

'I'll call you later.' He started to jog backwards. 'Gotta go or Coach'll torture me. Do you run?' he said to Suzanne.

'No.' She was still laughing almost too hard to talk. 'Man wasn't meant to run. Neither was woman. They were meant to bicycle.'

'One of *those* kind,' he said to me. He stopped to take a swig from our hose, and then he was gone.

Suzanne stared after him and then down at me. 'This is Eddie?' she said.

I nodded.

'He's crazy.'

I nodded again.

'He likes you.'

I was focusing totally on getting the leaves off the seat of my jeans, but my face smiled without my permission. 'He treats all the girls like that,' I said.

'He couldn't possibly! Nobody has that much energy. He'd kill himself.' She was looking at me curiously, taking note of the unfamiliar smile, no doubt. 'So, are you going to go for it?'

'Go for what?'

'Eddie. I mean, it's obvious to me. The ball's in your court.'

I looked at her sharply, but she was already strolling across the courtyard towards the garage. I was still looking at her when she turned around suddenly. Her face was at the tail end of changing its mind about something.

'If you want to get love,' she said, 'you're going to have to start giving it.'

Then she turned around and made for the garage again, waving her feminine fingers over her shoulder in good-bye.

Long after she'd taken off on her ten-speed, I was still sitting there, trying to put new locks on my Janice doors.

'Who asked her for her opinion?' I tried that one.

'He doesn't really like me. He's just being nice because his father's a preacher.' I gave that one a go, too.

Neither one of them worked. In fact, I had the slightly scary feeling that none of my doors had locks on them anymore.

Except the one marked 'GUTS'. That was hammered shut with industrial-sized thumbtacks.

Oh well, I decided with a contented sigh that came all the way up from my wounded heel, you can't win them all. But you can sure win some of them. Maybe.

8

'All right, Patriots, let's all get out there on Saturday and support our cross-country team in their first meet of the season. It's a home meet, folks, so be there . . .'

That's what the intercom said on Friday. On Saturday morning I decided it was a good thing it *was* a home meet. I think I would have thrown up if I'd had to ride in the car any further. I was so nervous I could have eaten my warm-up jacket.

Even though he was on call, Dad drove me, wearing his bleeper and an enormous proud grin.

Most of the other kids had ridden on the bus and were just piling out of it when we arrived at the course. None of them looked as nervous as I felt. The ones in the raspberry warm-up suits emerging from the Robert E. Lee High School bus looked even less nervous.

It was actually a perfect day for a race. Even though it was late September, it was the first time there'd been even a hint of autumn in the air. The breeze was brisk, and the sky was so blue it almost hurt your eyes. If I hadn't been so preoccupied with the fact that every one of the girls from Lee had legs going all the way up to her neck, the day and the place would have made me think of things like flags snapping in the revolutionary air.

While Dad went to introduce himself to Coach Petruso, I looked around for everybody and tried to figure out what

I was supposed to do now. Everything I'd been taught in the past three weeks might as well have been flushed down the toilet at that point.

I saw Tanya stretching and Chuck milling through the crowd of kids like he was at a fraternity party. I automatically started looking for Eddie, and jumped like a spooked cat when he came up behind me.

'Hey, Jan-Jan! You go to church. A bunch of us always like to pray before the meet. Come on.'

Pray?

I looked at him stupidly, but he had me by the wrist and was dragging me towards a set of portable bleachers before I had a chance to resist. I could feel Tanya and Chuck's eyes on all of us as we formed a little knot behind the temporary stands.

Eddie made no bones about bowing his head and carrying on a conversation with God, even with whistles blowing and people doing tendon stretches all around us. I hugged myself and turned at a slant so the casual observer passing by would be hard put to decide whether I was part of the group or not.

It wasn't that I didn't want to listen to Eddie pray. I'd been to the Sunday school class, and he prayed there and it was okay. But to stand out there in the middle of a bunch of gaping high school kids and do it? Out loud? Frankly it was pretty embarrassing.

I kept glancing up furtively to make sure no one was staring, and of course somebody was. Chuck had one hand on a hip, waist at a tilt, looking at me with amused derision. It was the third or fourth time in a week I'd caught him sizing me up like I was stripped, and it gave me the I-gotta-get-out-of-here's.

I turned completely back to the group and squeezed my eyes shut.

'Okay, God,' Eddie was saying, 'you know we're doing this for you. Please help us give it our best shot.'

Before he could get to the 'amen', Tanya's voice threaded through. 'If ya'll are *through* messing with your beads and holy water, Coach wants to talk to us.' She walked away in the wake of a unanimous dirty look.

We got into another semi-circle around Coach Spike, who showed no signs of anything but complete calm.

'Okay, folks,' he said, 'remember we're out here to run a sportsmanlike race and do the best job we can for the team and for the school. Stay calm. Stay loose. Concentrate.' He glanced over at Eddie. 'Anything you want to say to your team, Cap'n?'

I steeled myself for another prayer. Eddie, however, leaned forward and narrowed his eyes. 'Sweet Mother of Jefferson Davis,' he said through his teeth, 'let's get out there and kick some tail.'

I headed towards the starting line, but it became obvious at once that that was not the end of the preliminaries. A general hug-in commenced, which there was no getting out of. I was squeezed by just about everybody on the team, including the Wookie who put a half-hearted paw around my shoulder for a millisecond.

I wasn't the only one who didn't love that particular part of the opening ceremonies. 'Keep your preacher's hands off me, McBee,' I heard Tanya say. But when I looked — couldn't help it — I caught the flicker of a smile playing at the corners of her mouth as Eddie grabbed her up against him anyway.

Coach tooted his whistle before Eddie got to me. By then, it was time for business.

Eddie went into coach-mode as he walked me towards the start of the course.

'Okay, do you see this chick with the long dark hair tied back with the red rubber band?'

I nodded as said girl passed us, taking one stride to my three.

'Okay, she's the leader for Lee High. She's your biggest contender.' He jerked his head towards the girl who followed her. 'See that chickie with the brown hair — huh, she's got a red rubber band, too. She's your other big competition.'

I pumped my head up and down again, but my thoughts were starting to churn like a garbage disposal. Sweet mother of Jefferson Davis. They looked exactly alike. In fact, everyone on the team looked exactly alike.

'Now,' Eddie went on, 'those are the two that are going to be on Tanya like the stink on a piece of bad cheese. Keep them in your sight, but don't try to stay up with them until at least mile two. You remember the rest.'

As I moved away from him towards the starting line, I wouldn't have been surprised if, like some Dallas Cowboys football jock, he'd patted me on the backside.

By that time, my palms were sparkling with sweat and if I'd had just one more swig of water, I could have got the fibre-glass insulation out of my mouth. But as I lined up with the thirteen other girls, Tanya a few steps ahead of me, Tess beside me, Corie and the rest of the girls behind me, something dawned on me: for the moment at least, I was just like them. We all had on blue silky shorts and blue and white striped tank tops that boasted MADISON on the back. We all had the same destination, and we were all going to get there pretty much the same way. That wasn't a feeling I could say I'd ever had before.

'Hey,' somebody whispered from behind me. 'Janice! Good luck!'

I turned around to see Corie, dimples going just like always.

'I knew you for two months before I ever knew you had a dimple in your right cheek,' Jack had always said to me. I took a deep breath.

'You too,' I said. 'Good luck all of ya'll.' And then I matched her dimple for dimple.

Almost like it was coming out of a dream, the gun went off, and I left my case of nerves at the starting line. Now all I had on me was Eddie's strategy. Just as he'd said she would, Tanya scrambled away from the starting line as if a whole *band* of Christians were after her, and the two pairs of brunette ponytails and raspberry-coloured shorts were right on her heels, leaving me and the rest of the pack to scrap for the number four position.

I tried to concentrate on staying relaxed and remembering what Eddie told me: 'Look around a little bit and stay loose.'

The course really was beautiful. The top branches of the trees on either side met over our heads, forming a golden, shimmering tunnel for us to run through. The sun splattered in in spots, carrying me from pools of shade to puddles of sunlight. I could almost hear my feet splashing in them.

With a jolt, I heard Tony's voice yelling out the mile splits from the sidelines. I didn't hear what he said to Tanya, but I heard 7-oh when Tess and I went by. Tanya must be setting a 6 point 5 pace. It was only Eddie's voice pounding on my eardrum, 'don't pick up your speed until at least mile 2 — don't pass the major contenders until 2 point 5,' that made me hold myself back. I wanted to go for it.

At the next mile marker, as we were headed back the way we'd come, Lance yelled, 'thirteen point four' to Tanya and 'fourteen' to me. Right on cue, she was slowing down, and it was time for me to make my move.

I left Tess and caught up with the brunette who was in the number three place. Her legs were longer than mine, but she wasn't using them to their full extent. I hoped she didn't miraculously learn how in the next half-mile.

I watched ahead of me as the number two girl slid by Tanya, who instantly seemed to take a step backwards. Her shoulders sagged like somebody had poked the air out of her.

I dug in a little and passed the girl running next to me, and then just as easily passed Tanya.

She snapped up like a spring and she was right on my heels. She was gasping for air so desperately it was hard to distinguish words from half-sobs, but I know I heard her say, 'You little tramp!'

Eddie hadn't told me she'd do that.

The last fifty yards of the course was an uphill climb — the same hill we'd flown down at the beginning of the course. Pretending Eddie was at my elbow giving me instructions, I planted my eyes on the top of the hill, shortened my stride, and ploughed up. Chugging my arms almost to my ears, I pulled past Lee's number one long-legged girl, who was leaning back and struggling.

I could see Coach Spike out of the corner of my eye on the right, all six foot four of him stretched up like an exclamation mark — and to my left, a blur of blue male jogging suits.

They got closer and closer — until a faraway-sounding cheer brought me over the finish line alone.

Everything that happened from there was like one big blue blur that frankly I'd relive anytime without so much as a by your leave.

People told me I was 'awesome' and that I *had* 'kicked some tail'. Coach called out my winning time, and Tanya's second-place winning time, and our team's winning score — 22 to Lee's 34. Dad left on a call, looking like I'd just won an Olympic gold medal, for Pete's sake, and I even got to help Corie do Eddie's mile split. He seemed totally unaware that we were even there as he flowed by towards his first place, but I knew, like the veteran I now was, that he knew everything that was going on: how fast he was moving, who was behind him, where he was headed, and how soon he was going to get there — matching the county record, but not beating it.

I had to ride the bus back with the team, and if the driver had taken us directly to the Happy Valley Institute for the Certified Insane, I wouldn't have blamed him.

The kids pounded out cheers on the backs of the seats. They leaned out the windows screaming victory calls to passers-by who neither knew Madison had a cross-country team nor cared. They sang and did motions to bizarre songs, led by Eddie, of course. And I — squeezed into a seat beside Dixie — pounded, screamed, and sang too.

At one point, Eddie tried to get me to 'give a syllable or two for my adoring fans' and I came out with 'um' and 'uh' while everybody on the bus — *sans* Tanya — chanted 'First place! First place!'

Then Tony stood up on the seat, ignoring Coach's dry command from the back to 'park it', and shouted, 'We had a victory today, ya'll. What does that mean?'

'A party at Poe's!'

'What time?'

'Eight o'clock!'

' 'Til when?'

' 'Til whenever!'

' 'Til midnight,' Coach said calmly.

When we pulled into the school parking lot, Eddie stood at the bottom of the steps helping people down and giving them final hugs.

'You got a ride to the party?' he said to me while he was hugging on Dixie.

'I don't know if I'm —'

'I'm picking you up at seven forty-five. In my truck.'

He gave Dixie one last squeeze. 'Dix-ee! Awesome race!'

Dix-ee had come in dead-last. The boy was terminally nice. And I didn't care whether every single girl in Virginia had a share in him — at that moment I threw away the key to the Eddie Door. I was hooked.

Funny how that feeling was always haunted by a shadow, though. As I headed towards the locker room, the warmth of a body oozed up to my right. 'You are one good-looking little thing when you run,' someone said between his teeth.

My head snapped up and I met Chuck square in the nostrils. Before I could reply, even on the outside chance that I could have thought of anything to say, Tanya sailed up beside him and he was off with her like a Siamese twin.

Nope. I was feeling too good to take a chance. I skipped the locker room and walked straight home — get this — singing all the way.

9

I took our courtyard, the front steps, and the inside stairs
doing 'Chariots of Fire' in off-key la's, na's and da's. When
I got to my bedroom door, Suzanne stepped out of the
bathroom in a huge Minnie Mouse T-shirt, wearing five
dots of liquid make-up and an amused expression on her
face.

'Ya'll won,' she guessed.

'Yup,' I said.

'I'm impressed.'

My face wouldn't stop smiling, and my mouth was on
automatic pilot. 'I took a first place.'

She shrieked. 'Are you serious? That's great!' She was
still the only person I knew who could take a full five seconds to say the word *great*, but I didn't take the time to mark
it on my list of things to hold against her. Matter of fact,
my moment of glory was making me feel so magnanimous,
I said, 'Are you going somewhere?'

'To dinner with an old friend. What about you? You look
like you're headed in about ten different directions.'

By that time she had ducked back into the bathroom
and was transforming the dots into a layer of flawless skin.
I watched in fascination in spite of myself.

'I'm going to a party,' I said.

She lifted an eyebrow.

'With Eddie.'

She lifted the other one. 'Told you so,' she said.

'Well — he's picking me up. There'll probably be forty
million other kids along with him.'

'You're one in forty million easy,' she said.

I continued to watch her create eyelashes with a mascara

brush.

'I guess you need the bathroom. I'll be done in a sec. I do have a tendency to take the thing over.' Her voice trailed off, and abruptly she stuck the brush back in the tub and faced me, hand on hips. 'You are so darlin',' she said. 'With a little bit of this stuff, we could sure make the most of what you've got going for you.'

The woman was not stupid. She knew that, in the mood I was in, she could've suggested parading down Monroe Street in our birthday suits and I'd have gone along with it. And I have to admit, the next half-hour was probably the most fun I'd ever spent.

While I was in the shower, she assembled an arsenal of bottles and tubes. Once I was into a bathrobe and perched on top of the toilet seat, she twisted my hair into a clip on top of my head, removed, I'm sure, three layers of skin from my face with some kind of stuff on a cotton ball, and then went to work.

I watched in a hand mirror as spots disappeared under liquid make-up, cheekbones actually emerged at the end of a blush brush, and my eyes tripled their size with the magic of pale blue eye-shadow and a coat of mascara. Suzanne let me put the lip gloss on, and, after only two bad attempts, I was looking in the mirror at a stranger. She clucked like she'd just given birth.

'Now you just slip into some cute lil' old outfit,' she said, going after my left eyelid one more time with a cotton swab, 'and it won't matter if there are *sixty* million other kids with Eddie.'

I looked at her doubtfully. '"Cute little old outfit"?' I said.

I think she knew what I meant. 'Are you up for some more help?' she said.

I was.

Ten minutes later I was standing in front of the full-length mirror in her room, still staring open-mouthed at the reflection of myself in a mini-dress while Suzanne finished slinging a pink belt around my hips. 'Now with this tank top underneath,' she said, adjusting my neckline, 'you can just kind of slide this off the shoulders like this —'

It was incredible. Doors I hadn't even known were in me were popping open like there was an earthquake going. One of them, the one marked 'Feminine Instincts', jarred open, and without knowing why, I scooped my hair on to the top of my head.

Suzanne met my gaze in the mirror. 'Mmmm-hmmm. I was thinking the same thing,' she said.

'What?'

'You were considering cutting your hair?' she said.

I hadn't been, but the idea appealed to me.

'Let's do it,' I said.

'Seriously? Are you sure?'

I almost laughed out loud. From the look on her face, it was obvious she'd been wanting to come after me with the scissors ever since she'd moved in. But now that it was *my* idea —

I grinned at her. 'Let's do it,' I said again.

She didn't give me a chance to change my mind. I was back on the toilet seat wrapped in a sheet before I could draw the next breath. When she was finished, I absolutely gaped into the medicine chest mirror.

She'd cut it a little longer than chin length, with a fringe that slanted across my forehead. After a couple of twists of the wrist with the curling iron, it was shiny and bouncy and curvy — and short. I actually looked normal.

'Sweet Mother of Jefferson Davis,' I said.

Suzanne stopped sweeping up remnants off the bathroom floor. 'I just had an awful thought,' she said. 'What is your Dad going to say?'

I had an even worse one. I hadn't even asked him if I could go out. Matter of fact, I didn't even know what time to come home. The subject had never come up before.

Fortunately, nobody at University Hospital was having a kidney transplant just then, and I managed to get him on the phone. He'd obviously been regaling everybody in the operating suite with reports of my final time from the race, because he immediately started reviewing it with me like I'd never heard it before.

I waited patiently for as long as I could — approximately seven seconds — and then burst out with, 'Dad, I'm going out with Eddie — and some kids. Can I — what time — ?'

He switched from proud to ecstatic. 'Darlin', that's wonderful! Of *course* go, and you just have the *best* time, and now don't worry about when to come in — I mean you use your own judgment. Tell Suzy not to even wait up for you.'

'She won't be here.'

His ecstasy dissolved into panic. I think fathers are born knowing how to over-react.

'I don't want you coming home alone to that house at night,' he said.

'It's —'

'Where is Suzy going?'

That seemed like an irrelevant question, considering my entire social future was on the line. I reached for some hair to chew, and came up with air.

The monologue continued. 'How about asking Eddie to come in and stay with you until she gets home? He wouldn't mind that, would you think?'

I had a life-size picture of me asking Eddie to escort me in while the Madison High cross-country team waited in the truck, and I started to crumple.

'He's comin'!' Suzanne yelled from my window. 'He does drive green used parts, doesn't he?'

It was my turn to panic. 'Okay, Dad,' I said.

'Just have yourself a ball,' he said.

If I hadn't been so nervous, I would've stopped and imagined him hanging up and turning to the nearest defenceless X-ray technician, saying, 'My daughter is going *out* — with *friends* — to a *party!*'

As it was, though, I was having a breakdown. 'What if I spit on him when I talk or something?' I wailed as Suzanne steered me towards the stairs.

'Sugar, it'll be better than what I do on a first date, which is yak the poor boy to tears. You'll be precious.'

I took one last look at her, and ripped the Suzanne Door completely off its hinges. It just wasn't worth it, trying to hate her any more.

Eddie was loping across the courtyard to meet me when I emerged from the front door. He stopped in his tracks like somebody'd shot him from behind, and all elasticity left his face.

'Jan?' he said — as if I could have been anybody but.

He circled me, pigeon-style, then crossed his arms and nodded. 'Lance,' he yelled, still looking at me.

Lance's Wookie body popped out through the open window of the passenger side.

'You're ridin' in the back, Lance,' Eddie called to him.

As I'd known — well, there weren't forty *million* kids in the back of the pick-up, but close to it. They were all hysterical, but most of them got bug-eyed when they saw me.

Tony yelled, 'Hey, what did you do to your hair?' but Lance jabbed him in the ribs and said, 'Shut up, idiot. It looks hot.'

I went for the tailgate, but Eddie pulled me on to the cab and planted me in the seat next to him. 'You aren't riding in the back looking like that,' he said. His Virginia accent was thicker than honey.

I'd been to Poe's before when Dad and I had first moved in, before we'd found either the grocery store or our toaster oven. During the summer it had been a quiet, cosy little café where you could order a submarine sandwich with a name like The Thomas Jefferson Special and sit in a dark corner for hours, not caring that Jefferson had never had cold cuts in his life. Not so that night. Poe's was the hang-out for every student in three counties.

A couple of kids had got there early and reserved a table the size of a boxing ring. Chuck was at one corner of it, sulking about something, and Tanya was at another with some friends, flipping her hair around at a nearby group of pre-med. students. Even though I'd seen her with friends at the mall last summer, it startled me to realize she actually had some — people who liked her, people she might be decent to once in a while. It *didn't* surprise me, though, that they were all the type who wore two-hundred dollar sweaters and always looked like something in the room smelled terrible.

From the minute we arrived, Eddie was everywhere at once, giving Corie a piggyback ride around the table, braiding Tess's hair, and doing three-quarters of a barber-shop quartet with Tony and Lance that could set a person's teeth on edge.

Every few minutes he would dart over to where I was sitting and do something weird. He put two straws in a tanker-sized Coke, ordered me to man one of them, and made Dixie time us while we drank it. Eleven point five seconds. Later he came back to see if I wanted to have the burp contest he insisted always followed a Coke-drinking race. I passed on that one, but my face hurt from laughing.

In the course of the evening, I ate two Mondo Madison Burgers and drank at least one of the huge bottles of Coke that kept appearing on the table. Only Eddie could put away more. He drained two bottles single-mouthedly, griping all the while because Poe's didn't serve chocolate milk. I was leaned back in a chair patting my now-rounded stomach when Coach Spike dropped by.

Everybody looked at their watches at the same time.

'It's not twelve o'clock yet, Coach,' Tony said, bouncing from one foot to the other. The kid always looked as if he had to use the cloakroom desperately. I think Eddie went in his place most of the time.

'I just stopped by to see how you clowns were doing,' he said genially. 'I'm not checking up on you.'

He rested on the arm of the chair I was in. 'How's our champ?' he said.

I smiled up at him.

'Glad you joined the team now?'

'Glad I talked her into it?' Eddie said over our shoulders.

'Glad I talked *you* into talking *her* into it?' Coach said mildly.

99

'What do you mean talked *me* into it? *I* was the one who told you she ran like a gazelle.'

'And I was the one who told you to stay on her until she came out.'

For a second I think they forgot I was there. I expected the conversation to turn to, 'I'll see your Janice and raise you one Tanya' or something. Why people always ended up talking about me like I wasn't there was a thing I could never figure out.

Fortunately, Coach changed the subject.

'Where's Tanya?' he said.

'She split a while back,' Eddie told him.

'Too bad. I wanted to tell her she ran a heck of a race today. That's the best I've ever seen her run. We owe that to you.'

He was looking at me, but I still said, 'Me?'

'She always thinks she's burned out about three-quarters of the way through the race, but right when she hit that point today and sagged, you glided by her — and she got motivated.'

That explained how she'd managed to come in second when the last time I'd seen her she was flailing away behind the Lee girl in fourth place.

'Hey, Coach, look at this! Want a bite?'

Lance and another guy were holding up a six-foot-long meatball sandwich. Coach groaned and manoeuvred his long form around the table.

'Excuse me,' Eddie said to me. 'I'm gonna go check out the graffiti.'

As he headed off towards the cloakroom, I became immediately aware of a presence at my right elbow. That's what Chuck was, I'd decided. A presence. The guy was starting to give me the creeps.

'Are you and McBee a thing?' he said, sitting down in the chair next to me.

'No,' I said, although I wasn't convinced I knew what a 'thing' was.

'Good,' he said. 'That haircut's all right. It looks good.'

'Thanks,' I said, and started performing microsurgery on a straw with my fingernail.

'I see he was over here hobnobbing with the coach again.'

I shrugged.

'If Petruso spent half as much time with anybody else as he does him, we'd have a decent team.'

I didn't ask how much more decent you could get than first place.

'He might as well just hand McBee the scholarship and get it over with. I'd quit — except I know sooner or later he's gonna get out there and choke on his own —'

I made a frenzied lunge for a Coke bottle, knocking over somebody's half-empty Seven-Up in the process. Chuck caught it just in time.

'Was it something I said?' he asked, leering at me.

No, it was something you reeked, I thought. I knew I must have been visibly squirming in the chair.

'Have you got a ticket for that seat?'

If I hadn't turned around to look, I don't think I'd have recognized Eddie's voice. All the honey had been squeezed out of it.

Chuck stood up and looked down at me, eyes and mouth both in lecherous slits. 'Just keeping it warm,' he said. And then he walked out of the place.

'Time for a joint,' Eddie said. 'He's been unstoned for too long now. Has to have been at least two hours.'

He tried a laugh, but his eyes were still boring holes in the door. He looked pale and gaunt and hard. I figured it was as good a time as any for me to ask him to take me home and baby-sit me, as long as he was in a rejecting mood.

It amazed me that I got it out. It amazed me even more that he said, 'Let's go. I'll come back for these guys.'

By the time we climbed into the front seat of his truck, he was grinning again, and, tossing his arm lazily across the back of the seat, he cruised us into what he called 'the long cut' to my house.

'You had fun,' he said to me.

'I did. You guys are crazy.'

'*We're* crazy? Who pulled all the pepperonis off the pizza and wanted to use them for poker chips?'

'You did!'

'Oh. Well — who used Lisa's crusts for a moustache, huh?'

'*You* did!'

'Did I do all that stuff — really?'

'You did more.'

He chuckled and craned his face up towards the moon that was eavesdropping through the windscreen.

'Isn't God great?' he said.

God. How did he get into the conversation?

'You know what I've found out? You know why I do all that weirdo stuff all the time?'

I didn't have a clue.

'Because I *know* — for a fact — that if you believe in him, and set yourself on pleasing him, you've got it made. You can just be happy. Nothing bad is ever gonna happen to you.'

I stared at him as he pulled the truck up to the kerb in front of my house. Up until then, I think I'd believed every word that had come out of his mouth since the day I'd met him — and that had been a *lot* of words. But this — this was a little hard to swallow. Nothing could be as simple as that.

'What's the matter?' he said.

I could feel my face gaining about ten degrees, and, darn that Suzanne, I didn't have any hair to cover it.

'I never thought of it that way,' I said.

He turned the ignition off and settled back against his door. 'How *do* you think of it?'

'I don't know,' I said. Of course, I did know. God was Up There, I was down here. Once a week I went to church, but I never considered that it might guarantee me anything. God and I, like most people and I, didn't talk much.

But apparently 'I don't know' was a good enough explanation for the moment, because without warning, Eddie leaned towards me.

'You know what?' he said. 'I really want to hug you.'

My body functions went into code blue.

'But I know the minute I try, I'll get "No! No! Get away! Don't touch me!"' He was slapping his hands and squealing like a first soprano.

I spluttered, 'I don't say that!'

'Your mouth doesn't say it, but your eyes do. Your whole body does!'

'It does not!'

'Come here, then. Come *here*.'

He pulled my arms around his neck and held on to me, face buried next to my hair. For a magic minute — possibly two — all I knew was the clean smell of his shirt and the fruity odour of his breath and the warm strong feel of his leanness next to mine. For a magic minute — possibly two — I was Kylie Minogue, or at least some gorgeous facsimile thereof.

The minute ended, however, when, with the kind of timing my life is famous for, a car squealed up to the kerb, its high beams putting Eddie and me squarely in a spotlight.

We both gaped and blinked as the passenger door was flung open and a high-heeled foot groped for the kerb. It belonged to Suzanne, who, as soon as she could extricate herself from the bucket seat, slammed the door behind her and stomped stiff-legged across the yard. The car fish-tailed back into the street with an angry roar from the exhaust.

Eddie and I looked at each other blankly.

'What was that?' he said.

'Suzanne and her date.'

'Nice couple.'

'Oh — this is really gross!'

Suzanne's normally soft southern belle voice screeched from the porch like a fingernail on a blackboard.

'This is *dis*-gustin'!'

Eddie scrambled out of the truck with me right behind him. Suzanne jumped a foot straight up when she saw us, and then leaned against the doorknob, green-faced.

'Don't come any closer unless you have a strong stomach,' she said.

We didn't have to be told. As soon as the stench of rotten eggs and other unidentifiable garbage burned my nostrils, I backed up, gagging.

'Oh, gross!' Eddie plastered a hand over his mouth and retreated with me. The three of us stood staring down at a hefty-sized stack of several-days-old food waste, some of it teeming with white worms that looked almost fluorescent under the porch light. I could feel my face going chartreuse.

'Somebody loves us,' Suzanne said.

Eddie nodded grimly. 'Three guesses who.'

'If I hadn't been with him all evenin' I'd say it was my date.' Suzanne glanced ruefully down the street.

'Seemed like a nice guy,' said Eddie.

'Honey, he's a first-class jerk.'

As they chattered on, as only the two of them could do at a time like this, my mind did a double-time rewind. Eddie thought it was Chuck. Frankly, I thought it was Tanya. But either way, I'd just as soon leave it alone. And the way Eddie felt about Chuck, whether he'd admit it or not, the two of them didn't need to come face to face over it either. We were talking enough demerits to make both of them archive material.

'What are we gon' do about this, young'uns?' Suzanne said.

'Clean it up,' I said.

Eddie shook his head. 'I'd call the cops.'

I shook mine too.

'It's not a bad idea,' Suzanne said. 'After the incident with the back door, and then that fool who keeps hanging around here at all hours —'

Eddie looked at me sharply. 'I didn't know about all that.'

But I was already on my way to the garage. 'I'm going to get the wheelbarrow and a shovel and we'll get rid of this stuff. No police.'

I could feel them looking at my back like I'd switched identities.

'Jan, you gotta tell somebody.'

'And no Dad, either,' I hurled over my shoulder for Suzanne's benefit.

Eddie was practically crawling up my calves. 'If this has been going on for a while, ya'll oughta do somethin' about it.'

I stopped and turned around. 'We already have,' I said.

'That's what I'm supposedly here for,' Suzanne said. 'Fat lot of good I'm doing.'

'It's no big deal,' I said. 'Dad will just get hysterical. We can handle it.'

Eddie shook his mop. 'Nobody should get away with this, especially if it's who I think it is.'

'I don't want my dad upset.'

They looked at each other and then at me.

'Get the shovels,' Suzanne said. 'I'll help.'

'I'll keep my mouth shut,' Eddie said an hour later when the three of us were gathered at our kitchen bar with a pot of Suzanne's 'spiked' tea. He was on his fourth tumbler of iced water. 'But you two need a bodyguard.'

'You're it until the doctor comes home,' Suzanne said.

'I'll be it anytime you want me.'

I snorted. 'Some bodyguard. You left ten people stranded at Poe's tonight.'

'They'll live.' His face eased into a grin. 'Besides, I called while you guys were showering and told 'em they were on their own. Coach probably ended up carting them all.'

'You really can go home and shower,' I said. 'We'll be fine. Besides, you smell like old banana skins.'

'Nope. Can't leave you unprotected. A rotten cantaloupe could come flying through that window at any minute.'

'Sometimes Dad doesn't get in 'til 1.00 or 2.00.'

'No problem.' Eddie unwound his long legs from the stool and stretched out on the linoleum in the kitchen. We saw his feet rise slowly from the other side of the counter.

Suzanne lifted an amused eyebrow at me and then got up. 'Okay, stay all night if you want,' she said. 'I've got to turn in. An evenin' with a man who tries not to take "no" for an answer had me worn out before I even *saw* that little present on the front porch.' She went towards the hall, feigning a yawn. 'Love ya'll. Call me if you need me.' She gave me a thumbs-up over her shoulder and disappeared.

'Hey, Jan-Jan, can you do this?' Eddie called from the floor.

I leaned over the counter. He was wound up in a complete coil, knees touching his shoulders, head stuck out between his legs, teeth shining.

I shook my head and let out a laugh. Doors were opening like nobody's business. Taking my place on the tile beside him, I hoped I'd remember to throw away all the keys the next chance I got.

10

Eddie was true to his word, and for the next three weeks, every time Dad was on call he'd show up at our door at dusk with enough books under his arm for three kids, spread them out on our dining-room table, and study until 10.30, when he would crash on our couch until Dad got home. The boy followed training rules like there was a guillotine over his head.

Suzanne made herself scarce, except when she was tempting us with left-overs. It had become a regular routine: she cooked the 'dinnahs' and I cleaned up. I was eating things I couldn't even pronounce, and I know my taste buds thought they'd died and gone to heaven. If Dad and I didn't polish something off at the dinner table, Eddie got it for a snack, and he devoured it like a starving refugee. The beast never gained an ounce, either. In fact, he just seemed to get skinnier and skinnier.

Me — I *didn't* make myself scarce. I studied at the dining-room table too, in case Eddie might want to propose marriage or something. I still hadn't figured out if we were a 'thing'. I definitely made myself visible in the halls (seeing how I had his timetable memorized) and made sure I was the first one out of the shower after track practice every day so I'd be available to hold the stopwatch while he and Coach worked out. He didn't seek me out, as far as I could tell, but he always had a big ol' hangin' grin ready when he saw me. One thing was sure — I was freeze-dried, fat-fried, head-over-heels crazy about the boy. And I was just as sure he didn't even know it.

Our conversations certainly didn't tend towards the romantic, although Eddie told me as much about himself as I'm sure the average wife knows about her husband. But I hung on every word like it was a sweet nothing being whispered in my ear.

'I have to get a scholarship or college is out for me,' he told me one night. 'My dad's a great preacher, but he doesn't make enough to shout about. Both my brothers had to win grants and work to get through. Bobby'll probably be paying back student loans until *his* kids are in college. It's gonna have to be a track scholarship, too. I mean my grades are okay, but I'm no brain.' He grinned a slobbery grin at me. 'Not like some people I know.'

I said nothing, naturally.

'I reckon I could go to community college, but that isn't gonna do, Jan-Jan. I've got my eye on Furman. They've got a track programme there —'

He gave one of his whoops.

'You'll get a scholarship,' I said. 'You're a great runner.'

'But I'm not a cert. I'm going to have to do something like break a county record. And there's competition.'

'Who?'

'In the county — Albemarle's got a couple of really fine runners. Slade's being considered, I think. He needs it, too. He likes to make people think he's in Tanya's parents' tax bracket, but his folks aren't any better off than we are.'

My eyes were widening, not only because as far as I was

concerned Chuck Slade was just a hot-dogger, or because he'd definitely had me fooled in the financial department, but because a shadow was passing over Eddie's face and twisting his features into an expression I would've thought was hatred if I'd seen it on anyone else.

'You can't stand him, can you?' I said.

Immediately the shadow took off, and Eddie was looking at me defensively.

'I don't judge anyone.'

'I know, but —'

'He's got his problems. But I don't hate him. That's wrong.'

Methinks the preacher's son protests too much, I thought. But I just nodded. The good Lord notwithstanding, Eddie could curl his upper lip with the best of us.

I even loved that about him.

The only night we didn't use his bodyguard services was the Friday we had off from school for a teacher's workday. Suzanne cut classes and took me to Richmond with her, where I proceeded to spend half my stashed-away clothes allowance on a re-do of my room. After getting a good look at it the night of the party at Poe's, she'd commented to me that she — ahem — 'liked what I'd done with it'. Once you let Suzanne get started she wasn't too subtle.

Dad was baffled when he saw what we came up with. He didn't say so, of course, but I know he expected to see Colonial Period lamps and Martha Washington curtains and at least a pewter candlestick holder or two. He took one look at the brown mini-blinds and the beige wallpaper with the big-eyed tiger up in the corner over my bed, and gazed at me like I'd just announced I was going to pierce my ears in four places. It was similar to the look he'd given me the first time he saw my haircut.

'It's different,' he said.

'You don't like it?'

'Oh, I don't have a problem with it, I just — if *you* like it, darlin' —'

He left the room — in search of the Settlers, I'm sure. It

was a good thing he and Suzanne had started going antique hunting on Sunday afternoons. That satisfied his urge to make the whole house look like the set of *1776*.

The rest of the time, I was either running, thinking about running, or keeping my grades up so I could keep running — and that *did* make Dad happy. He'd even dropped 'darlin'' for 'my little leather lunger'. I thought it lost something in the translation, but it showed his appreciation.

Running with Eddie was, of course, the best way to go as far as I was concerned. He could pull three miles out of me even after my insides had decided they were ready to collapse. The whole time, I just kept smiling.

It was funny, though, because he'd be jacking his jaws about the 'high' he got from running and how he could feel a closeness to God. I nodded a lot, but I really didn't get it. Me, I liked the way our feet sounded crunching out the same rhythm in the gravel, and I got into the feel of my hair swinging back and forth, and the burn of the sun on the backs of my legs. Stuff like that.

We had two more track meets during those three weeks, one in Roanoke and the other in Lynchburg, and, although it seemed as natural as blinking while I was out there following our strategy and pumping my way to the finish line, I was flabbergasted both times when, as the intercom voice on Monday mornings blurted out, I 'brought in first-place honours for the Patriots'!

Tanya wasn't flabbergasted. She was furious — even though she took a second and a third — according to Coach the best times she'd ever done.

Her attitude was haunting me more and more, maybe because for the first time ever, everything else in my life was coming together. One spot always stands out more on a clear complexion.

I wrote to Jack about it one morning.

> *She really scares me, and so does her boy-*
> *friend. He takes a different approach, of course. She*
> *says things like 'You wait until we meet Albemarle*

109

County. Those girls'll rub your nose in the dirt.' He
just slithers out of shadows and ogles me like
I'm auditioning for a porno film. About three times
now I've been just standing at my locker and suddenly
felt this breath right at my earlobe. I can't understand
what he's saying — partly because my whole body
freezes, including my eardrums, and partly because he
talks like he's afraid moving his lips will mess
up his hair. All I can catch is words like 'Baby',
'nice' and 'let me know'. I don't even want to
guess what the words in between are.

I've never done anything to either one of them,
but they both hate me, and it seems like they're
doing everything they can to get me off the track team.
But then when I think that, Jack, I wonder
if I'm not just being paranoid. I mean, Tanya treats
just about everybody like they're dirt. She already has
three demerits in track — one for deliberately cutting
Corie off on the sprints and two for, shall we
say, alluding to Dixie's weight problems in untactful
terms. Okay, she called her Jabba the Hutt —
in front of Coach.

And I am trying a new approach. Eddie says
if you just believe in God and do what he wants you
to do in your life, nothing bad will happen to you.
I wasn't too sure about that at first, but I decided to
give it a try and ever since, I mean, things have been
going better. So maybe God isn't going to let Tanya
and Chuck mess everything up.

'All right, Patriots,' the squawk box said. 'Go directly to
your second period class. No first period today. Have a great
day.'

I scribbled my signature at the end of the page.

Out in the hall, on the way to Fruff's freshman science
class, somebody wheezed 'Janice' from behind me. I turned
around to see Dixie chugging up to me from the stairwell,
red in the face and gasping. It blew me away that she could

run track at all, but I sure had to give her credit for trying.

'Has anybody talked to you yet?' she said.

Yes, I thought, a few people have talked to me in this lifetime, miracle of miracles. But I shook my head. 'About what?'

'Tanya and What's-His-Name.'

'Chuck?'

'Yeah.' She stopped to take an asthmatic breath. 'There's some stuff going around — about you and Eddie being out all night — or something. Everybody thinks him and her are spreading it.' Her eyebrows were crocheted together in concern. 'I think Coach knows about it — at least I saw him talking to Eddie, and they weren't smiling.'

She patted her chest and waited for me to answer. My brain was too busy doing battle with itself to tell me what to say, and luckily the bell rang.

'Thanks,' I said, walking backwards. But I was anything but grateful. Paranoia or no paranoia — this did not sound good.

Fruff's ninth-graders were already at work, and Lincoln was sitting in the back of the room drumming his fingers on his desk. With a sinking feeling I remembered I was supposed to help him with his oral report that day. Mrs Fruff had turned him over to me almost completely, saying I was the best thing that could happen to him — besides maybe a daily bath and some jeans that didn't hang off his derrière like a deflated balloon. I spent at least two class periods a week helping him read through the assignments. It wasn't easy concentrating on scientific methods with a pint-sized Eddie Murphy.

'No,' he said to me when I got back to his seat.

'No what? I haven't even said anything yet!'

'I don't know nothin' about no chemical reactions, and I ain't gonna stand up in front of the classroom and give no report.'

'Too bad. I had an idea for you — but if you're not going to do it —'

He rolled his big brown eyes up at me. 'What is it?'

'These,' I said, pointing to the rectangular bulge in his T-shirt pocket.

He pawed protectively at the hidden pack of Marlboros, and his eyes narrowed to slits.

'You crazy.'

'Smoking makes a chemical reaction.'

He slung his arms over the back of the chair and looked off in the other direction. 'I still gotta stand up in fronta a bunch of *people*. I don't like that.'

'Neither do I,' I said, more to myself than to him. And in my case, it didn't even need to be a 'bunch' of people.

He was looking at me sideways.

'Do it and I won't tell Fruff I've been helping you read all the chapters,' I said.

'Who gives a —'

'You do,' I said quickly.

He glared at me.

Fruff gave her approval for the report, although not without insisting on keeping Lincoln's visual aids in her desk. But that didn't keep him from following me out of the classroom and down the hall when the bell rang.

It was lunchtime by then, and I was headed outside. I still couldn't bring myself to go into the cafeteria, plop myself down at Eddie's table and say, 'Hi, gang. Here I am!' Besides, Suzanne's left-overs beat anything the school lunch menu had to offer.

Lincoln was right on my trail all the way, and he sat down on the step above me as if he'd been invited.

'Why you eat out here, girl?' he said.

'I like to be alone,' I said pointedly, unwrapping a crab salad sandwich.

He just grinned with his two rows of teeth clenched together.

'You pretty strange, you know that?'

'I know. You tell me four times a day. Is that your lunch?'

He'd produced a greasy brown paper bag from under his jeans jacket and was emptying out two Marathon bars,

112

a box of Sweet Tarts, and three tremendous chews. One of the latter went into his mouth, creating a squirrel-like bulge.

'You want some?' he said, almost unintelligibly.

'No thanks.'

'Why not?'

'Can't. Training rules.'

'You trainin' not to eat candy?'

'No. Cross-country track.'

'What for?'

''Cause I like it.'

'That is crazy, girl,' he said with authority.

'And that —' I thumped his bulbous cheek '— is a chemical reaction.'

But even that didn't get rid of him. He stayed, sucking on his chew and telling me I was the weirdest white chick he ever met. Somehow I knew he was going to become a daily fixture.

The rest of the school day, I didn't hear anything more about my supposedly having been out all night with Eddie, and by the time I got to the gym area for track practice, I'd decided it was all a figment of Dixie's imagination. That's when Coach Spike stuck his head out of his office and said, 'Would you join us, please?'

My insides dissolved.

Eddie was leaning on the office wall, one foot propped up against it. He looked skinny and chalky, and he was chewing at the chapping on his upper lip. I could see the muscles in his face twitching.

I'd never been in trouble in school. It just doesn't happen to you when you make straight A's and never open your mouth. But I recognized this scene as 'in trouble'. Maybe it was the way Tanya and Chuck were sitting bolt upright in two chairs in front of Coach's desk, looking like Hot Lips and Major Burns filing their latest complaint report. I think I swallowed the part of my heart that was beating its way up my throat.

Coach motioned for me to take his chair and positioned

113

himself on the corner of his desk. He looked down at his hands for ever. I looked at Eddie, hoping for a big ol' hangin' reassuring smile, but he looked as ashen as I felt.

'You know, folks,' Coach said finally, 'I've had about as much of this little game as I'm going to take. This is a track *team*. You're supposed to be working *together* — and all I've heard since this season started has been "Eddie did this" and "Janice did that". I've had a thumbtack show up in somebody's shoe —'

'Are you saying one of us is responsible for that?' Tanya said icily.

'Not necessarily.' He stood up and flung his big hands on to his hips. 'But what am I supposed to think, Tanya?'

She didn't answer.

'Chuck?'

Chuck just looked at the floor.

Coach glanced at Eddie and me, but he didn't continue that line of questioning. I was so confused I couldn't have even wrung out an 'I don't know'.

'The two of you,' he said to Tanya and Chuck, 'have some kind of case you want to present against Janice and Eddie, and I'm going to let you make it. But I tell you what — if there's any funny business about it — look out.' He took a place on the wall beside Eddie. 'Okay. Go for it.'

I still didn't have the slightest hint of what was going on, but my knees started banging against each other anyway. I glanced at Eddie again, but he was just standing there chewing his lip and boring a hole through the back of Chuck's head with his eyes. This was the guy who didn't hate anybody? I'd never seen him look that mad, and I hoped I never did again.

'So go ahead,' Tanya said to Chuck.

His hard blue eyes glinted. 'McBee's been breaking training rules,' he said.

'McBee,' Coach said. 'Corie? Eddie?'

Chuck gave a disgusted grunt. 'Eddie.'

'Okay. Go on.'

'He's broken curfew four — no, five times in the last three weeks.'

Eddie tossed his head angrily and recrossed his arms.

'You have specific dates? Witnesses?' Coach said.

'I heard his truck's been parked in front of her house 'til 1.00 in the morning — on school nights.' He moved around in the chair, looking at nobody.

'Who's her?'

'Her,' he said, pointing at me and, as if by remote crayon, turning my face bright red.

'Janice Kennedy?'

'Yeah.' Chuck was really getting impatient by now, and his voice hung precariously on the edge of disrespect.

'You say you "heard". From whom?'

'Friends.'

'Friends who cruise around town at 1.00 a.m. on school nights?'

Chuck didn't say anything.

'Have you "seen" as well as heard?'

'No, man, I *follow* the training rules!'

'Watch your tone, son.'

All four of us snapped our heads up. Even Tanya, I'm sure, had never heard that kind of sternness come out of Coach. We were talking serious business here. I sat on my fingers to keep them from shaking right off the ends of my hands.

'You come in here and tell me I ought to kick both these people off the team because they've broken curfew based on something somebody *told* you?'

It was a voice not even Chuck would lie to. He shook his head. 'I was with 'em one night when we saw his truck out on Main and we followed him home. I didn't exactly see him parked at *her* house, but he was out after curfew —'

Slowly taking his eyes from Chuck, Coach turned to Eddie. 'Is that true?'

Eddie had by then drilled completely through Chuck's head and was working on widening the hole. I didn't know the voice that answered, 'Yes, sir, it is.'

'Wonderful.' Coach slammed his clipboard on to the corner of the desk — and I jerked several inches into the air. I'd long since stopped breathing.

'But I have an explanation,' Eddie said tightly, 'and I don't think what I've been doing qualifies as breaking curfew.'

Coach just looked at him.

'Dr Kennedy doesn't like for Jan and the lady who lives with them to be alone, so I volunteered to stay with her on the nights when he can't be there. I go over, we study, and when the doctor comes home, I drive back to my house.'

'At 1.00 in the morning,' said Coach.

'Yes, sir.'

Coach looked like he'd rather have had Eddie announce that he was going to die soon. His voice went from angry to defeated in two syllables. 'That's a violation of training rules all right. You're supposed to get a certain number of hours' sleep every night — that's the whole reason for them —'

'I do.'

'How do you manage that?' He looked over his shoulder at some imaginary ally he wished was there. 'I don't even want to hear this.'

Eddie finally looked at me. 'I sleep over at Jan's until Dr Kennedy gets home.'

Tanya snickered, Chuck gave an X-rated sneer, and Coach looked like he wanted to cry.

'Tell me he's putting me on,' he said to me.

I tried to untie my tonsils. 'Well . . .' I said fluently.

They all waited.

'That doesn't tell me much,' Coach said.

'Well — after we do homework, about 10 o'clock, he goes to sleep on our couch — and — I go up to bed. I don't even know when he leaves.'

Tanya was practically crawling up the back of the chair. 'If that isn't curfew violation I don't know what is, and if you don't nail them for this —'

Eddie came off the wall. 'Ease it away from the kerb! What are you, the moral majority?'

Coach put up both hands in exasperation. 'Bag it! Both of you!'

They went back to their corners, and Coach looked at each one of us in turn like he expected some sordid confession to come bursting forth — from somebody. The three of them looked at me. I stared at my lap and wished I'd never cut my hair. It would've been nice to have a place to hide.

'All right, this is how it is,' Coach said, 'because I haven't got either the time or the desire to sit here and sort this whole mess out. Number one —' he erected a finger '— five demerits for each of you. Slade and McBee, you each broke curfew. Jan, you and the hero could've filled me in on what was going on, so you're as much at fault as he is. And you —' he pointed the finger at Tanya '— can add the demerits to the three you already have to keep you honest until next week's meet, because number two —' he produced another finger '— on Monday after practice, Tanya, you and Jan will spend one hour sorting junk in the lost and found, and, Mr Slade, you and Mr McBee can spend an hour picking up garbage out on the infield. Now — we have interval training this afternoon. You have a ten-mile run tomorrow morning. If I get a *clue* — I mean even if it *smells* like any more of this trash is going on — all four of you will wish one hour of duty were *all* you had coming to you. Am I understood, folks?'

Of course Tanya's mouth came open. That girl was programmed for automatic retort. Coach, however, deprogrammed her. 'Are you interested in more?' he said.

She closed her mouth.

'If you want to appeal, we have a court in this school. Meanwhile, I want you changed in five minutes.' He picked up his clipboard and slipped his whistle over his head.

Nobody had to tell us the case was closed. Tanya and Chuck left, eyes spewing bile, and I reluctantly pulled myself out of the chair. I'd rather have stayed there and died.

As Eddie reached for the doorknob, Coach caught him by the shoulder. I'd never thought I'd see the man with a smile again, but one was already coaxing the corners of his mouth. 'Boy, you're more trouble than you're worth,' he said.

Some of the colour had started to come back into Eddie's face, and he was grinning. 'I got one more question for you, Coach. Can I still go over to Janice's house and play?'

'Get outa here!'

When we got out into the hall, Eddie was chuckling, and he tugged at the strip of hair I'd finally managed to stretch to my mouth. 'Don't look like that,' he said.

'Like what?'

'Scared half out of your mind.'

'She'll probably try to strangle me with somebody's dirty shoelace.'

'Stuff an ol' sock in her mouth!'

I turned towards the locker room.

'Hey.' He grabbed my arm and raked my fringe down into my eyes with his fingers. 'Let's go out tomorrow night.'

I looked at him stupidly.

'Maybe it'll stop the nagging.' He went into his operatic mocking voice. ' "You never take me anywhere. All we ever do is sit around this house." '

'I never said that!'

'I know. I'm talking about me.'

He put his arm around my shoulder and ushered me towards the locker room. 'I know this neat drive we can take, and then I might even part with some cash and buy you a stick of gum or somethin' —'

I took a swat at him — and decided maybe I'd put off dying, at least until after Saturday night.

11

I changed my clothes about twelve times the next evening. In the first place, I didn't know what you wore on a 'drive', and in the second place I was so jittery about doing the right things on this first real, *official* date with Eddie, nothing looked quite good enough. In spite of the fact that Suzanne had talked me into spending some more of my money on decent clothes, my wardrobe still looked pretty grim to me. I was fussing with the collar on a blue jumpsuit and, ridiculously, wondering what kinds of clothes Tanya had worn when she used to go out with Eddie, when Dad tapped on my door.

Until I'd redecorated, he'd always knocked and then just poked his head in, but ever since the arrival of the tiger on the wallpaper, he practically waited for me to come out into the hall and talk to him there.

He glanced warily at it now as I let him in. But then his eyes hit me, and his face started to shine.

'You look precious,' he said, his voice all soft with emotion. 'You don't look like my little leather lunger at all.'

'Thanks.'

'I won't keep you, darlin'. I just wanted to say a couple of things and then I'll go and let you finish your girl stuff.'

I sensed the obvious relief in his voice that I had actually turned out to be a girl who had dates and looked in the mirror and did something besides chew her hair.

'Now,' he went on, 'I want to give you some money. Eddie's parents aren't rich, and times have changed, and there's nothing wrong with you offering to pay for some Cokes or something.'

He reached for his wallet while I turned fourteen shades of scarlet.

'Dad. You don't have to do that —'

'Call it mad money then,' he said, tucking a twenty-dollar bill insistently into my palm. I could have choked thinking about how much Coke that would buy. 'You never know when the car might break down and he might not have that much on him.'

He was right on both counts, so I gave up and stuck the money in my pocket.

Dad, in the meantime, had stuffed his hands in *his* pockets and was looking as if the next thing he'd come in to say wasn't going to be as easy. Matter of fact, he chickened out completely.

'There are some other things I'd like to talk over with you — how about we go for a run tomorrow?'

'I ran a ten-miler this morning. We're supposed to rest tomorrow.'

'Oh.' He jangled his keys uncomfortably inside his pocket. The look on his face yanked on one of my heart-strings.

'A nice easy jog wouldn't hurt, though,' I said.

But he had the door open and was backing out of the room. The sounds of Eddie making his entrance below drifted up the stairs. 'I need more than an easy jog,' he said, patting his already trim middle. 'I'll catch you, though, darlin'. It'll keep.'

Then he winked at me and nodded his head towards the bed, where my other eleven changes of clothes were heaped. 'You look just right,' he said. 'Don't change a thing.'

I did, of course. I hated the lipstick I'd put on, and my hair wouldn't co-operate, and I realized in horror that I'd somehow got mascara on my high-tops. I was sure I was the only person over three years old who could manage to get make-up on her shoe.

By the time my sweaty, shaky, clumsy fingers scrubbed off the lipstick, recurled the hair, and rubbed off the mascara with saliva, Eddie had had time to make himself at home at our kitchen bar.

Suzanne had produced a bowl of popcorn big enough for all of them to bathe their feet in, and Dad had Eddie deep in a discussion. I just hoped he wasn't asking him how he intended to support me or something.

'They're just now scratching the surface of sports medicine,' Dad was saying when I came down the back stairs into the kitchen. 'What they've found out about running alone just blows your mind.'

Eddie, of course, was hanging on every word while stuffing popcorn in his mouth with both hands and preparing for *his* next contribution to the conversation. As soon as there was a break, he started in, cheeks packed to maximum capacity.

'I don't even think we've come close to using the body to its fullest —' He stopped in mid-bite and mid-word to gaze at me, and I started going crimson from the neck up.

'— capability,' he trailed off. 'Hi, Jan.'

'Hi,' I said. I was at my usual effervescent best.

'Well,' Dad said, standing up. 'Enough of that. I know you all have places to go, and you've both been working hard. You deserve it.'

'Ya'll have fun,' Suzanne said. She glanced at me, Dad, and the door in rapid succession, and I almost laughed out loud. That was Suzanne-shorthand for, 'Get out of here before this man fathers both of you to death.'

'I'll have her in by 11.00. Curfew and all that, y'know.' Eddie was still staring at me and making zero sense.

'I wasn't even worried about that. I probably won't even wait up.' Dad went for his back pocket. 'Now, do ya'll need money —'

'Loren, how about going down to the basement and getting us another six-pack of Seven-Up out of the fridge down there. I feel a powerful thirst comin' on.' Suzanne was talking to Dad but looking at me with eyes that said, 'Get *out* of here, girl!'

I looked up at Eddie, who was looking down at me fuzzy-eyed. 'Ready?' I said.

'Yeah. Oh, yeah.'

In spite of Suzanne's attempts, Dad walked us to the front door. I saw her throwing up her hands in the background.

'You sure you aren't overtraining, son?' he said as he trailed us through the foyer.

Eddie looked at his body innocently. 'Just the usual. I've got to trim at least fifteen more seconds off my time if I'm gonna break the county record at the Albemarle meet.'

'You look mighty thin — *mighty* thin. I'd watch it.'

He was using his doctor voice, the calm, authoritative

one I'd always loved. But I looked at Eddie and giggled. 'Don't worry about it, Dad. He eats all the time.'

'He's eaten up half our popcorn,' Suzanne called tautly from the kitchen. 'Loren-get-in-here-and-get-some-before-I-finish-the-other-half.'

Eddie grinned at me and pushed me out the door. 'Night, Dr Kennedy,' he said. Dad was still talking as we took the steps at a trot.

'Sit over here by me,' Eddie said when we got in his truck and I slid towards the passenger door.

'Why?' I said, and immediately wished I could rip my tongue out by the roots.

'Because I can't hear you over there — because you talk so soft — and because I want you next to me and because —' He grinned. 'Sometimes that door flies open without any warning. I've lost a lot of friends that way.'

I let him pull me to the middle of the seat and give me a hug. 'You look good tonight,' he said into my hair.

'You do too.' That was definitely true. Except at church when he wore nondescript cotton shirts with button-down collars that I was sure his mother bought and forced him to put on once a week, I'd never seen him in anything but jeans and sweatshirts. That night he had on a rust-coloured sweater that burnt at his brown eyes and made them sparkle behind his glasses. If I hadn't known from track that he was the jump-out-of-the-shower-and-go-for-it type, I'd have even thought he'd blown his hair dry. The wonderful combination of his newly-washed sweater and the sweet smell of his breath filled up the cab — and I thawed right there in his arms. Suddenly he squeezed me and let go.

'You're gonna love this drive,' he said, wiggling in his seat and tapping on the steering wheel as he started the truck. 'Last time I was up here I had about thirteen kids in the back and we —'

He launched into one of his famous stories, and I followed every word with my eyes. As he drove and talked and produced a supply of granola bars and apple juice out of the glove compartment, he was more delightfully hyperactive than ever. His eyes and smile both flashed and his right hand talked with him, touching my arm and squeezing the back of my neck for punctuation. He was alive with the night, more so than I'd ever seen him, and I'm not sure quite at what point it dawned on me, but —

Eddie McBee was nervous.

He drove us to the outskirts of town, out to the old plantations and up the winding roads that crawled in and out of the Blue Ridge foothills. In the dark the friendly eyes of the mansion windows smiled down at us, and their big trees, older than the legend of Rhett Butler himself, reached out inviting arms. Eddie must have seen them that way too, because abruptly he swung the truck to the side of the road and grabbed my hand.

'I want to climb that tree!'

'Now?'

'Yeah. Come on.'

I didn't refuse. It wouldn't have mattered if I had — he'd have slung me over his shoulder and carried me to the nearest branch and hoisted me up on to it.

'Meet you at the top,' he said. His mouth was bubbling over — literally and figuratively.

I'd never climbed a tree in my life. You don't run across many opportunities when you grow up in a Chicago apartment. But it was the night that made me do it: it was sparkly and exciting, and, for the moment, so was I. That alone took me right to the fattest sprawling limb, where Eddie was already lounged against the trunk.

'What took you so long?' he said.

'I had a phone call,' I said.

I settled in on the branch beside him.

'Wow,' he said. 'Isn't God great?'

'You asked me that before.'

'It's true. Look at me. I have friends. I have a great family. I can do the thing I love more than anything — and that's run — whenever I want. And if I keep on like I'm going — maybe break that record next week — I'll get

123

my scholarship and be able to run — for ever! God's keeping his half of the bargain, I'm tellin' ya.'

I was just sitting there smiling at him, but he closed his eyes and pounded his forehead with the heel of his hand.

'There I go again!'

I looked around. 'What?'

'How long have we been sitting up here — and all I've done is flap my lips about myself. That's all I ever end up doing when we're together.'

'I like it.'

'Well, I don't! I mean, just because you're the best listener ever created — no, I want *you* to talk. Miss Kennedy, speak into the microphone, please!'

He curved his fingers around an imaginary mike and thrust it under my chin. I slapped it away, but I was laughing.

'No!' I said.

'Do you think I'm going to let you down out of this tree until you tell me your entire life story?'

'You better!'

'I've known you since September. It's now the end of October — and I don't even know what your favourite cereal is.'

'That's vital.'

'It *is*. Now spill it!'

'Eddie!'

'It could be a long night up here.'

'Sugar Puffs.'

'Sugar Puffs. O-kay.'

He looked over his shoulder. 'I knew she was different, but this is incredible.'

I stared down into my fingerprints. 'Did you really think I was different?'

He looked at me, and his face went soft. 'I did. And I was right. But I wanna know why. I really want to know about you. I do.'

An impatient little gust of Virginia night air tossed a small twig aside for a moment, and the moon flooded on

124

to his face. It was a wonderful face, of course, but it was also pale and wan-looking, the face of someone who'd tried all his tricks and didn't have any left to perform the magic he'd set out to do.

'I'll tell you,' I said.

I never knew Eddie *could* be quiet for more than a minute at a time, but as I talked, on and on, for the rest of our stay in the tree, he listened with his whole face.

I told him about my mother — what little I remembered — and about the struggle Dad and I had had to survive without her.

I told him about the combination nursemaid-army sergeants who'd taken care of me, and, ashamedly, about my instant hatred for Suzanne when she'd moved in.

I told him about Lincoln, and how much I liked Corie and Dixie and Coach Spike.

I even took a step I vowed I'd never take with anyone. I told him about Jack.

'What's it like, seeing a — psychiatrist?' he said. He was straddling the limb and leaning insistently towards me.

I shrugged — but it was only the first time that night. 'It's neat, I guess. He never made me feel like I was a weirdo. I liked that.'

Eddie sat up straight. 'You *aren't* a weirdo. Where'd you ever get that idea?'

'I don't know.'

'Well, give it up, okay? You're not a weirdo. Or even close, so stop it.'

Incredibly, he'd run out of words, and there we sat, looking at each other and groping inside for what to say next. I exhaled a laugh and choked on it as it came back in, and Eddie just kept watching me.

Another funny little gust teased at the tree, and the last of the leaves chattered against each other. I caught at two and snapped them from the branch.

'How do I look?' I said, tucking them behind my ears. 'Do I look like Mr Spock?'

Eddie laughed, a little, and slowly, as if he didn't want

the moment to happen at all, he cupped his hands around my face — and he kissed me.

I'd been kissed before — once in second grade when Billy Barnes told me he loved me in the art corner and then splashed blue tempera paint in my face, and once in front of a water fountain at my high school in Chicago when some guy I didn't even know jumped out from behind a row of lockers and planted one on me, while his friends howled and hooted down the hall and yelled, 'Is she frozen, man? Did she freeze-dry your lips?'

Needless to say, neither of those kisses had floated me down out of a tree, wrapped itself around me in the front seat of a truck and wafted me up the front steps of my house. And neither of them had made me want to be kissed again.

When we got to my front door, Eddie put both hands in my hair and searched my face. I was looking at an Eddie I hadn't seen before — an Eddie who suddenly wasn't on top of the situation, an Eddie who suddenly was just as vulnerable as I was. And I knew from the half-sad way his eyes were looking at me, it was an Eddie he hadn't seen before either.

'I hate to bring you home so early,' he said.

'We have curfew.'

'It's not even that yet. I'm just so tired.'

I nodded. Just in the past half-hour he'd sagged so much I thought he was going to curl up at the wheel.

'I really had a great time tonight. I really did,' he said.

'Me too.'

'You are —' He smiled straight out to his ears and back. 'You are so special. Come here.'

I did, and opened every door I'd ever invented — and then some more.

From inside our front door I watched him go, his hands in his pockets, his legs swaggering under him, and then I squeezed my eyes shut as hard as I could so the moment and the feeling and the vision of Eddie's tender eyes wouldn't go away.

126

Tender eyes, I thought. Not teasing eyes. Not the runner's cunning eyes. But eyes that wondered just as much as mine did what in the world was happening to us here.

That's what I wanted to wonder all night, curled up under the tiger, looking out of my window at the Virginia moon, and being in love.

And I would have, too, except the most unearthly noise was coming from the living room. I knew what it was before I even got there.

It was the man who wasn't even going to wait up — stretched out on the Early American sofa and snoring his nose hairs back and forth.

So much for romantic thoughts. But who cared? Didn't I have it all? And wasn't God great?

12

Saturday night, life was absolutely perfect.

Monday morning, life was bordering on perfect, but losing ground fast.

In fact, on Monday morning I decided life was like trying to fold down a box with four flaps. Just when you get one or two or even three of them tucked in, the fourth pops up and gets you right under the chin — at which point the other three come loose, too.

Monday morning, Lincoln gave his oral report and it was, to be kind, nothing short of a disaster. He mumbled into his Marlboros, forgot three-quarters of what I'd told him to say, and basically only had the class's attention when, while demonstrating the exhalation of smoke, he blew several smoke rings. When it was over — and I thought it never would be — he slunk into his desk, looked at me like I'd perpetrated the whole thing, and said, 'I *told* you I didn't like gettin' up in front of no class.'

His attitude changed completely when at lunchtime on the steps — where my prediction that he would be joining me daily proved true — I produced half a batch of Suzanne's home-made fudge. I didn't tell him I'd originally meant for it to be part of a celebration for the success of his oral report.

But I needed more than chocolate to dispel the gloom that was gathering around me. I had my afternoon duty with Tanya hanging over my head, and Eddie wasn't even there to keep me from falling apart over it.

He hadn't been in church the day before either, and his little sister Carla had run up to me after the service to report that he was sick in bed. From the way she'd been wiggling in the row in front of us during the sermon, I knew she'd been waiting since we walked in to be the one to give me the news.

When he didn't show up in first period PE, butterflies began to reproduce at an amazing rate in my stomach. I kept envisioning Tanya fashioning a noose with old shoe-laces while Chuck stood by leering. Only Eddie could have turned that image upside down and booted it out.

Besides, it bothered me that Eddie was so ill he was missing school and practice just five days before an important meet. I knew he must be at death's door.

That's why I stayed close to Corie while we changed. If my calculations were correct, it would take her about seven seconds to volunteer something about his condition.

I was wrong.

Six seconds.

'Why weren't you at registration?' Tess said to her as she dashed into the locker room, tripped over a bench, and made a three-point landing in front of her locker, gym clothes sprawling everywhere.

Corie looked up at us sullenly. 'I'm not having a good day.'

'Evidently,' Tess said.

'I get up late to begin with — look at this hair — it's still wet! So I *run* all the way down to Eddie's — and then I get there and Aunt Elizabeth tells me he's still sick and he can't drive me to school.'

'Don't they have a phone?' Tess said. 'She could've called you.'

Corie was by this time firing her shoes into her locker. 'Yes. But when I got there, she looked at me at first like she'd never seen me before. I almost went, "Earth to Aunt Elizabeth — it's me — Corie — your niece?"'

'What was her problem?'

'I don't know. I've never seen her like that before. She must've really had something on her mind. If it were *my* parents, I'd say they'd had a fight and she was —'

I couldn't stand it any longer. 'What's wrong with Eddie?' I burst out.

They both looked at me in surprise.

'I don't know,' Corie said. 'He hasn't called you?'

I shook my head.

'Call *him*. And when you do, tell that dum-dum to get back over here.'

A whistle nagged at us then from the doorway — Tanya announcing that it was time to fall in for roll call. I followed Corie and Tess miserably out of the locker room.

'She's in a good mood today,' Tess said to me over her shoulder, nodding towards Tanya.

Involuntarily I glanced at our self-appointed sergeant, whose eyes were drawn so close together in a sulk, she almost looked like a wasp. Wonderful, I thought, rubbing the neck where the shoelace was sure to be wrapped. And Corie thought *she* wasn't having a good day.

By the time track practice was over that afternoon, I was really coming unglued. I was completely off on the distance run and shuffled in behind Tess and Lisa at fourth. It would have been the perfect set-up for Tanya to sneer, 'Concentration bad today, *Miss* Kennedy?' But she didn't say anything.

And I mean she didn't say *anything* — to *anybody* — the whole afternoon.

Corie snickered when Tanya left the locker room after

showers. 'I wish Coach would get her up to eight demerits more often. She's easier to live with.'

I wasn't convinced of that, and my walk to the lost and found was like heading for Cell Block 14. I'd just about taken my last anguished step when Chuck materialized in front of me.

As usual, he got in my space and breathed out of his flared nostrils right at my upper lip like he was performing mouth to mouth resuscitation.

'Reporting for duty?' he said to my nose hairs.

I stepped back, and he followed like we were ballroom dancing.

'Y'know, Coach blew it,' he said.

I turned my head to the side, and I could feel the mercury rising on my face. 'Why?' I said.

'He should have put you and *me* in that room together. We could've had a *good* time.'

My head went to the other side, and so did his. Though I didn't even know the script, he wasn't missing any of *his* lines.

'Actually, we don't need a room. We can just start right here.'

To my horror his face got even closer, and I realized he was trying to kiss me. Practically retching, I clawed past him and lunged for the door. A dry, empty 'cheeee' and derisive laughter hissed in the hall behind me.

When I slammed the door to the lost and found behind me, Tanya looked up with disinterest from a cardboard box full of odd shoes. 'It's not that bad,' she said. 'Just do it and get it over with. Here —' She shoved a pile of jackets in my direction. 'Coach says these go to the Salvation Army. Put them in one of those plastic sacks.'

I was amazed at how organized she was. It would have taken me a week of afternoons to decide how to sort out three years' worth of lost stuff. She had four different piles going and was efficiently starting a fifth in the trash can. The fact that she was hurling unmatched shoes into it like they were lethal projectiles didn't help me stop shaking, but at least she hadn't seen her boyfriend putting the moves on me or I'd have *been* a lethal projectile.

As I stuffed the trash bag, I tried to calm myself down. I was working on getting my teeth settled when she said, 'Don't you ever talk?'

I just turned around and looked at her.

'Guess that answers that question.' She made a 'cheeee' sound, too, and tossed the now-empty box into the corner. 'How do you and the preacher communicate if you never say anything? No — never mind. He jacks his jaws so much he probably doesn't even notice you never open your mouth.'

It took me a minute to realize she was talking about Eddie. I was still getting over the shock that she was speaking to me at all. Funny though — it irritated me, and I turned abruptly towards a stack of assorted T-shirts and shorts that smelled of old sweat.

'What do I do with these?' I said curtly.

'See if there's anything worth saving. Throw the rest out.'

'Aye aye,' I muttered.

'What?'

'Nothing.'

'When you do talk you won't even admit it. What — do you have speech anorexia or something?'

'No.' I was fighting down unfamiliar anger. 'I just don't have anything to say.'

'To me, you mean.'

She'd stopped sorting the towel pile and was surveying me with her bottom lip hanging down. There were times when Tanya looked awfully pretty to me, but just then she was less attractive than any girl I'd ever seen — including the one I looked at in the mirror every day.

'Yeah, I guess so,' I said.

Our eyes caught. 'At least you're honest,' she said.

We worked for a while in silence, until it was as if she couldn't deal with it. She was like Eddie in that respect. They must have driven each other nuts when they were dating, I thought, both of them expressing their so-sure thoughts at the same time — all the time.

'The only reason I can't stand you is because you came in here like some prima donna on the track team and had Spike and PM and everybody fallin' all over you.' She was pelting socks into the trash can.

'PM?'

'Yeah — Preacher McBee. Or haven't you noticed he has a terminal case of religion? I've worked my butt off for going on three years now for the track programme at this school, and then somebody new strolls in off the streets and I'm out like — one of these.' She gestured with a sock.

I sucked in some air. 'You're not out,' I said timidly. 'You're really running well.'

'Oh! Thank you, Cross-Country Queen, for those pearls of encouragement.'

Her voice had risen to a dangerous level, and I glanced nervously towards the door.

'Coach'll hear you,' I said.

'You think he thinks we're in here making a pact to become college roommates or something? He knows this isn't gonna work, and besides I'm so sick of his judgmental —'

I took in more air. 'We need you on the team.'

'Spare me! You sound just like McBee. I'm the *second*-best runner and I'm supposed to *thank* you for that? You breeze in and get the individual coaching I used to get and I'm supposed to smile and say "Yea team"?' She hurled the last sock in the direction of the trash and missed. 'Rah, rah,' she said.

I thought I caught the threat of tears at the end of her sentence, and I almost felt sorry for her. Almost.

'I didn't know Eddie coached you before,' I said.

'Now you do. It didn't last long. He told Spike I argued with him too much, so Spike took him off and worked with me himself.' She looked at me, and I think she laughed. 'He said Eddie was right, I did argue too much.'

She picked up a plastic bin fastener and started to chew on it. I went to work on the miscellaneous junk, but I kept

132

a close watch on her. She pretended to be rambling absently, but she was watching me too.

'I hate having somebody tell me what to do — especially McBee. He's so condescending. You can't see that because you're one of those churchie kids. It's all a bunch of lies.'

I didn't say anything.

'Do you and him actually date, or do you just pray together?'

I still didn't answer. I didn't like her tone.

'I used to date him. What a jerk he turned out to be.'

I looked up sharply — and she was watching. 'You haven't caught that yet, I see. Wait until you really start to like him and show him you like him. He'll be gone so fast all you'll see is the dust in your eyes. As long as he's doing all the chasing it's great. But give him an inch and he'll take a mile — in the other direction.'

She stopped. We both realized her voice had changed in the course of her monologue, and she'd been talking in something besides a malicious rasp. There'd been hurt in her voice. She knew it, she knew I knew it, and she didn't like it. She slapped the lid on the trash can.

'I don't know why I'm telling you this — you'll probably tell *him*, and then he'll want to pray over me or something.' Her index finger headed for me. 'But look out. He flirts. He does cartwheels for you — and then all of a sudden he turns around and starts doing them for somebody else.' She shook her auburn mane at me. 'No wonder he's going out with you, though. You listen to everything. He could talk for days.'

It was the closest she'd ever come to being civil to me. I said, 'Thanks.'

She laughed harshly then and picked up two of the stuffed plastic sacks. 'Get the rest and we'll take them to His Majesty. Oh —' She halted at the door. 'And I intend to win at Albemarle, by the way. That's the way it is.'

But the cutting edge was gone from her voice, and I had the feeling an unspoken truce had been declared between us.

With that ordeal behind me, I should've been overjoyed — but Eddie didn't call that night, and he wasn't in school again on Tuesday. Naturally, I had myself convinced he was staying home to avoid me — before Corie got to class and broadcasted that Eddie was 'about out of it, ya'll', and he refused to go to the doctor, and Uncle Edward was out of town, and Aunt Elizabeth was 'tearin' her hair out' because Eddie was 'so bullheaded' and swore he was going to be in school Wednesday and run in the meet Saturday.

Aunt Elizabeth wasn't the only one threatening self-imposed baldness. Corie had to be exaggerating, of course. But I was worried about Eddie, and I missed him.

It was almost dark when I got home from track practice, and the only light in the house was the flourescent bulb over the stove pointing a big blue finger at the note Suzanne had magneted to the stove hood.

Janice-Sugar — Had to finish a paper at my office. Be home around 7.00. How does some of that left-over vichyssoise sound for dinner?

How should I know how it sounded? I couldn't even say it. Miserably I searched the refrigerator and then slammed its door. The sound reverberated eerily through the empty house.

Now, Janice, get a hold of yourself, I said mentally. Don't start imagining somebody's crashing the back door. Nobody's bothered us for weeks. Just go up to your room and start your homework. Or make yourself a tuna fish and vichyssoise sandwich. Or, better yet, put your jacket on and get your body out of here!

I was halfway to the university campus before our back door closed.

I'd never been to Suzanne's office, and finding it was no easy matter. Inside the building, a graduate student with terrific shoulders asked if he could help me, and when I charmingly blurted out, 'Suzanne St Claire's office, please' he showed several pairs of dimples and escorted me right to her cubicle.

Suzanne was curled up in a chair behind her desk, madly scribbling across the page of a spiral notebook and twisting a tendril of blonde hair. Her face softened when she looked up and saw me.

'Sugar, for ever more! What are you doin'?'

'I didn't mean to bother you. I just —' Suddenly I felt ridiculous and would've bolted out of there if she hadn't already squeezed me once and wasn't toppling a pile of books off the only other chair in the cubicle.

'I've been dyin' for somebody to bother me. I've been at this wretched paper for so long I was fixin' to ask the janitor in for a cup of coffee. I haven't even seen you for three days. How are you, sugar?' She studied my face with her black-eyed-Susan eyes, as she had a habit of doing. 'Not good, huh? You want to talk about it?'

In spite of how lousy I felt, I laughed. 'If I *wanted* to talk, would you even give me a chance to get a word in?' I said.

She grinned at me. 'I've created a monster. I draw you out of your shell and then you turn on me.'

For a second she looked as if she'd said something she wished she hadn't, but before I could figure out what, she was on to the next topic.

'Have you eaten anything?'

'You mean the vichyschmutz?'

She wrinkled her nose. 'You obviously haven't. Let's do somethin' disgusting — how about if we order subs from Poe's — loaded up with onions — you think that's drastic enough?'

'I want mine with meatballs.'

'They deliver.' She picked up the phone and then pressed the receiver against her leg. 'Do you have any money?' she whispered.

I dug into the pocket of my blue jumpsuit — which I'd worn to school *certain* Eddie was going to show up that day — and, to my own surprise, pulled out the twenty-dollar bill

Dad had given me on Saturday night. For some reason, it made me sad.

But Suzanne grinned. 'We're in business,' she said.

While Suzanne made the call, I looked around her 'office'. Even that six-by-six cubicle, with partitions that didn't even go up to the ceiling, had her personality flashing from every inch: a tasteful abstract painting, chrome desk pieces, photos of her family, and even my eleventh-grade school picture in acrylic frames. It seemed funny now to think I'd been intimidated by how beautifully she'd decorated her room at home. Now being near anything with Suzanne's touch was like being soothed by a cool, comforting hand.

'What's on your mind, sugar?' she said. She'd hung up the phone and was surveying me softly from her perch on the edge of the desk.

I looked at her sheepishly. 'It was too quiet at home.'

'Gave you the heebie-jeebies, huh? I'm sorry. I thought you might like some space for a change.'

I shook my head. 'Not today.'

'Trouble?'

'I don't know.'

'That's the worst kind.'

She tucked her arm into mine. 'Come on. Let's go meet the delivery boy at the front door. You could have cold meatballs by the time he finds this hole.'

We walked down the hall arm in arm, the heels of her boots tapping cleanly on the tile floor in rhythm with the squeal of my rubber soles.

'So how was your date with Eddie Saturday? I've been so tied up with riboflavin, I haven't even had a chance to ask you.'

The colour brushed over my face. 'It was — wonderful. He — it was wonderful.'

She squeezed my arm. 'I love young love, I love to hear about those feelings.'

'But that's just it.' My shoulders were up in a permanent shrug. 'I don't know what the feelings are!'

'So what else is new, sugar! Does anybody? What does Eddie say?'

'Nothing. I haven't talked to him since. He's really sick.'

'Well, honey, haven't you called him?'

I didn't have to answer. She stopped inside the front door and leaned against the brick wall, arms folded into her big sweater. She shook her head slowly. 'Janice, what are we gonna do with you?'

Unexplained tears were starting to make my throat ache. I swallowed hard and stared down at her toes.

'You know, he's not the only one allowed to make a move,' she said. 'All you have to do is pick up the phone and call the boy — especially if he's sick.'

'I'm scared.'

'I know.'

I looked up in surprise, and she caught me by the shoulders in her warm hands. 'I started to say this to you once before, but I quit because that was back when you detested the very sight of me.'

I opened my mouth to protest, but there wasn't much point in it.

'Like I tried to tell you then, no matter how scary it is, if you want love, you're going to have to give it. It's not just Eddie's responsibility — or mine, or your dad's. You've got a lot to give — and if you've found somebody darlin' like Eddie, sugar, I say go for it. Believe me, those kind are so hard to come by. I know.'

Her eyes were so full of concern, I almost started bawling for real.

She pulled me into a hug and laughed into my hair. 'I love you, sugar,' she said.

'That's nice, lady,' said the Poe's delivery boy. 'That'll be $7.04.'

'Now, that cocky little jerk from Poe's is like most of the guys I dated in high school,' Suzanne said when we were back in her cubicle, tearing into the sandwiches. 'My ex-husband was him — times about thirteen.'

I stared at her, tomato sauce drooling from my chin. 'You were married?'

'Haven't I ever mentioned that? Oh yeah, sugar — Vince Loria — the finest little old Italian boy who'd ever crossed the Mason-Dixon Line. He swept me right off my Georgio Bertini's. I quit college for the man — gave up my dream of really doing something with my life — to marry him — and I do mean I gave it *all* up.'

I put my meatball sandwich down so I wouldn't drop it in shock.

'He treated me like I was a fairy princess, and I just let him make all the decisions and call all the shots. I was totally in his hands.'

'You?'

'The me I used to be. After we were married, he continued to do everything. My name wasn't even on our bank account, if that tells you anything. I was slowly demoted from fairy princess to medieval serf. I was a little slow in those days. Took me three years to realize I'd married a monster — and by then I was a mess. It was three more before he left and I put myself back together. Thank the Lord — literally — I learned somethin' from the whole mess.'

I was practically in a trance. 'What?' I said.

She leaned forward into my face. 'You can't wait for somebody else to make your life for you. In fact, if you get somebody who even wants to — watch out. And if you find somebody great that you want to *share* with, you don't sit there drummin' y' nails and hopin' he'll pick up on what you're thinkin'. I'm not makin' that mistake again.'

She looked at me for a minute, almost as if she wanted to say more, but was afraid she'd blurted out too much already. I picked up my sandwich and then plunked it down again.

'Do you really think I should call Eddie?'

'If you need to talk to him, call him.'

I ran my finger along the edge of the bun and put the

drippings of tomato sauce into my mouth. 'What if he doesn't feel the same way I do? You know, what if I dreamed the whole thing up? He could tell me to get lost.'

Her eyes widened over the top of her sub. 'Frankly, my dear,' she said, her mouth full of salami, 'that's always the risk.'

13

I called Eddie as soon as we got home. I was so nervous, I dialled the wrong number the first time and got the answering service for some paediatrician. After assuring the lady that I didn't want to leave my name, my number, and my child's temperature, I hung up and tried again. By then a lump the consistency of cream of wheat had formed in my throat, and I could barely say hello when Bernadette answered the phone.

'May I speak with Eddie?' I got out.

'Who's this?' she said.

'Janice Kennedy,' I said, heart sinking. Were there that many girls calling Eddie?

'Oh. Hey. Eddie's asleep — as usual. For you I could wake him up.'

'Oh, no!' I said. 'That's okay.'

'Whatever he has, I wish I'd get it,' she said. 'He's slept through two whole days of school.' She gave a junior-high snicker. 'Did he get it from you?'

'No,' I said idiotically. 'Bye.'

I almost wished I had whatever Eddie had if it meant getting to sleep. I lay awake for at least an hour that night, thinking.

The longer I went without talking to Eddie, the less real Saturday night seemed. It had been so different between us that night. It hadn't been super-Eddie who was so sure of himself, and nothing-Janice, who could barely breathe without asking somebody's permission. We'd been two equal people, talking about our dreams and our plans and our feelings. I wasn't blind; I had seen the tenderness in his eyes and the confusion on his face. He'd felt everything I'd felt. I knew it.

But the doubts were creeping in like mildew. Was he so sick that he couldn't pick up the phone or send a note with somebody — or let me know somehow that he hadn't changed his mind? Or had he decided I wasn't 'special' after all?

I propped myself up impatiently on my elbow and peered out of the window. Jack would've told me I was building up my defences so I wouldn't be disappointed. Dad would've assured me, 'Darlin', everything is going to be all right.' Eddie himself would've said, 'If you believe in God and do what he wants you to do, nothing bad is going to happen to you.'

Never having Eddie look at me that way again — now *that* would be bad. Every inch of the ground I'd gained in the past two months would be lost for ever. Not even Suzanne could talk me out of that — or Dad — or Jack — or God.

I looked up at the moon, the same moon that had chaperoned Eddie and me in the tree. 'For once in your life, Janice, don't expect the worst, okay?' I said out loud. 'What possible difference could three days make?' I sighed up into the window. 'Okay, God,' I said. 'I'm counting on you.'

It sure sounded good. But when I walked into the gym first period the next day and saw Eddie sprawled across the bleachers with his clipboard, my heart tried to slam right out of my chest. 'I say go for it,' Suzanne was whispering in my ear. Shaking all the way to the earlobes, I headed for him.

'Hi,' I said, practically inaudibly.

He looked up.

'How are you feeling?' I said.

'I feel great.'

You do not, I thought.

'I oughta feel great. I've been asleep for three days.'

'Are you sure?'

'I'm pretty sure I was asleep.'

'No! I mean, are you sure you're all right?'

He stood up. 'Does this look like a sick body to you?'

Actually, it did. His skin had a waxy look to it, and I'd have sworn he'd lost another ten pounds since Saturday. His legs looked like pathetic popsicle sticks jutting out of his shorts.

'I'm running that race Saturday,' he said. 'I'm not sick.'

'Okay,' I said. I tried to giggle. 'I'm not arguing with you.'

He looked down at me without smiling and nodded. 'I know. I'm sorry.'

Coach blew his whistle and, as if to prove his state of health, Eddie vaulted over the bottom three rows of bleachers. 'Let's get to class,' he said.

I spent the rest of the day debating with myself.

'It isn't the same,' I told me.

'Don't be paranoid,' I answered back. 'It's obvious he's sicker than a dog. What do you expect? Some big passionate scene right in the gym?'

'That'd be nice. Or at least something more than "hi".'

'Maybe he's scared too.'

'Of what?'

'I don't *know*! What are *you* scared of, for Pete's sake?'

Lincoln poked me during lunch while I was in the midst of that mental dialogue for about the fortieth time.

'What's wrong with you, girl?' he said.

'Nothing.'

'Liar.'

I gazed at him. 'What are you, the DA?'

'Does that stand for dumb a—'

'No!'

He looked at me shrewdly. 'Somebody been messin' with you?'

I shrugged.

141

'You want me to fix him?'

'What are you going to do, step on his toe?'

'Whose? Give me the name, girl!'

I yanked his jeans jacket up over his head and told him to mind his own business, but for the moment at least I felt enormously better.

At track practice, Eddie didn't work with me, which was understandable with all the catching-up he had to do. We were doing intervals, and from what I could see he was so far off his form I wanted to crawl into a hole for him. Chuck was almost kicking dirt in his face at the starting line — and, of course, he was smirking every step of the way.

'PM's having a bad day,' Tanya said at my elbow.

'He's been sick,' I said curtly.

'Looks like he still is. He shouldn't even be out here.'

Her tone was strangely soft, and my hackles settled. We looked at each other for a second before she slipped back into the Tanya mode and strutted off.

Coach Spike signalled the end of practice then, and Eddie let out a too-loud whoop. I waited ultra-casually at the edge of the track, but Coach got to him first. They walked past me towards Coach's office, Spike with his hand on Eddie's shoulder, his head bent earnestly almost into Eddie's face. Eddie was laughing and tossing his head back, just like always.

Or was it like always? As I showered, I kept picturing his face, his posture, his whole attitude all day. He seemed like Eddie, but it was an Eddie who was trying too hard — and not just with me. It was as if he were trying so hard to be Eddie, he didn't have much time to think about anyone else. If anybody would know what *that* was like, it was me.

The only thing that went right for me that day was that I emerged from the girls' locker room just as Eddie was finishing a long drag on the water fountain outside the door — though later it was debatable whether I wouldn't have been better off not running into him at all.

He finished drinking and, obviously unaware that I was behind him, braced his hands on the sides of the fountain and let his head sag. Putting his weight wearily on one leg, he let out a sigh that seeped out from somewhere deep inside him. I stood there feeling as sick as he looked.

When he turned around and saw me, he drew himself up and grinned deliberately.

'Don't drink this stuff. It'll kill ya,' he said.

Scrapping for every ounce of courage I could find, I said, 'Do you want to come over? I'll make you a sundae.' I took a stab at a giggle. 'We have good water.'

He actually shrugged his shoulders. I'd thought *I* had the corner on that particular gesture.

'I was gonna run home,' he said, '— do a little catch-up. But maybe I oughta rest first. Okay, let's do that.'

The house was mercifully empty when we got there. Eddie immediately collapsed on the couch in the den. This was the boy who'd intended to *run* all the way to his house?

'Had any uninvited guests lately?' he called to me as I went after our sundaes with a whipped cream can.

'No. Since you haven't been here, Suzanne's been leaving every light in the house on when Dad's out.'

'So you don't need me anymore, huh?' Eddie's eyes were trying to tease behind the puffiness that had set in. I handed him his sundae and sank uneasily on to the couch beside him. He dug in like it was his first meal in a week.

'I say go for it,' Suzanne was still whispering. 'If you want to get love you're going to have to give it. It's not all Eddie's responsibility —'

'We need you,' I said suddenly. 'I mean I — anyway —'

'So does the track team, and I feel like a real idiot for letting everybody down. I'm gonna stink in that meet Saturday.'

That wasn't the direction I'd been heading, so I didn't say anything. An awkward silence hit us like a slap. For once things were going even *worse* than I'd expected them to.

Then, ridiculously, I said, 'I had fun Saturday night.'

Eddie concentrated on setting his empty sundae glass on the coffee table. 'I'm glad,' he said. 'I wanted you to.'

Silence. I ploughed on.

'Thank you — for listening — to all that stuff about me — and everything. I don't tell that to very many people — well, nobody.' I tried to swallow the lump of cream of wheat and waited for Eddie to grin and start finishing my sentences for me. He didn't. He just leaned on his knees and looked down at his hands.

Feeling like I was somebody else, I charged on even further. 'You told me I was special, and I —' I practically gasped. 'You're really special to me, too.'

Eddie's head came up, and he stared at me out of a colourless face. A noise started in my ears, and I stared back.

'Aw, Jan,' he said in a wire-thin voice, 'I wish you hadn't said that.'

That made two of us.

He pawed to reach my hand. His palms were clammy against mine, and it was all I could do not to yank it away — yank all of me away.

'Jan, I like you so much,' he was saying, barely over the din in my ears. 'You *are* special — and you're my friend. Don't ever forget that.' He ran his tongue over his dry lips. 'I guess I got a little carried away the other night, but I didn't mean to give you the wrong idea —'

He stopped and dropped my hand so he could put both of his into his hair. I couldn't even hear him anymore, but as he leaned over his knees again I knew he was saying, 'I'm a rat.'

'I'm sorry. I never meant to hurt you. Let's still be friends.' That was probably coming next, but the sound of Dad's Golf pulling into the garage cut him off. Eddie stood up and wiped his hands on the seat of his sweat-pants. 'I wanted to help you, Jan. You were like a challenge to me, you know, so all wrapped up inside yourself the way you were. And maybe I did bring you out, or maybe it wasn't me. But anyway, you're okay now.'

Everything stopped, including my heart, my breathing, and the noise in my ears. I stared, frozen, at the stranger with the white face and dry lips and no smile who was telling me I'd been a project he now felt he'd completed. My face, I knew, didn't register anything. But for an instant the pity faded from his, and he looked so sorry it was pinching his cheeks.

'You're gonna find somebody who can love you to death. Somebody who's not a jerk like Eddie McBee.'

'You're not a jerk,' I said in a voice so tiny and scared it almost squeaked.

'Maybe not,' he said. 'But I sure feel like one.'

When the back door opened and Dad came in grinning, the noise started in my ears again and all I wanted to do was get away — upstairs — anywhere. Somehow I got it across to Dad that Eddie needed a ride home, and somehow I got them out the door, Dad ready to discuss the latest in sports medicine at length and Eddie so anxious to get out of there he wouldn't even look at me again.

Somehow I got up to the bathroom before the ice-cream sundae, the lump of cream of wheat and just about everything else inside me came up. Too bad I couldn't have vomited the pain out too. Or the memory of Tanya saying, 'Wait until you really start to like him and show him you like him. He'll be gone so fast all you'll see is the dust in your eyes.' Or Coach saying, 'I was the one who told you to stay on her until she came out for track.' Or Eddie saying, 'I wanted to help you. You were like a challenge to me.' That all stayed as I threw myself down on my bed, jammed my pillow over my ears, and cried and cried and cried.

When I woke up, it was dark and cold, inside of me and out. There weren't any tears left — just a hard empty space somewhere in the pit of my stomach. Oddly I thought about Jack always talking about 'the worst that could happen'.

'What's the worst that could happen if you do that?' he'd say to me when I was agonizing over some ridiculous thing. 'When you get it down to something concrete, it's never as bad as you thought it would be — even at worst.'

Shows how much you know, I thought. I pulled my blanket around me and started to go for my desk. I'd write to him. I'd tell him what he could do with his advice.

But I stopped in the middle of the floor. That wasn't going to do it. I was so empty, I needed more than a bunch of words on a piece of paper. I needed somebody. I needed Dad and Suzanne and our cosy kitchen downstairs and a big plate of pasta with a name like a foreign car. I needed to sit down at the dinner table with them and tell them all about it. I had that, at least.

I glanced sympathetically in the mirror at the swollen face that looked pitifully back at me and, drawing my blanket up under my chin, headed down the back stairs.

I could smell the food before I even got to the den, but there were no lights on and no forks clattering. If it hadn't been for the fire in Dad's favourite fireplace and the two fat candles burning a glow on to the shiny surface of the coffee table, I'd have thought they'd both headed for Howard Johnson's.

I took two steps across the den and screamed to a silent halt. More candlelight flickered from the dining room, and through the partially opened door I could just discern the shadows of Dad and Suzanne's heads bent together over whatever it was they were eating.

Only they weren't eating. From what I could see, they were just looking at each other — like they never wanted to stop.

I'll never know to this day why I did it. It was as if my body and mind went on automatic pilot. Not even feeling like a sneaky little brat, I crept closer and stood in the shadow of the refrigerator, listening shamelessly.

'I've tried a couple of times, but it just hasn't come together,' Dad was saying in his soft Virginia voice.

'I wish it would,' Suzanne said. 'I've almost slipped twice. Loren, please don't wait for all the conditions to be right. It's never going to happen. The longer you wait, the harder it will be, and that isn't fair to her.'

'She loves you so much, I really don't think she's gon' mind all that much.'

'My incurable optimist,' Suzanne said. And she laughed softly.

It got quiet. It wasn't because I didn't know what I was going to see that I leaned stealthily around the door. It had only been a few days since I'd experienced that magic silence myself. I already knew I was going to find them in each other's arms.

And then I ran without making a sound and closed myself in my room and hugged my arms around myself and shook.

Yeah, I knew the minute I heard them talking that I would see them kiss. What I hadn't known was that they were going to look so natural doing it, as if Dad *belonged* with his hand on Suzanne's cheek and Suzanne *should* have her fingers entwined around Dad's arm. As if they had done it many times before in their secret world.

Suddenly I tore across the room to my window and, eyes blurring, yanked on the cord, bringing the blinds down with a startled clatter. 'You're not invited, God,' I said. 'You didn't hold up your side of the bargain.'

Then I had to pull the pillow over my ears again because the noise was back, louder than ever.

I realized what it was, of course. It was the angry slamming of a thousand doors.

14

My luck just wouldn't let up. The first person I saw the next morning when I went to the gym to put clean socks in my locker was Eddie. At least that solved the problem of which rotten thing to think about: Eddie dumping me or Dad and Suzanne falling in love and hiding it from me like I was some emotionally unstable basket case.

Of course, by then I felt like one again. I'd barely slept all night, and I was moving towards the locker room door like a zombie when I almost mowed Eddie down. He caught me by both arms to keep from being ploughed under entirely — and then just as quickly let go of me. He plastered on a big smile, but his eyes shifted uncomfortably. 'Are you all right?' he said.

'Yeah,' I said.

'Okay. Well, I've gotta go.'

And he left me standing there. No playing with the ends of my hair. No threat to carry me piggyback to class. No throaty chuckle to send the chills up my spine. I forgot the socks and dragged off to class.

First period PE was almost unbearable. Corie and Tess chattered on in the locker room as if the world had not come to an end in the last twelve hours. By the time we were dressed, their giggles were crawling under my skin. I got away from them as soon as roll call started and volunteered to take the bench for the first round of volleyball.

I was staring vacantly at everyone's tennis shoes when I felt Tanya at my elbow. It was funny how I always sensed her and Chuck before I even knew for sure it was them.

'What's wrong with *you*?' she said.

I snapped my head towards her. 'Nothing!' I said.

We looked at each other. I think I was as surprised as she was.

'You lyin' sack of cat litter,' she said finally.

I turned away.

'Well, let me see,' she went on, 'I see the preacher in class starin' at his government book instead of talkin' everybody's ear off — only he's not really reading it, because he doesn't turn a page for ten minutes. And then I come in here and you're countin' the hairs on your legs and looking even more suicidal than usual. So I figure that can only mean the preacher has made the Big Dump.'

I didn't intend to turn around and stare at her. My body just did it automatically. And my mouth, bless its heart, said, 'Why don't you ever just mind your own business?'

As soon as it was out, I could feel all the colour running in terror from my face, and I immediately looked at the floor. But Tanya gave a satisfied snicker.

'But, you see, Kennedy, it is my business. Because now, at long last, you and I have something in common.' She started ticking things off on her fingers. 'I'm a life-time runner and you're a flash in the pan, so that didn't work. I'm a big mouth and you're practically a deaf-mute — no go there. But —' She narrowed her eyes at me like we were about to embark on some international conspiracy. 'Now we are both victims of the wonderful but fickle Eddie McBee. How does it feel?'

At the moment it felt angry, but when I looked up at her again, it was obvious she wasn't being snide. Her eyes locked with mine in an instant of understanding.

'Don't say I didn't try to warn you,' she said.

'You did.' I shrugged. 'It wasn't him, though. I blew it.'

She snorted. 'Oh, spare me. What did you do — make the fatal mistake of telling him you liked him? I told you that too, you idiot.' She pulled her red mane up in a bunch and tossed it impatiently over her shoulder. 'What's that stupid thing Corie's always saying — "dum-dum"? That's what he is — a real dum-dum. The minute — no, the second — you stop playing hard to get, he's history.'

'Tanya, could we have some line calls, please?'

Coach Spike was suddenly standing over us, his big hand slanted over his hip. I stared down into my lap and felt Tanya getting up. 'He may have had you convinced he's the most perfect guy in the world,' she said hoarsely over her shoulder, 'but there are better ones, believe me.'

When she'd moved away, I looked after her. Flipping her hair around at some junior guy on the back line, shrieking the whistle at Corie, levelling her eyes at Eddie's back — yeah, it was Tanya, all right. But for a few minutes there, you could have fooled me.

I knew Eddie wasn't going to talk to me again unless we were locked in a locker together or something, so I didn't even make myself available in the halls. I went straight through the rest of my classes in a semi-coma. Fortunately,

149

second period science was taking a test, so I didn't have to live through Lincoln's third degree and could shut myself up in Mrs Fruff's office and file stuff. It would have been perfect if I could have managed to get out at the end of the hour without having to talk to her either. No such luck.

'Don't tell me you're coming down with that flu everyone's getting,' she said without looking up as I was making for the door.

I stopped. 'No, ma'am. I'm okay.'

'You don't look okay.'

Reluctantly I turned around. The steely blue eyes were studying me closely. Naturally I shrugged.

'What are you doing for lunch today?' she said.

I shrugged again. 'Nothing,' I said. For once that was the truth. I'd made it a point to get out of the house before either Suzanne or Dad was up — and I sure hadn't reached for any of Her left-overs today. I wasn't about to eat anything made by the person who'd just destroyed my life by talking me into throwing myself at Eddie, and then turning around and throwing *her*self at my dad behind my back.

Uneasily I realized Mrs Fruff was still looking at me, probably waiting for me to do something besides mutter and shrug. 'I'm not doing anything,' I said.

'Join me then,' she said matter-of-factly. 'I always have enough for a small platoon anyway. Why don't you meet me here and then we'll try to escape from this mayhem for half an hour or so.'

It was a command actually, and although I'd just as soon have accepted an invitation to a concentration camp, I think I said okay.

Lincoln called me 'Teacher's Pet' when I told him I was lunching with Fruff after fourth period. Then he went off sulking. I was on my way to the lab when I ran into Dixie. It's hard not to notice Dixie coming at you down the hall; that's how preoccupied I was.

Her big round eyes were drooping down at the corners as she grabbed my arm. 'I heard you guys broke up,' she said.

'Who?'

'You and Eddie.'

'Oh.' I hunched my shoulders and avoided her eyes. They made me want to cry again. 'We were never really "going together" anyway.'

'Yes you were!' she said, bobbing her head.

'No.'

'You *were*. Why'd you drop him?'

I blinked at her. 'I didn't —'

'He's so bummed out. He looks like he's dying.'

'He's sick —'

'Are you going to lunch?'

I blinked again. I was having a hard time keeping up. 'I'm eating with — I'm not going to the cafeteria.'

She then entrapped me in a huge hug, in the middle of the hall. 'Well look, now that ya'll aren't together, any time you want to eat with us, just come on, all right? We've got to take care of you.'

Wasn't that everybody's job? I thought grimly as I walked into the lab. To get Janice to 'come out of her shell', 'feel good about herself', 'get her started' — and then tell her she's okay and kick her out on her own. I picked up a petri dish and peered into it. I know what it's like to be a 'project', I said silently to the culture. Just wait until you start getting it together. Then you're outa here.

'You're doing an excellent job with those,' Mrs Fruff said, appearing out of nowhere and gesturing towards the cultures. 'Your lab technique is superb — but then, I'm repeating myself. That's what I wanted to talk to you about, though. Are you ready?'

Whether I was or not, she led me to a courtyard on the west side of the campus I hadn't even known existed. Neither did anyone else, apparently, because it was quiet and empty. It was November cold too, but Fruff parked us at a cement table in the sun and broke out a thermos of herb tea. I watched in amazement as she peeled the lid off a Tupperware container to reveal a work-of-art salad that made Suzanne's look like paint-by-numbers. A couple of paper plates, some forks, and a container of vinegar and oil dressing also appeared, followed by a stack of bacon-flavoured crackers. Mrs Fruff motioned for me to help myself.

'What are your plans for after school?' she said.

Why is everyone so concerned about my every move? I thought bitterly. But I said, 'I have track practice.'

She smiled faintly. 'I meant much after. After graduation.'

'Oh.' I could feel my cheeks starting to sizzle. 'I haven't thought that far ahead.'

'I know the feeling. Sometimes I can barely think past the hot bath I'm going to climb into at 4 o'clock.'

I tried not to imagine Fruff sliding into a bubble bath. I didn't have the energy.

'With your grades and your aptitude, you can be very competitive. But the time to start planning is now. What about science? How would you feel about going at it seriously?'

I looked at her helplessly. She didn't have a clue, obviously, that all I could think about right now was the way the bottom had just dropped out of my life. The future meant nothing at the moment. In true Fruff fashion, though, she didn't go on. She was waiting for me to answer. I toyed numbly with a cherry tomato.

'I like biology a lot,' I said.

'It shows. And you have the perfect temperament for the laboratory. You work steadily. You don't have to be engaging in constant conversation. You learn extremely quickly.'

'Thank you,' I said.

She broke a cracker in half thoughtfully. 'I don't mean to pressure you, but I find so few students who are ready to settle down and take anything seriously. Natural for the age, I suppose. But when I find academic maturity, I like to try to grab it for the sciences before those language and art people get a hold of it.' She smiled her stern smile. 'But you have other interests, I know. Your track prowess is making a celebrity of you. I try to avoid listening to that wretched PA routine every morning, but I have picked up on your name.'

152

'Yes, ma'am.'

'I've never been a sports woman myself. I don't even like being a spectator. I guess the orderliness of the lab has me spoiled.'

'But there's order in running,' I said, and then stopped.

She cocked an interested eyebrow. 'How so?'

'I don't know,' I said. I crumpled my napkin.

'Certainly you do, or you wouldn't have said it.'

Her eyes were twinkling. Looking right into them, I said, almost curtly, 'You know just what to expect when you're running. If you breathe the right way and move your arms right — all of that — you're going to get where you're going, and you're going to get there fast. With strategy — it's very — orderly.'

She watched me as she chewed, and took her time wiping her lips. 'There isn't much else in life where you do know what to expect, is there?' she said.

I shook my head.

'Hold on to your running, then. It's hard enough just being alive without being a teenager too. You have my respect.'

I nodded.

'Promise me one thing, though. Two things. You won't let those PE people woo you until I've taken you to a few colleges myself.'

'Yes, ma'am,' I said.

'And that you won't let just plain living get you down. There are good days and bad, no matter who you are. Just accept that. End of sermon.'

Are *you* going to get brownie points for saving me, too? I thought. But out loud I just muttered, 'Amen'.

At track practice that afternoon Eddie, according to Corie, was locked in Coach Spike's office 'rehydrating' on a litre of Diet Coke because Coach wouldn't let him run looking as awful as he did.

That was a blessing. And so was the fact that Chuck wasn't loitering around the water fountain when I came out of the locker room. Tanya was.

153

She fell into step beside me. 'If we're gon' beat Albemarle Saturday it's gon' depend totally on you and me,' she said. 'The preacher's really sick.' She stopped and rolled her eyes. 'And you know the rest of the team except for Chuck is about as worthless — well, worthless. We're gon' have to work together.'

I wanted to ask her what in the name of Jefferson Davis Coach Petruso had been trying to drill into her head all season, but I didn't.

'Do you have any suggestions, or am I gon' have to do all the thinkin'?' she said.

Without mentioning that we already had a strategy, created by Eddie, I nodded mechanically. 'I have a plan that might work,' I said.

'That's a miracle. So what is it?'

So on the run that day, I showed her. And we beat the Adidas off all the rest of the girls, plus Tony and the Wookie. It was a photo finish. Anybody would've had a hard time telling which of us came in first. She never once recognized it as the strategy Eddie had designed. The chick must've been running in her sleep since September. Me? Running didn't fail me. The rest of the world was the pits, but when I was out there it all came together — at least for a few miles, a few minutes.

After practice I stayed in the shower until the tips of my fingers shrivelled up. There wasn't much to hurry for. It wasn't worth rushing to try to be with Eddie for five more delicious minutes — and I sure wasn't anxious to get home and watch Dad and Suzanne pretend they'd never touched each other.

By the time I got out, the locker room was quiet. I jumped a foot when I rounded the corner to the mirrors, blow-dryer in hand, and found Tanya standing there.

'You took a long enough shower,' she said when she saw my gaping reflection over her shoulder. She was experimenting with her hair and not liking the results.

'Is everybody gone?' I said.

'No. They all shrunk up and climbed into their lockers.'

Deliberately avoiding her eyes, I plugged in my dryer.

'You hate it when I say sarcastic stuff like that, don't you?' she said.

I shrugged. 'Kind of.'

'I am pretty much of a smart mouth.' She glanced at me out of the corner of her eye. She had her auburn hair pulled up on top of her head, and she let it fall as she sighed. 'Ugly mouth. Ugly face. Ugly hair. The only thing I got going for me is legs.'

She propped one up on the counter, and we both looked at it like it was a museum piece.

'Chuck likes my legs.'

'That isn't true,' I said.

She snorted. 'How do you know whether Chuck likes my legs?'

'I didn't mean that!' The old tongue was at its usual best. 'I mean you don't have an ugly face or ugly hair.' I flicked the dryer on in self-defence.

But she was grinning slyly. 'I have an ugly mouth, though, right?'

I didn't answer. She poked me in the side. 'Right?'

I bent hurriedly over at the waist and started drying the underneath layers of hair. 'Right,' I said.

She let out a hoot. 'You have the potential to be a smart mouth too, Kennedy. Being a bitch can take you far. Work on it.'

I stood up and looked shyly at her in the mirror. 'You're not really that bad. You just want people to think you are,' I said.

'Bull.' But she was fighting back a smile. Personally, I was fighting back a faint. I couldn't believe I'd actually said that to her.

'See ya, Kennedy,' she flung over her shoulder, squealing her Reeboks across the floor. 'You're still weird. But you have promise.'

I watched her retreating reflection and listened as her heels squeaked to the door and she yelled into the hall, 'Slade, you better be out here waiting for me.' If it had been anybody but Tanya I wouldn't have thought so, but in her case I was convinced: she was actually trying to be friends with me.

Going home was hard, but since there was only a note when I got there, saying Suzanne had gone to Savannah for a few days and Dad would be home soon, I holed myself up in my room with homework, fed myself before Dad arrived with a bucket of fried chicken, and feigned early sleep. I started to write a letter to Jack, but two lines into it I tossed the pencil and ripped the paper into confetti. What was I going to tell him — that I was going to be somebody's case or client or patient for ever? He'd be really happy to hear that.

I got into bed and lay there for a long time, expecting Dad to come in and try to have 'The Talk' with me, at which point I planned to be a complete brat and let him suffer through it before I told him I already knew. But he stayed in the den all evening. Even as numb as I was by that time, it made me mad.

'Why'd you have to eat lunch with that ol' Fruff woman yesterday?' Lincoln said to me Friday on the steps. 'You got some kinda problem or somethin'? Runnin' all around on the road. Gettin' all snotty, eatin' with some ol' teacher. Girl, you are strange!'

I smacked the chocolate-brown hand that was reaching for my cold chicken. 'If you think I'm all "strange", why do you hang out with me?'

'Because *I'm* strange.'

He was grinning broadly, and I couldn't help myself. I smiled — for about the first time in two days. Jack may have been wrong, though — my face did feel like it was going to crack.

'Tell me something, Lincoln,' I said.

He laid down full-length on the step, hands behind his head. 'Shoot,' he said.

'Am I some kind of project to you?'

His face squirmed into a question mark. 'I don't know nothin' about no project.'

'Do you hang out here at lunch because you think you're going to "save" me or something?'

'What I'm s'pose to be savin' you from?'

I looked at him — stretched out like a small, brown psychiatrist, sucking on a chew — and I splattered a laugh all over him. He sat up.

'What is wrong with you, woman? First you all bummed out. Then you start laughin' and askin' me weird stuff —'

'Why do you sit here every day at lunch-time?' I said.

'I want your body.'

'Come *on*!'

'I don't know!'

'Yes you do, or you wouldn't do it.'

'I ain't gonna do it no more if you gon' keep askin' me so many questions.'

The smile drained off my face. Miserably I tossed a half-eaten chicken leg into the trash can and wiped my hands on my trouser legs.

Lincoln was watching me sideways.

'Did I make you mad, girl?' he said.

'It wasn't you,' I said.

'Who was it then? I tol' you I'd get him for ya.'

I looked at his warm brown face. His eyes cared, and suddenly I wanted to tell him everything. He couldn't fix it, I knew. The point was, he wouldn't try to, and just then I wanted somebody who wouldn't try.

I started with, 'When I came here, I was just really shy and I wanted to be left alone, but nobody would leave me alone.' I ended with, 'I thought they liked me for me, you know? Now I find out I was just some challenge or something. I should've known better.'

He didn't say anything. He just shook his head. It was all I could do not to hug him. Instead, I went into the girls' cloakroom and cried.

While I was changing for practice that afternoon, I made a decision. As much as I loved to run, the heck with being on a team. As soon as the season was over, I was going to go back to running for fun, the way I'd wanted to do in the first place. Just me and Dad —

I stopped, mid-thought, and felt the anger welling up in me again. Okay, fine. He could mess around with What's-Her-Name. I'd run by myself, darn it.

That's the frame of mind I was in when I stepped out of the locker room, and straight into Chuck Slade's arms.

'Hello,' he said into my nose. If snakes could talk, they'd have sounded a lot like him. My flesh started to ooze disgust.

'Alone at last, huh?'

'Let go of me,' I said, trying not to throw up on him — though later I wished I had. It would have got rid of him at least.

'Come off it, Kennedy. With McBee out of the running, why don't you let somebody show you how it really is?'

Both of his hands were gripping the elastic at the back of my shorts, and he had me pulled so hard against him I could feel his ribs digging into me. I jerked angrily away, but the instant I put space between us, he wrenched me forward again. My head snapped back, and he skewered a kiss on to my neck. My saliva glands started to ache.

'You'd be so fine if you'd loosen up. Somebody needs to work on you.'

Retching, I tried to wriggle free. I ended up with my back to him, his arms around my waist in a vice, his hot breath in my ear.

'Kiss me back one time and I'll let you go,' he said.

The word 'no' was out of the question. My vocal cords were paralyzed. But I shook my head as hard as I could. On its final swing, he caught my chin with his hand and pressed his mouth hard against mine. Screwing my eyes and mouth shut as tightly as I could, I fought against him from the outside, and against the rising sickness from the inside.

Then just as suddenly as he'd been on me, he was off. Grabbing my mouth with both hands, I opened my eyes.

There was Tanya.

158

Her face was so white, her freckles stood out in bas-relief. Her eyes prickled with hurt. But in the instant it took for Chuck and me to register that she was standing there, the ache went out of her eyes and the hatred came in. And she wasn't aiming it at Chuck. She was firing it straight at me.

'You little tramp,' she said.

I started shaking my head.

'You have to have everything, don't you? You have to be the star on the team. You have to have the special coaching — because you can't make it on your own. You have to have Eddie because he used to be mine. And now you have to have him too.'

She jerked her head towards Chuck, who, it seemed to me, was taking the whole thing very coolly for a guy who was about to have one if not both of his eyes blackened.

'You little Christian hypocrite,' she went on. 'I loved him. I loved him so much. All I wanted was just him, all the time. He made me feel like I wasn't this self-centred little witch. He made me feel like I could be — sweet.'

I could feel my chin dropping practically to my chest. For one thing, Tanya was actually crying. And for another, I realized she wasn't talking about Chuck. She was talking about Eddie.

Still shaking my head I said, 'It's not like you think, Tanya. I didn't try to take either one of them from you. Eddie hurt me too, remember?'

'What do you think, I'm Helen Keller? I just saw you. You were standing here suckin' face with him right in the middle of the hall.'

Of course, if Chuck had come out with the truth at that point I'd have died of shock. But for some reason I couldn't come out with it either. The tears were pouring down Tanya's face in mascara rivulets, and her eyes were screaming with confusion and pain. I couldn't dump any more on what she was already feeling.

A small, buzzing crowd was gathering, so I started to push past Chuck. Still sobbing wildly, Tanya snatched at my arm.

'Everybody thinks you're so quiet and sweet,' she said. 'Bull! Do you hear me? Bull!'

'Stop it,' I said quietly.

'No. I want everybody here to know what you did to me. How I tried to be your friend and how you — *puked* on me.'

'Stop it!'

The buzz stopped. Not surprising, seeing how Janice Kennedy had just raised her voice. That wasn't surprising either, really, because somewhere inside the door marked GUTS had just sprung open, and all the rotten, ugly things that had happened to me in the past five days were shoving their way through it. For probably the first time in her life, Janice Kennedy was really angry.

'Stop it!' I said again. 'Just knock it off. I haven't done anything to you. All I've done is try to stay out of your way. *You're* the one —'

'Oh! The Christian martyr!' Tanya grabbed my arm and roughly shook it. 'Listen to this —'

'Don't touch me,' I said evenly.

'Stop me.' She lunged at me, and I was ready for her. Drawing back, I started to hurl myself forward. But clammy skin met mine from behind, and someone pinned my arms behind my back.

'Get her out of here, Slade!' Eddie barked in my ear.

'Let 'em go for it,' Chuck said.

'Get her out of here!'

'I'll get myself out,' Tanya said. Arching her chin, she swallowed hard. 'You've had it now, chick,' she said to me. 'You're history.'

The Tanya veneer was safely back in place as she squealed her shoes on the hall floor and left, with Chuck strolling behind her. Tess, Corie, Dixie, and Tony all looked anxiously at Eddie, who nodded them after her. Couldn't anybody do anything without his permission? I pulled my arm away from him and started to leave too, but he caught my wrist. Still pumping inside, I yanked it back and looked up into his face. A skull with a paste of white skin looked back at me.

'What's the matter with you?' he said. 'If Coach had seen that, you'd have been demerits in the *hole*. What got into you?'

'Anger, okay? Is that all right with you?' Tanya had got my mouth going, and, Sweet Mother of Jefferson Davis, I wasn't going to stop it now. 'I'm tired of being manoeuvred around! I have feelings. I'm a *person*! I'm not a project!'

Poor Eddie. He didn't know what I was talking about. For that matter, neither did I. And since I couldn't stand looking any longer at his sunken eyes and his sad mouth that used to smile all the time, I turned around and walked away. I didn't even turn around when he called 'Jan' after me. I was crying too hard.

15

The intercom announcement during registration Friday morning had blabbed that the Albemarle meet was the most important one of the season. That if the team won we'd have the county championship. That Eddie was going for the county record. That things like scholarships and 'careers' hung in the balance. It even said something about me going for a spectacular finish to a great first season.

But when I dreamed about it in the eerie early hours of Saturday morning, it went on about Eddie dying at the finish line, literally, and me being chased out of the course and all the way across Virginia by Tanya and Chuck and even by Eddie's ghost. It was exhausting. I got off the bus at the meet looking like I'd been running all night.

We prayed like usual, but I wasn't tuned in. I'd held up my end of the bargain, and so far God was reneging on his. Besides, I had OD'd so much on emotion the day before, I was like a stick. All I was really aware of was

Tanya looking at me constantly, and Eddie not looking at me at all.

Under any other circumstances, of course, that wouldn't have hurt me so. I knew this meet was everything in Eddie's mind, and he was concentrating. How he was even going to get one mile into it, I didn't have a clue. He was a skeleton. A dried-up, hollow-eyed skeleton.

The boys' race was first this time, and since Eddie asked Corie to do his mile split instead of me, I wandered towards the finish line. I was suddenly aware of a warm little form beside me.

'What are you doing here?' I said down into Lincoln's big, grinning mouthful of teeth. 'I thought you said running was weird or something.'

'You think *this* weird,' he said, thumb to chest, 'guess who else showed up today.'

My eyes scanned the bigger than usual crowd strung out along the sidelines at the start. 'Who?' I said.

He stiffened his neck. 'Miz Fruff herself.'

'You liar!'

His voice switched to falsetto. 'I ain't lyin', girl.'

He wasn't. There was Mrs Fruff 'herself', standing next to Coach Petruso, wearing wool slacks and a sweater tied just right under her neck, and a pair of wire-rimmed sunglasses. Even as I gaped, she turned towards me and gave me a thumbs-up sign.

Dad was there, of course, having just made it from the airport after picking up Suzanne. But at that moment, having Mrs Fruff and Lincoln there was about all the encouragement I really needed. For the first time it dawned on me: they never tried to 'draw me out'; they liked the qualities I *already* had.

The gun popped, and Eddie and the pack headed off down the hill and into the trees. I could see him taking the lead from the jump. Perhaps he really was going to kill himself.

It seemed like several for evers before the spectators further down from me started shrieking and the leaders came into view, heading for the finish line. By then I'd wrung my hands into two saturated dishcloths and was gnawing on my hair from both sides. When I saw green shorts I cringed.

But they weren't first. Blue shorts were first. Chuck Slade's blue shorts.

I suppose I'd known hate at some point in my life before that. Maybe I'd hated the witch in *Sleeping Beauty* or something. But real hate — the kind that makes you want to spit — reared up in me then for the first time. I couldn't come up with anything vile enough to think, so I just stood there, rooted to the ground, and hated.

They were only a hundred yards from the finish, steadily chugging up the hill, when I saw Eddie come over the crest. He was struggling, there was no doubt about that. It wasn't the Eddie-thing-of-beauty I loved to see run. His head was tilted back as if it were too heavy for him to support, and his arms flailed helplessly at his sides. But his legs kept going, kept reaching, kept driving like taut pieces of elastic band.

As I screamed myself crimson, he moved ahead, taking the green shorts like a ghost floating by. By then I could see his face, colourless and twisted with pain, and my screams started coming out in big old hangin' sobs.

'Come on, Eddie,' I heard myself crying. 'Come on, sugar. Kick some tail. Come *on*!'

He tried. Mother of Jefferson Davis, he tried. If almost had counted for anything, he'd have been a winner. Straining desperately forward, he could nearly touch the number on the back of Chuck's shirt. He reached the finish line in second place, and then collapsed.

I got to him first, but Coach Spike and Dad pulled me off him. Not before I saw his face, though. Not before I saw that although he was biting savagely at his bloody lip, he was crying out loud — a dry, raspy cry.

It was a bad dream, it had to be — the way Dad snapped into his professional self and ordered the paramedics around, the way Mrs McBee climbed into the ambulance shaking all over, the way Dixie came up and put her arm around me and Corie came at me head-on and cried all over the front of my warm-up jacket. I didn't even bother to snub Suzanne when she came and stood quietly beside me for a while. Why bother? It had to be a dream.

I woke up when Coach Spike came up and put both big hands on my shoulders. His eyes soaked into me like a drug.

'Are you all right, hon?' he asked.

'No, sir,' I said.

His mouth went up kindly on one side. 'I know. But can you run? You don't have to.'

I closed my eyes because nothing else seemed to be wiping the whole miserable nightmare out. But all I saw inside my eyelids were Chuck and Tanya: standing at the bottom of the bleachers saying, 'We don't need her.' Hovering around my locker with a thumbtack hidden in their clothes. Sitting in Coach's office accusing me of being a tramp. Kissing me. Grabbing me.

Making my Eddie lose everything.

My eyes snapped open and I looked at Coach, who, as always, was still waiting.

'I do have to,' I said.

As we jogged to the start, the usual nervous, happy chatter of the team was missing. Corie was sitting the race out. Tess was tying her hair up and staring straight down at the ground. Tanya was keeping her distance. Only Dixie could connect. She trailed me all the way with her hand touching my back.

As we passed the crowd, I looked up once to find Mrs Fruff. She didn't smile at me. She just nodded. There's order in running, I'd said to her. You always know what to expect. I sure hoped I knew what I was talking about.

Ever since the day Tanya and I had practised strategy together, I'd had such high hopes for this race. I'd imagined it so many times — us working the course like a well-oiled machine. That, of course, was out of the question now. But it still surprised me that she didn't turn around in the line-up and start her psychological thing on me. She just crouched, hands resting on her tilted upper thighs, and zeroed in on the course ahead. At least she was concentrating. That was more than you could normally say.

When the gun went off, I had to force myself to focus. I had to get Eddie and Tanya and Chuck and everybody else out of my head. I was going for it because it was there to be gone for. That was all that mattered.

The crowd thinned away, and we tunnelled down into the trees, which were bare now but still reaching out their friendly arms. It was quiet at last along the sidelines, and all I could hear was the heavy patter of feet, the sound I loved so much. I could already feel the tension going out of my shoulders. I was running. It was good.

My first clue that all was not well came at the turn-around. Although the two leading Albemarle girls were well ahead, Tanya wasn't snapping at their heels. As I rounded the curve from behind a row of now-naked trees, she was there, right in front of me. Her pace had slowed dramatically.

Concentrate, Janice, I told myself sternly. Remember your strategy. Putting my feet firmly out in front of me, I moved up beside her. It was way too early in the race to pass her, but by then she was practically moving backwards.

Don't listen to her, I chanted in my inner ear. Just go past her. Don't listen to her.

But she didn't say anything. Taking in air as much from relief as to gain speed, I started to go by her. Then I felt a pressure on the side of my foot, and a split second later I was on the ground.

She seemed to run on in slow motion. Everything was in slow motion. The pounding of feet coming faintly up behind me. The bounce of my arms and knees against the ground. The spin of the branches over my head.

'Come on, girl,' I heard somebody say.

Get out of my dream, I wanted to tell it. I can't do this anymore. Just let me lie here.

'Get your white self off that ground, girl! Come on,' it said again. 'You ain't no quitter. *Run!*'

Run. Run. My own voice took over. Run or you're nothing. Run, honey, or you don't have anything.

I was up off the ground and in one lean into the curve had Tanya in my sights again. It felt like I'd been down for hours. But it couldn't have been more than a few seconds. I was by her in an angry, white-hot flash before she even felt me behind her.

But the air wasn't there. I hadn't taken the time to get back what had been knocked out of me in the fall. And when I got to the final hill, my legs wouldn't kick in. I had nothing to drive them with.

By sheer desperate will I got by one pair of Albemarle green shorts. But the other one took first place ahead of me. I trailed in behind her through a blur of tears. I hurtled into someone's arms, but to this day I don't know whose, because immediately everything went black. When I opened my eyes, I was on the grass like a pretzel, head being pushed gently between my knees. I struggled to straighten up and saw Suzanne, crouched in the knot of people around me.

'Will you take me home?' I said.

'You bet, sugar,' she said. 'Anything you say.'

But as soon as we got in the door, I told her I wanted to be by myself. My knee was starting to hurt, and I had a jumble of things in my head all screaming to be sorted out. Besides, I remembered that she was the last person I wanted to sort anything out with. I told her to let me know the minute Dad came home from the hospital, and then I headed upstairs. I must have looked pretty awful, because she just let me go.

But when Dad came into my room ten minutes later, I forgot he was the *second*-to-last person I wanted to be with. I reached up both arms from my bed and buried my face in his neck.

'Darlin'! You okay, darlin'?'

I nodded feverishly. It was the first security of any kind

166

I'd felt since a certain tree in the country. But with a start I pulled my face away from his jacket.

'Eddie . . . ' I said. 'Dad, is he dead?'

He pulled me back against him. 'Darlin', of course not. He's okay. He's gon' be all right.'

I squirmed out of his grasp. 'Really? Are you sure?'

He cocked his head to the side and looked at me curiously for a long time. 'Yes, darlin',' he said finally. 'I'm tellin' you the truth. He isn't out of the woods, but he will be. He's gon' be just fine.'

'He's *going* to be? Dad, what's wrong with him?'

His head began to bob, as if nodding would somehow soften the blow. 'Eddie's got diabetes,' he said. 'He was almost in a diabetic coma when we got him to the hospital. But he's conscious now,' he went on quickly, head still nodding adamantly, 'and they'll have it controlled in a day or two — no problem.'

Diabetes. The word wove through my mind like an unreal tendril of smoke. Flu and strep throat and pneumonia — those were the things kids got — and got over. But diabetes. I knew nothing about it, but the dread in the word alone clamped down on my throat.

'What about you — are you all right, darlin'?' Dad said.

No, I thought. 'Yes,' I said — because what was the point really? Putting it all into words wasn't going to make it any better. Drained of everything, I sank back into the pillows.

He stood up slowly. 'I have to get back to the hospital. I think the best thing for you to do is get some sleep. Suzy's here if you need anything. Y'know that.'

I nodded and closed my eyes. When the door closed behind him, I opened them again, and all the things I'd thought I believed started to torment me.

If you believe in God and do what he wants you to do, nothing bad is ever going to happen to you.

Ha. Then why did Tanya hate me? And why had Chuck practically tried to rape me in the hall? And why had Eddie almost died? Huh? Answer me that!

167

*If there's one thing you can do and feel good about, you know
you're worth something. You have a reason to be here.*

Ha. Was that why I'd blown the race today? Was that
why out of nowhere I'd just flat fallen down on the track?
I mean, did that make sense?

Oh, yes, and the ever-popular *'if you want to get love,
you're going to have to give it'*.

Indeed — that was a real jewel. That must be why Eddie
had slapped me down when I told him he was special to me.
That must be why I'd let Suzanne into my life — so she
could get her hooks into my father and hide it from me.
That must be why I'd opened myself up to everybody: so I
could find out I was nothing more than a challenge to them
— some project to make *them* feel good.

That must be it, right?

It took me a minute to realize I must be talking to God.
Like everyone else, he'd disappointed me. But unlike everyone else, I was still talking to him.

Correction. I was screaming at him. I hadn't really
known I was doing it until my bedroom door flew open
and Suzanne came at me. By the time she had her hands
on my arms I was gasping, and my words were coming out
in chokes.

'Janice! Hey! Come on, sugar! Stop it!'

'No!' I screamed at her.

'Yes.'

'Don't, don't, don't —'

But she did, and I only tried for a second to get out of her
arms before I was sobbing into them. I could feel her body
relaxing, and she began to gently stroke my hair.

'That's better,' she said softly. 'That's better. Just let it
all out, sugar.'

'I don't want to.'

'I know. It hurts. But let it go. Come on, just let it
go.'

I don't know how long I cried, but the minute I went
limp, she pushed me firmly away from her and held on with
both hands.

'Now, you listen to me, girl,' she said quietly, right into my eyes. 'And you listen to me good.'

Whether I'd had a choice or not, I think I would have. The southern belle was temporarily out to lunch, and a serious, in-charge woman had come in to take her place.

'First of all, it doesn't take runnin' or looks or Eddie or some teenage snob at some school to make you worthwhile. You are Janice. Period. Full stop. Were you meant to be Miss Madison High or run your mouth and charm the socks off every man, woman, and child? Why can't you be Janice? You're quiet. You're smart. You think before you talk — and if you don't have something important to say, you don't say anything at all! What in the name of Moses, sugar, is wrong with that?'

There was no stopping her.

'The only thing wrong is when you don't tell the right people when you're so miserable about something you can't even hold your head up. What's going on? Tell me!'

I was ready to tell her, all right. The problem was where to start. I went for the throat. 'Why didn't *you* tell *me*?' I said.

'Tell you what?'

'That you were having an affair with my father?'

Her eyebrows went up. 'I'm not.'

'What good does it do me to be honest with other people if they can't tell me the truth?' I cried, pounding my fist on the bed.

She caught it in mid-air. 'I love your daddy, Janice. But I'm not having an affair with him.'

'I saw you kissing,' I said stubbornly.

'People in love kiss.' She touched my face lightly with her hand. 'Don't tell me you don't know that.'

I was swallowing hard. 'But why did I have to sneak up on you to find out? Why couldn't you have shared that with me?'

'I wanted to. But your daddy was waiting for the "right time" to tell you — and he wanted to be the one. I guess the right time never came.'

She put her pretty hands on either side of her face and sighed.

'You come by it honest, sugar, I'll tell you that. He tells me he doesn't think you'll mind, that you'll be crazy about the idea. But he's scared to death to confront you with it, and he won't admit it.' She shook her head tearfully. 'What am I gon' do with the two of you?'

I had tears, too. 'I don't know,' I said.

'Don't hide from me,' she went on. 'Don't hide from anybody.'

'You told me that before.' I drew my knees under my chin. I was starting to wind down. 'It didn't work.'

'You mean Eddie?'

I nodded miserably. 'I did what you said. I told him how I felt about him. And you know what? You were *wrong*! He looked at me like I was some poor baby who'd just lost pin-the-tail-on-the-donkey at a birthday party and said he was sorry, but he hadn't meant that at all —'

'Bilge water!'

I stopped.

'That is trash, sugar! That boy is so crazy about you he can't even stay right side up — and don't try to feed me that baloney about him treatin' all the girls that way. I know lovesick when I see it.'

'But I blew it.'

She puffed out her fringe with a disgusted sigh. 'Honey, you aren't the only one with hang-ups. Eddie must be about as scared of commitment as any guy I've seen.'

'Scared? Eddie?'

'Yes, Eddie. The point is, sugar, you can't stop trustin' just because one person with problems burns you. Honey, if that were true, I wouldn't be in love with your daddy.'

I squirmed.

'I was married to a man who started out feedin' me every meal by hand out of a silver spoon and ended up beatin' the stuffings out of me every time I got out of line. It took me three years before I'd go out with anybody after the divorce, and the minute I did, with an old friend from home, the jerk fed me Chesapeake Bay shrimp and then tried to unbutton my blouse in the restaurant parking lot.'

I choked, but by then she was laughing.

'You remember that night we found the garbage on the front porch?' She nodded. 'That was the one. That good ol' "friend" in the sweet little red sports car. But you see?' She took hold of both my hands. 'I can't stop lovin' because a couple of men have done me dirty. Your daddy is the kindest, most lovin' man I've ever known. All he wants is a good family life. And that's all I want, too. He has his problems — as I'm findin' out — but I'm willing to open up and let him in so I can help him, and he can help me. And even that doesn't make everything perfect. I went home to Savannah this week to tell Mother and Daddy about Loren. Mother didn't say a word. Daddy told me I must be out of my mind, carryin' on with an "old man" with a half-grown daughter.'

'Old!'

'That's exactly what I said. And when he told me I should find some nice boy my own age, I just turned on my heel and high-tailed it back here to ya'll.'

'You're upset, though.'

'Oh, you bet. That's life, sugar. Even with God on your side, there is no guarantee everything is goin' to go your way. But if you let people in, if you tell 'em how you feel — ugly or pretty — a lot more things are gon' go your way —'

'Ha!'

'— in the long run.'

I was too tired to cry any more, so I just sadly closed my eyes. 'How long is the long run?' I said.

'Oh, sugar, if I knew that, I'd be rich.'

A silence settled over us. She kept her hand on my hair for a while, and I kept my eyes shut, partly to close it all out and partly to hold in what I knew were finally some answers.

Somewhere in the quiet she said, 'So you want something to eat?'

'A meatball sandwich,' I mumbled.

'You've got it.'

Actually, I don't know if she ever ordered it or not. I was asleep before she even got off the bed.

16

They didn't wake me up for church on Sunday, which was fine. I had my own service, peeking out through my blinds at the crisp, Virginia-November day and talking to God.

If I were going to start anywhere having the guts to let someone in, it ought to be with him. I'd never known there was a God Door before, but that morning I guess it opened.

The first thing I did was apologize to him.

I wish I could say I knew you were there all along and you'd help me in the end, I said silently, but I can't. I was convinced you didn't really care about *me*, the way Eddie said you did. But I do believe now. Maybe not the way Eddie does, but somehow I believe. I've let you down, will you forgive me?

As I prayed, and as I drifted in and out of sleep, I started remembering things.

Like Corie saying, 'I bet you look gorgeous all the time.'

Like Mrs Fruff saying, 'I like the way you handled yourself in this lab today.'

Even Tanya saying, 'You're a good listener.'

But like Suzanne had said, the ugly came in with the pretty. I'd lost Eddie, for one thing, no matter what the reason.

And I'd lost the race too. I'd just fallen down, right at the crucial moment, like some spastic.

But had I? That was the question that kept pestering

me. Like it or not, I had to force myself to mentally rerun the race.

I'd been concentrating. I'd been determined to win that race — if for no other reason than to make up for Eddie's not winning his. Everything had been fine until I'd rounded the curve and seen Tanya.

No, even then I'd had it together.

I'd tried to pass her, and *then* I'd fallen, and then she'd gone on.

No. I'd felt a pressure on the side of my foot — and *then* I'd fallen.

A pressure on the side of my foot.

Like somebody had side-stepped me or knocked my foot sideways so my knee would buckle and I'd fall. Somebody like Tanya.

I sat up, wide awake, with my heart pounding. She'd made me fall on purpose, just like she and Chuck had done everything else to try to keep me from winning. It was as clear to me as anything had ever been.

But wearily I sank back into the pillows. For some reason, it didn't give me any great thrill to have something concrete on Tanya. In a nagging kind of way, it made me feel sad.

Besides, I couldn't prove it. It was the sabotage on the shoes and the sexual harassment and the psychological needling all over again. There wasn't a thing I could do about it.

I was still mulling over that when I heard the phone ring from very far away and a few minutes later saw Dad peeking through the crack in my door.

'Hi,' I said.

'You up for a phone call?' he said. 'Somebody named Dixie?'

I could picture Dixie's round eyes all filled with concern as I picked up the receiver. Her voice was brimming with it, too.

'Are you all right?' she said, trying to catch her breath as usual.

173

'I've been better.'

'You must be *all* bummed out. I would be.'

'Did you hear about Eddie?' I said.

'I can't believe it. And you know, Janice, all this week I just thought he was so miserable because you'd broken up with him. He was really sick, wasn't he?'

'But he broke up with me!' I said.

'Nuh-uh.'

I found myself giggling. 'Dixie, I oughta know. He did.'

'That doesn't make any sense. He was with you longer than I've ever known him to be with a girl. He quit flirtin' with *everybody* else — and if you know Eddie, you know that's sayin' somethin'.'

I was beginning to think I didn't know Eddie at all.

'Well, whatever,' she said. 'You know you have your friends, girl. Now you *better* eat lunch with me tomorrow. Tell you what, I'll bring some —'

She went off on a detailed description of the feast she was packing, most of which I missed. All I heard was the friendship in her voice, and I loved her for it.

When we hung up, I pulled off my covers and examined my knee. Basically I just had a bunch of grazes down the side of my leg. The joint itself wasn't even tender anymore. Wriggling out of the sweatshirt I'd been sleeping in, I went for the wardrobe, and in five minutes I was down in the den, perching on the edge of Dad's chair. His face lit up.

'Let's run, Dad,' I said.

'You shouldn't today, darlin'.'

'I'm fine. Now come on. You're getting flabby on me.'

Sparkling a smile at him, I pinched his midriff.

'Let me get changed,' he said.

Naturally he wouldn't let me get past a slow jog, but even the rhythm of that was soothing. He whistled his breathing beside me, and I settled in. Now was the perfect time to bring some matters up.

In the true Loren Kennedy fashion, though, he was too busy making everything okay to give me a chance.

'You know, Eddie's going to be fine, and the two of you

will be out here running together again before you know it,' he said.

My spirits immediately flagged.

'That won't be happening, Dad. We aren't going out any more.'

'I don't believe that!'

'He didn't really like me that much, anyway.'

'Now, darlin', don't be silly. This boy and girl stuff has its ups and downs when you're young. It'll all work out —'

'Dad.' I stopped dead on the side of the road. 'It isn't going to work out.'

'Honey—'

'It isn't! It's awful, okay? I hate it!'

Grabbing on to a street lamp, he looked at me helplessly. 'What do you want me to do, darlin'?' he said.

'Just let me tell you I feel rotten and don't try to cover it all up! Just tell me I'm not making your whole life a mess if I get sad or something. Just tell me life's gonna be tough sometimes.' I was stomping my foot on every accented syllable. 'Don't tell me everything's wonderful. Just tell me I'll make it when it isn't!'

Dad and I have never looked alike, but just then I could tell he had the same expression on his face that I had on mine. An anger he never vented on me was right there behind his eyes.

'It works both ways then, my dear,' he said tightly. 'How can I tell you those things when I don't even know you're hurting? You pretend just as much as I do.'

We stared at each other. If he was surprised at my outburst, I was flabbergasted at his. I'd just asked him to show me some real stuff — but I'd never expected him to actually do it. It made the ground feel very safe for going on.

'I didn't fall in love with somebody and try to hide it from *you*.'

'Janice —' he said sharply.

'You could've told me about you and Suzanne, Dad.'

He folded his arms uneasily across his chest. 'She told you.'

175

'No. I saw you two together. But why *didn't* you tell me?'

The anger was still clinging to his jawline, but he looked as miserable as I'd ever seen him as he gazed off down the street. It was as if he hoped to find a good answer lying out there somewhere.

'I did try once. But then, you had so much going on in your life already, darlin', I didn't want to get you upset when things were just beginning to happen for you.'

I took a deep breath and searched where he was searching. 'Am I that messed up that you think I'm going to break or something?'

'Of course not —'

'I'm getting tired of everybody thinking of me as a case. You sent me to a psychiatrist so I could get better. Now I'm better, and you and everybody else are still acting like I can't handle anything. I'm a person!'

'I know that.'

'You don't act like it.'

'That's enough!'

Our eyes locked for an angry moment, and to my immense relief there was no apology on Dad's lips.

'I should have given you more credit,' he said. He sounded as if he were controlling every word. 'But I didn't want to upset you.'

'I can handle it. I've been handling a lot of other stuff.'

'How am I supposed to know that? You hide things.'

'So do you.'

He closed his eyes and let out a weary puff that, oddly, ended in a chuckle. 'You sound just like Suzy.'

'Why?'

'She says I hide, too.' He looked at me sadly. 'She's good for us, darlin'.'

'I know that. Why did you think I'd be upset anyway? I loved her. I still do.'

'Me too,' he said, as he reached for me.

A tearful hug on the corner of Monroe and Main doesn't solve all your problems — but it's sure a start.

In class the next day, Corie was, shall we say, not her

176

usual bubbling self. She looked like she'd been crying most of the weekend. Dad had assured me that Eddie was out of danger and that the doctors were getting his diabetes under control, but my veins started pumping anxiety the minute I saw her.

I slid into my desk beside her. 'What's wrong?' I said. I was talking over the false gaiety of the intercom, a no-no in Mrs Garner's class, but I really didn't want to hear that bozo's version of Saturday's fiasco anyway.

'My cousin — that's what,' Corie said.

'Eddie's gonna be okay,' I told her, as much to convince myself as her.

'Not if he doesn't co-operate. He says all the insulin — or whatever that stuff is — in the world isn't going to make him a world-class runner, and if he has to count every bite that goes into his mouth for the rest of his life, forget going to college or bein' a coach or anything. 'Course without the scholarship, he can't go anyway.' Her eyes filled with tears, I was sure for the hundredth time since Saturday. 'He won't even talk to Uncle Edward —'

Suddenly she leaned across the desk and looked at me like she'd just realized it was me and not merely the next person she could get to listen. 'Janice — *you* talk to him. He'd listen to you.'

I squirmed against the back of my seat. 'No, he wouldn't.'

'Idiot! Janice, go to see him! Here.' She flipped open her binder and ripped out a sheet of paper. 'He's in Room 203,' she said, racing a purple felt tip across the page. 'Talk to him, okay?'

I took the paper, but I shook my head. 'He won't want to see me. I'd probably just make things worse.'

'Come on, Janice.' Her brown eyes were direct. 'Eddie tried to help you when you first moved here. The least you could do is help him.'

When the bell rang, she left. I stayed in my desk, looking after her. The Eddie Project, huh? It didn't have a bad ring to it.

I got up with a jolt, and tossing everything except a pencil and a spiral notebook into my locker, I tore down to the gym. It only took a minute to convince Coach that I was fine, but not fine enough to do PE — only fine enough to have a hall pass to the library.

It gave me infinite pleasure to present one of the Brown Brogue Twins with a bona fide pass and start attacking her precious encyclopedias with a vengeance.

You can only find out so much about diabetes in fifty minutes, but it was enough to show me that Dad's assurance that Eddie was going to be perfectly okay wasn't entirely accurate. But then, bless his heart, that was Dad for you.

Eddie's pancreas, which normally produced insulin to get the fuel in his cells going, wasn't doing that any more, so energy was being drawn from his body fat, and its breakdown products were accumulating in his bloodstream. Every symptom I read turned on light bulbs in my head.

Extreme thirst. That explained why he could never pass a water fountain without draining the thing. All the empty milk cartons and Diet Coke cans in our trash can made sense now, too.

Frequent urination. Coach Spike had mentioned that Eddie peed more than a puppy.

Increased appetite. Yeah, life was one big meal to Eddie — but then he'd just kept losing weight. Dad had been on the right track that night he'd questioned Eddie about training too hard.

Fruity odour on the breath. With a pang I realized that was one of the things I loved so much — being close enough to him to smell his clean clothes and sweet breath.

Weakness and listlessness. I got a lump in my throat just thinking about that. He'd tried so hard to fight it. Who else would've kept *walking* around, let alone tried to run a three-mile cross-country race?

The worst part of it all was that even though the disease could be controlled with diet and insulin injections, there were so many complications that could occur down the line no matter how carefully he took care of himself. Things like blindness, kidney problems, high blood pressure, nerve damage, gangrene. Just when he was really beginning to live, he'd have to be thinking about how he might die.

I was starting to wish I'd never found all that stuff out when I came across one sentence that saved me. 'Exercise,' the book said, 'is the invisible insulin. Diabetics can stay healthier and extend their life span if they exercise consistently.'

Eddie *could* still run, it told me — as hard and as competitively as he wanted. He *had* to run. Somebody had to tell him that.

Second period I was in Mrs Fruff's room before anyone else.

'May I work with Lincoln in the library?' I asked her in lieu of 'hello'.

She just nodded as she wrote out two passes. But as I was ushering him out the door, she said, 'Janice.'

'Yes, ma'am?' I said.

'You may not have won that race Saturday, but you were superb. Those PE people may get you after all.'

Not surprisingly I didn't know what to say. 'Thank you for coming,' I managed to get out. And then I pushed Lincoln off down the hall.

'What is this?' he said as I half-dragged him by the collar of his jeans jacket.

'See this word?' I pulled an index card out of my notebook and poked it in front of his face.

'Dia-what?'

'Don't worry about how to say it or what it means. Just find it in every book you can and bring it to me.'

'You crazy, woman!'

'Oh, shut up,' I said.

Lincoln Lewis had never worked so hard in his life, I'd bet on it. The creamy whites of his eyes were bloodshot by the time the hour ended. But I had ammunition, and that made me happy.

'I heard Eddie McBee has been diagnosed diabetic,' Mrs Fruff said to me when we slid back into class just before the bell rang.

'Yes, ma'am.' My face went crimson. 'That's why I was in the library — to look stuff up about it.'

'Wise move.' She arched an eyebrow approvingly. 'Tell you what. Skip the quiz fourth period today. You can spend the hour in my office. I have pamphlets galore back there. Just help yourself to the files.'

I did, and by track practice that afternoon I could've pulled anybody out of insulin shock or recognized a diabetic coma from a hundred paces. There were at least ten million questions I wanted to ask Suzanne about diet, and several thousand more I could probably get Dad to answer. I was so engrossed I didn't even see Tanya until she was standing behind me in the line for the workout.

The season was all but over now, except for the regionals. We hadn't done that well Saturday, but we were still in the running. In the end, Tanya had won what she was after. Maybe that was why it didn't give me the usual heebie-jeebies to have her parked behind me. Our feud had to be all but over, too.

Chuck was another matter. I still looked anxiously for him, but he'd stationed himself way down at the other end of the pack. Tanya obviously hadn't pinned *all* the blame on me. I was amazed he didn't have a black eye.

We just did a light run that day, and Coach even held everyone back on the end sprint. There was such a hush over the team, none of us probably could have put out much anyway. I was walking around the track with Dixie, cooling down, when Tanya trotted by us. I'd been wrong about the truce.

'Think you can remain vertical today?' she said.

I didn't hesitate. 'I usually do,' I said.

'Was that a mirage I saw Saturday then?' She was jogging backwards in front of us, hands coupled into the front pocket of her turquoise sweatshirt, red hair bouncing tauntingly on her shoulders.

I didn't answer. 'I'm sorry I missed lunch today,' I said to Dixie. 'I was in the library.'

'You liar! You were probably sleazin' around, lookin' for

180

some other girl's boyfriend to steal.' Tanya snorted at Dixie. 'Good thing you don't have one. She'd be after him.'

Dixie's face was the colour of cabbage. 'Why don't you shut up, Tanya?' she said.

Tanya, of course, didn't.

Instead she stopped in front of us and spread her feet apart. Sighing, I tried to go around her. She blocked my way.

'We didn't get to finish what we started the other day. As *usual*, the preacher was there to clean up everybody's act and absolve their sins or something.' Her eyes narrowed into nasty incisions. 'But he isn't here today — and I'm gonna kick your tail.'

Dixie stepped away, but Tanya halted her with a look. 'Forget it, Tubby. Just stay right there.'

I probably should have been mad or scared or had some other normal feeling, but all I was was very, very sad. I just wanted to get away from her before she messed things up for herself any more.

'Come on,' I said to Dixie. 'She's all talk.'

A cold hand closed over my arm. 'Am I talking now?' Tanya said.

I jerked away — and *then* I got mad. I could hear my voice coming out, and I could see it reflected in the shock on Tanya's face. 'You don't know how to win without hitting somebody or tripping them on the track or something. But you're gonna have to back off me — right *now*.'

She was paralyzed, but I didn't push my luck. Before she could recover, I grabbed poor Dixie by the sleeve of her warm-up and fled. We were almost to the locker room when I finally started to shake and Dixie found her voice.

'She's still standing there,' she whispered.

I didn't turn around to see.

'You're not even scared of her, are you?' she said.

'Right.' I gave her a look.

'Well, you sure didn't act like it. You know, she's been like that ever since *kindergarten*. She was the kind of kid who'd only give Valentines to three or four of her friends, and then *bite* the kids who didn't give *her* one.'

I snorted shakily. 'She bit?'

'Is that so hard to believe?'

'No.'

'Well, it's about time somebody stood up to her. Eddie's about the only one who ever does. The rest of us are such wimps around her.'

'I'm not that brave when I'm by myself.' I looked at her shyly. 'Thanks for being there.'

'Did I have a choice?'

I grinned at her, but her big round eyes had taken on a serious shine.

'Janice, was that true, what you said to her about her tripping people on the track?'

My grin disappeared. Suddenly I desperately wanted to get out of there.

'Is that so hard to believe?' I said lamely.

'No.' She plumped her hands on to her hips and started breathing hard. 'I know you fell down in the race. We saw you getting up. She did it, didn't she?'

'I can't prove it.'

I started drawing a box on the dirt with the toe of my shoe, but I could feel her eyes on the top of my head.

'Well, somebody's got to get her sometime. I'm probably not even gonna be on the team next season. She just makes it a complete drag for me — and Robin and Lisa feel the same way.'

I wanted to shrug, but I controlled myself. When I finally looked up she was still staring at me.

'I'd go with you to tell Coach,' she said.

I shook my head as she bore into me with her big eyes.

'Whatever,' she said after a long, awkward silence. She turned towards the locker room door. 'But you aren't scared of her like the rest of us wimps. If you don't do it, nobody ever will.'

Then I guess nobody ever will, I thought. So much for the GUTS Door. I could feel it closing, even as I stood there.

But then I could feel somebody putting their foot in it and springing it open again.

Was it Dixie? Eddie?

As I turned slowly towards Coach Spike's office, I realized whose foot it was. It was mine.

17

The word travelled fast. I was surprised the intercom voice the next day didn't say, 'Good morning, Patriots. Yesterday cross-country runner Janice Kennedy lost her mind and made a ridiculous accusation against long-time Madison track star Tanya Early.'

By lunch-time everybody and his brother-in-law knew I'd gone to Coach Spike and told him not only that Tanya had tripped me in the race, but that she'd tried to start two fights with me, was probably responsible for the thumbtack in my shoe, and had otherwise harassed me the whole season. They all knew we were taking it to the school court and that our court date was Friday, after school. They also knew that Tanya and Chuck were back together and that they intended to 'change my mind' before Friday.

I didn't even know that last part myself, until the delegation on the front steps told me.

I was just opening the aluminum foil on one of Suzanne's sandwiches — with Lincoln slavering over my left shoulder — when our steps suddenly filled up with bodies. Dixie, Amy, Lisa, Robin, Tony, Tess and the Wookie were led in front of me by a very triumphant-looking Corie.

'It's gettin' crowded out here,' Lincoln muttered.

'You are great,' Corie said, twinkling her face down at me. She was obviously the spokesperson for the group because everybody else nodded behind her. Dixie's face was bright red, and she was puffing happily away.

'Thanks,' I said. I looked quizzically at Lincoln, who shrugged in disgust and started eating my sandwich.

'We heard what you did and we're impressed.'

'It blew us away,' Tony said. 'But now that we've recovered from the shock — we're impressed.'

The Wookie poked him.

Corie was practically doing the Funky Chicken by this time. 'Of course, we all feel like total wimps for not standing up to Tanya and Slade ourselves —'

'Well, not *total* wimps, do you think?' Tony said to Tess. She smacked him.

'— but now that you've started it, we're going to help you finish.'

'Okay,' I said. I wasn't sure what I was agreeing to, but I was sure it didn't really need my endorsement. They'd obviously already made up their minds about it.

Dixie couldn't contain herself any longer. 'Tanya and Chuck don't run the team. They can't infect everybody with their — bile.'

'Ooh. Nice word!' Tony said.

'So,' Corie said, 'you've inspired us to form a support network — a sort of gang — to keep the good stuff on the track team. No more pussyfooting around. No more kow-towing to their threats —'

'*And* —' Corie sat down beside me, nearly pushing Lincoln right off the step. He snuffed indignantly and stuffed the rest of my sandwich into his mouth. 'We're going to stand behind you every inch of the way and see that you win this trial. What can we do?'

My face was about the colour of the now-devoured corned beef, and I spluttered around for words. 'I don't know,' I said. 'It's basically my word against hers on everything.'

'We saw you getting up from the fall,' Dixie said.

'All that shows is that she fell,' Tony said. 'Don't try for law school, okay, Dix?'

'We were there the day she put the thumbtack in your shoe,' Tess said, motioning to Corie. 'We saw her by the lockers when we came in.'

'Purely circumstantial,' Tony said.

'Would you please shut him up?' Tess said to Lance.

They were all looking at me then, and I just looked back helplessly. 'Just be there for me,' I said. I could hardly get the words out, but they were all nodding eagerly. 'I guess just think of every piece of evidence you can, and then just be there so I'm not by myself.'

Corie squeezed my hand. 'You're not alone, okay? You've got all of us.'

There was a funny silence, during which Tony cleared his throat loudly and Dixie gave Corie a nudge. Corie wrinkled up her nose. She sure didn't want to say what was coming next.

'We also have a confession to make,' she said when Dixie poked her again. 'When you first came here, Eddie was all hepped up about making you feel at home and all that.' She glanced around uncomfortably at the rest of the group, but they'd all started examining their Reeboks with unusual interest. 'We all said, you know, 'Yeah, yeah, Eddie, we'll be nice to the chick.' But you were so shy, and we couldn't get you to even look at us half the time. When Eddie was around we tried, but most of the time it just kind of turned into his thing.'

'We were all a bunch of dum-dums, okay?' Tony said.

'But — now, Janice, this is for real.' Corie leaned her sparkly little face close to mine, and her Eddie-like eyes were squinted with sincerity. 'It's crazy, but slowly you've just become a part of us. I mean, you aren't half as rowdy as any of us —'

'Who could be?' somebody said.

'— but you're one of us — and not just because Eddie said you had to be.'

'Yeah. Matter of fact, the minute we all get to be friends with you, he dumps you.'

Lance clapped a hand over Tony's mouth and lifted

him over the cement banister. We heard him clatter into the bushes below.

I probably should have been crying or shaking or trying to crawl into my lunch bag at that point, but all I could do was laugh. I knew I was bright red; I could feel the steam coming off my face. But I just kept giggling at all of them.

'It's okay,' I said. They leaned forward to hear me; that's how softly my voice was squeezing out. 'I know I'm not the easiest person to get to know. But thanks.' I took a good hard look at *my* Reeboks. 'I really like you guys, too.'

'Why not? We're great.' It was Tony, vaulting up over the side.

'Well.' Tess tucked her purse under her arm. 'I don't know about ya'll, but I'm starved. Do you think there's anything left in the cafeteria?'

'We sure had a hard time findin' you.' Corie said to me. 'Why do you eat out here?'

I suddenly remembered Lincoln, but when I looked around, he'd disappeared — with the remains of my lunch.

'Come on, I've got loads of stuff,' Dixie said, pulling me up by the hand.

'Got enough for me, too?' Tony said, sniffing at the nappy-bag-looking thing she carried over her shoulder, bulging with interesting food-like shapes.

'We forgot somethin'.'

Everybody stopped, because it was Lance who had spoken. I'd realized early on why he and Eddie were such good friends. He never talked and Eddie talked all the time. But when Lance did open his mouth, everybody listened. I looked up the six and a half feet to his face and listened too.

'Tanya and Slade are lying in wait for her,' he said. He looked down at me. 'Me and Tony are gonna be your bodyguards 'til Friday. You don't go anywhere in this school without us, and we don't leave until you're in your house in the afternoon.'

I'd have laughed except I wasn't sure if that was within the rules he was laying out. Instead I nodded.

'Then let's go,' Tony said.

He took one elbow and Lance took the other. I got to the cafeteria without either of my feet ever touching the ground.

I'd planned to do some important shopping that afternoon, but Tony and the Wookie wouldn't hear of it unless they went along.

'The mall? You gotta be kiddin'!' Tony said. 'If Tanya's gonna show up anywhere, it's gonna be there.'

I couldn't argue with him on that, so piling into Eddie's truck — the 'green spare parts' Eddie'd said they could use while he was in the hospital — they took me to the mall.

I don't have to mention how self-conscious I felt, walking up and down the aisles in the health food store with the two of them trailing behind me. It didn't seem to bother them, though. Lance bought twenty carob and sesame seed bars he thought were chocolate candy bars, and Tony spent the whole time looking for natural vitamins that would pump up his muscles.

'What's all this stuff for anyway?' Tony said when the clerk loaded thirty bucks' worth of granola bars and the like into a bag.

'Eddie,' I said.

'I thought you guys broke up.'

Lance groaned.

'We did,' I said. I headed out of the store with Tony scrambling at my heels and the Wookie strolling behind us, cautiously checking out the environment. 'But we're still friends.'

'Oh yeah, the old "let's still be friends" line, huh?'

I stopped, and he ploughed into me.

'Shut up, would you, Tony?' I said.

He made a face, but for the first time I saw Lance grin.

187

'I like you, lady,' he said to me in his big moaning voice. 'You're all right.'

By the time we picked up a gym bag at the athletic store, a medic-alert bracelet and about a year's supply of Life Savers at the drugstore, and a personalized T-shirt at the T-shirt shop, they were getting a little restless. If they were anything like Eddie, food was the only cure for that.

'I'll treat you to meatball sandwiches,' I said shyly.

They carried me bodily to Poe's.

I was doubled over, laughing, through five sandwiches and a bottle of Sunkist. But the minute they dropped me off at the hospital — where I assured them Dad would take custody of me at the front door — the giggles were swept away by the worst case of nerves I'd had since my first day at Madison High.

There was no turning back now, of course. I'd come too far for that. But what I'd told Corie was true. I was probably about the last person Eddie wanted to see.

Just as he'd promised me the night before, Dad was waiting for me by the front door, and so was Suzanne, dressed in a designer lab coat and ready to squeeze the ever-lovin' breath out of me.

'You're doin' the right thing, sugar,' she said. 'I'm s'proud of ya I could squeak.'

'You are squeaking, Suzy,' Dad said. And then he pulled her up against his face.

I shook my head at both of them. They were worse than a couple of teenagers in love. If I weren't so happy for them, for all of us — if the three of us hadn't had a talk last night that lasted until 2 in the morning and ended in a huge group hug — I'd have thought they were kind of silly.

But love isn't silly, I thought as I walked down the endless hall towards Room 203. It can hurt a heck of a lot, but it isn't silly. If it were, why would I have spent my whole month's clothing allowance, plus an advance from Dad, on a gym bag full of it?

My first fear, that Eddie was still going to look like the skeleton he'd been last Saturday, disappeared the minute I crept into his room. Dad, Mrs Fruff, and the books had all been right. Physically, he looked better than I'd *ever* seen him look.

The only thing missing was the smile. I was tempted to bolt out of there when all he said was, 'Janice. Hi.'

Only sheer nervousness kept me rooted to the spot. At least he didn't say, 'What are *you* doing here?' as I'd been sure he would.

'Hi,' I said. 'How are you doing?'

'Terrific.'

Liar.

'Why shouldn't I? They've fed me enough stuff that's good for me. I feel like Mr Clean, you know?'

I knew I was staring at him, but I couldn't stop. It sure looked like Eddie, swinging his legs over the edge of the bed in Madison High sweats. But the voice that was coming out of him was the voice of a stranger. A Chuck Slade maybe, or a male Tanya. The bitterness was so sharp I thought it was going to reach out and slash me to ribbons.

I opened my mouth and hoped something would come out. 'In a lot of ways, you'll be healthier than the rest of us from now on.'

'Good. I can sit on the sidelines, healthy as a horse, and cheer the rest of ya'll on.'

'Why?' I said.

'Why what?'

'Why should you sit on the sidelines? Why can't you run?'

He laughed, but it wasn't his deep throaty chuckle. It came from some pit inside him. 'Because halfway through a three-mile race I'd have to stop and take my blood sugar or something. "Uh, could we stop the race for a second. I need to pull out my Auto-let here, yeah, oh, I'm still normal. Okay, hit it!" '

'You're feeling sorry for yourself,' I said between my teeth.

189

'How did you guess?'

I'd only seen that expression on his face a few times, and it had always been directed towards Chuck Slade.

'I'm an expert on it,' I said. 'I've been feeling sorry for myself my whole life. But then this friend came in and took me over and made me stop it and made me turn my life around.' I took my first step forward since I'd entered the room, and plopped the gym bag on to his tray table. 'So now I figure I owe him the same thing.'

His eyes went dull. I looked down at the tray table and started reciting the speech I'd been rehearsing for the last twenty-four hours.

'First of all, if you don't run, you'll be in big trouble. If you do, it could save your life. You won't have as many shock experiences, the insulin will stick better to your tissues, and you'll metabolize glucose better. You just have to take some precautions.

'You'll need less insulin because you're active, but you'll need to monitor it closely. An electronic meter would be nice, but that costs $340.00. You haven't got that. Dad can get it for you wholesale, and he'll let you work it off helping out in his office.

'You won't have to stop in the middle of a race for anything, but you'll need to eat beforehand. Any of this stuff would be fine.' I dumped a myriad of bars on to the tray. 'And afterwards, keep the Life Savers around. In fact, keep them around all the time. And the apple juice and the crackers.' I was plunking things down and talking as fast as I could.

'Just remember not to inject your insulin in your legs the morning of a race or you'll use it up too fast. And always wear this so people who don't know you can be aware that you have diabetes and won't complain about you eating at unauthorized times or something.' I laid the bracelet down with the rest of the stuff. 'Of course, you'll have to keep your cool, because getting all angry will only make your sugar go up. Luckily, you're not the angry type.'

'I'm angry now, Jan,' he said.

I looked up and a pang went through me. His eyes were bright red and streaming.

'It's not fair, Jan. I'm a good person. I did everything I was supposed to. It'd be different if I was somebody like Slade. But he's still out there running. Winning the scholarship I wanted so bad I could just about touch it. Why did God do this to *me*?'

I shook my head. I knew if I tried to talk, I'd start crying too.

'My father comes in here preachin' at me about "acceptance" and "God's will". It almost makes me sick! I can't accept somethin' I don't deserve. I mean, this is not a broken leg. This is for ever.'

'I know.'

'No, you don't.'

'Yes, I do!' Without intending to I'd punched my fist on the tray. He looked at me sharply.

'I do too know what it's like. I've been crippled all my life.'

'Crippled?'

'It's like I'm emotionally and socially crippled,' I said. 'That's what Jack always told me. I'm going to have to fight it all my life, just like you. I can't just wake up one day and say, "I'm not going to be shy any more." To me, it would be easier to get up and take insulin.'

He was shaking his head and swallowing against more tears as if he hadn't heard a word I'd said. 'I get up and cry in the shower. I'm seventeen years old, and I have to control everything I do because of what might happen to me when I'm fifty.'

'You can still go away to college.'

'Wearing a bracelet.'

'You can get married and have kids.'

'And maybe die before I see my grandchildren, if I don't go blind first anyway.'

'But maybe you won't.'

He looked down into his lap, and his face contorted. I looked uneasily out the window. The campus was out there, looking as staid and calm and secure in all its history as it had every time we'd run through it together. Why, then, was everything upside down in here?

'Thanks for coming, Jan,' Eddie said. His voice was thick. 'But I need to be right by myself — okay?'

The last two syllables barely came out. I nodded without looking at him and left.

Nice work, Kennedy, I thought through my own tears. Just what he needs.

Suzanne was at my side from out of nowhere, but she didn't ask how it had gone. She didn't have to.

18

Student Court, the squawk box announced on Wednesday, was scheduled for Friday after school. That set everyone in the student body gaping at me. Only a couple of things got me through the next two days.

One was finding out Mrs Fruff was going to be the faculty advisor on the jury.

'I can't vote, and I can't play heavy-handed when they're making their decision,' she told me on Wednesday. The freshmen were working in groups, and she'd drawn me out into the hall. 'But I usually make my opinion known, and nine times out of ten they listen.'

I bet they do, I thought.

Another thing was the fact that Chuck and Tanya were making themselves scarce. Dixie told me that Tanya's counsellor had advised the two of them not to even think about talking to me until after the trial. By that time, I knew better than to doubt Dixie's word where good gossip was concerned. She might exaggerate the juicier details from time to time, but basically she was accurate.

Tanya's friends, however, weren't under the same mandate. Three of her eye-rolling, lip-curling, mall-type cronies crowded behind me in the girls' toilets — about the only place besides class Tony and Lance let me go by myself. Even at that, they stationed themselves outside the door like storm troopers.

'Why'd you bust Tanya Early?' the blonde said.

Don't beat around the bush, I thought, looking at their reflections sneering over my shoulder into the mirror. Just get right to the point.

'Everything you've said's a lie,' said the brunette. 'You're going to end up off the team *and* out of this school.' She flipped her hair. She must have learned that from Tanya.

'Tanya's been in this town since before you were even born. Nobody's going to believe you over her.' I looked at the girl who said that. *Her* hair looked like it had been curled with a waffle iron.

I gave my own mop a flip. 'I guess we'll find out,' I said.

They were still making comments to me when I swung out of the door, which was already partially opened because the Wookie had decided I'd been in there long enough and he was coming in to see what was going on.

'Tanya's back-up,' I said, jabbing a thumb in their direction. 'But I handled 'em.'

He and Tony grinned at each other.

The icing on the cake was a card from Jack on Wednesday afternoon. I hadn't heard from him in weeks, but then I hadn't written to him in almost that long either. He didn't know what was currently going on in my life — which made his comments pretty freaky.

> *When I got back from vacation your last letter was waiting for me, and I don't guess I have to tell you how* ecstatic *I was to find out that things are going so well for you. I was especially glad to hear that you've begun to open the door to God. It's the most important thing you can do. I'd have said so before, but your dad wasn't paying me to make a religious experience*

part of your therapy! But, Janice, I have to say
that what your friend Eddie says about God isn't
right. Faith guarantees a lot, but it doesn't guarantee
that there will be no breakdowns. However, God does
come with a lifetime warranty for parts and labour.
That's where the good stuff comes in.

Whatever that meant.

The only person in my life who wasn't being supportive
— besides Eddie, who was really no longer in my life anyway
— was Lincoln. He would barely talk to me in class, and he
didn't show up on the steps Wednesday for lunch. I had to
share my cold crab quiche with Lance and Tony.

'Where were you yesterday?' I said to him second period
Thursday.

He scowled and, if possible, his face darkened.

'You got your new friends to eat with,' he said.

'I didn't go in the cafeteria with them!' I said. 'It stinks
in there — like rotten bananas and salami. Besides, I hate
waxy milk cartons.'

I nudged him, but he kept frowning.

'Too cold out there,' he said.

'Pooh! It's barely even winter yet. Wimp.'

'Don't be callin' me no wimp!' he said. Then pulling up
the collar of his jacket, he buried his face in his book.

Things went steadily downhill from there.

Friday morning, Dad was called in for an unscheduled
surgery for that afternoon. I already knew Suzanne had an
important class and couldn't be at the trial, but I'd been
counting on Dad.

'You won't need me, darlin'. It's all gon' go smooth as
silk,' he said.

'Dad, don't try to pacify me, okay?'

He looked at Suzanne and sighed. 'I'm sorry. Be patient
with me, darlin'. I know you need me there. I know it's gon'
be hard on you no matter how it turns out.'

'Confrontations like that are never fun,' Suzanne put in.

'But —' Dad squeezed the back of my neck. 'We'll all

be home by 6.30 and we'll go out and celebrate. Where to, darlin'?'

'Poe's,' I said. But I was unenthusiastic. There was a real good chance I would *be* a meatball sandwich by then.

That was the thing that was nagging at me and had *been* nagging at me all night, even when I'd been trying to talk to God about it.

Actually, my thoughts had been so rambly, I'd resorted to writing him a letter.

> *Dear God,*
>
> *A lot of good stuff has been happening to me since I started getting to know you, and I believe what Eddie used to say — that it's because I'm counting you in on my life. But some fairly ugly things are going on too, and although I don't blame you for those, I just wonder what are we going to do about them?*
>
> *If I win and Tanya loses, she'll be out to get me for the rest of my high school career — and probably then some.*
>
> *And if she wins, aren't I going to look pretty stupid? Are people going to think I really did lie?*
>
> *I could use some help!*
>
> *Janice*

Mrs Fruff only made that dilemma seem more real second period. She called me over to her desk as soon as I got there.

'Have you managed to put together any concrete evidence against the Early girl?' she said. Her brow had furrowed her face out of its usual calm.

'No,' I said.

'I wish you could. An eyewitness to *something*.' She put a hand on my arm. 'It isn't that you don't have credibility, but my sense is that your word against hers isn't going to get more than a slap on the wrist for Tanya. I'd thought earlier in the week that something would come to light and we could see some justice done here.' She let go of my arm. 'It isn't impossible. I just don't promise anything.'

I nodded heavily.

'Mr Lewis, is there something we can do for you?'

I followed her gaze to where Lincoln was loitering a few feet from her desk, unconvincingly pretending to examine the progress of our latest bacteria culture. I didn't know how long he'd been standing there.

'No, ma'am,' he mumbled, and moved away.

'I don't know what you see in that child, Janice,' Mrs Fruff said.

My instructions were to report to Coach Spike's office after school and, since he was my court sponsor, we would walk down to the library together. Lance and Tony, of course, delivered me there themselves, and Tony went into a deep bow at the door.

'It's been a pleasure serving you, ma'am,' he said. 'But after today's trial, you won't be needing us anymore. Those thugs will be behind bars.'

'Get real,' Lance said, taking a chip at the top of Tony's head.

Tony ducked and took off down the hall with him. 'We'll be there. Good luck!'

Feeling oddly empty, I watched them go until they disappeared around the corner. The Wookie came back around, gave me a thumbs-up, and was gone again.

I dragged myself into Coach's office, where he was just unfolding his long legs from the top of his desk.

'Sit down for a couple of minutes, hon,' he said. 'We've got some time.'

I'd rather have paced, but I sat down anyway. He perched on the edge of his desk like always and looked down at me out of his big, kind face.

'It seems like a hundred years since you came in here at the beginning of the year — all scared and shaky.' He grinned. 'But you aren't even the same girl you were then.'

'I'm still scared!' I said.

'Sure you are. But you aren't letting that keep you from doing what's right. That's the difference.'

I was turning red, I knew.

'I'm real proud of everything you've accomplished this season, hon. Real proud. But I think what you're doing today makes me the proudest.'

'Thank you,' I said. My face was totally on fire.

'Fruffie says we don't have much hard evidence —'

'We don't have *any*.'

'But that's not really the point. Nobody knows better than I do that you're telling the truth. Even if they don't nail Tanya's little tail to the wall, we know you tried.' He looked at me for a minute and then squeezed my shoulder. 'You ready?' he said.

I nodded and stood up as he did. If I wasn't ready then, after that vote of confidence, I never would be.

From the noise level in the library, we could tell several yards away that there was standing room only. A couple of kids were even hanging around outside the door.

I'd never seen Lincoln anywhere but in second period science and on the steps at lunch, but somehow I knew these must be his friends. Only one was black, a chubby kid with an earring, but they all had Lincoln's certain air about them.

'Better get in and take a seat, fellas,' Coach Spike said to them.

'We ain't goin' in, Coach,' the stout one said. 'We just waitin' for our friend.'

They weren't lying. Lincoln was the first person I saw when I walked in. He wouldn't look at me, though. He was trying to make himself invisible in a back corner.

There was a table front centre where six kids and Mrs Fruff sat. They were the jury. Coach and I sat at a table facing them, and a few feet away there was a table for Tanya and her sponsor. Dixie had told me that none of the teachers would stand up with her, so the guidance counsellor had to. Sort of like a public defender.

I looked over at Tanya as I was sitting down, but she was staring straight ahead and fingering her hair. As Suzanne

197

would have said, she was looking puny. I hated the position I was in today, but I'd sure have hated worse being her.

I glanced nervously around the library-turned-courtroom. The gang all waved from the fourth row of chairs. The rest of the cross-country team was behind them, and Tanya's friends were behind them. Blondie curled her lip at me.

'I've never seen this many kids at a "trial",' Coach whispered to me.

Everybody, it seemed, was there. Except Chuck. He'd been conspicuous by his absence all day. The least that slime could've done was be there for Tanya, I thought. He was probably the one who'd got her into this whole mess in the first place. That was the thing that made me mad. At least I'd detected a little good in Tanya — once or twice. But Chuck was almost a complete zero as far as I could see. And yet she was the one I'd had to end up accusing. I hoped someday he'd get what he deserved.

The Student Body President came in to preside over the court, and to my amazement everybody hushed. From that moment on, I believed we were really in court and that somebody's future was actually in the balance.

The proceedings were strict, but they were fairly simple. First, the guidance counsellor asked a few people to speak on Tanya's behalf. They amounted to Blondie, Waffle Hair, and the Brunette whose flipping rivalled Tanya's. She called Chuck's name just for the record, and a buzz went through the crowd. It had been common knowledge that he wasn't going to show. I stole a look at Tanya. She was gnawing on her bottom lip.

All the witnesses said was that Tanya was a 'real sweet girl' and that she'd never do anything to hurt anybody. In fact, they felt sorry for her because 'that Kennedy girl' came in at the beginning of the year and tried to take 'poor Tanya's' hard-earned place on the track team. When Waffle Hair started going on about how Coach was giving me all the attention and Tanya was being tossed to the side of the track, the 'judge' said that was irrelevant and told Waffle Hair to step down.

'Well,' Coach whispered to me, 'they can't prove she didn't do it. Now we have to prove she did.'

Coach had a whole sheet of legal paper full of names to call, but he deftly picked out a few with his pencil and called them to the 'stand'. A firm sense of nausea was rising up in me, and I kept sighing to keep it under control. I knew Tanya must have felt even worse.

Dixie told about seeing me get up from my fall, and about witnessing Tanya trying to pick a fight with me out on the track. She even quoted Tanya saying, 'Think you can stay vertical today?' The girl had watched enough soap operas to know how to be a star witness.

Tess and Corie both testified that Tanya had been hanging around my locker the day of the thumbtack incident, and that she was constantly needling and harassing me. Corie told about the fight Tanya had tried to get going with me in the hall the day before the race, but when the guidance counsellor asked her if I'd fought back, she looked at me painfully and said, 'She started to, but somebody broke it up. You couldn't blame her . . .'

I closed my eyes as the counsellor cut her off and told her to step down. I wouldn't have wanted her to lie, but I could feel the shudder of doubt running through the room, and I wanted to dissolve.

Coach, however, had a couple of surprises. He called some guy to the stand whom I'd only seen in the halls once or twice with Chuck. The only thing I knew about him was that he swore a lot and called girls 'babe'.

'Tell me what you know about Tanya Early and Chuck Slade,' Coach said to him.

The Student Body President cleared his throat. 'Uh, Coach, does this have anything to do with Janice Kennedy's accusation?'

'I think so,' Coach said.

Everybody snickered.

'Go ahead,' the judge said.

The kid in the chair, whose name turned out to be Kip, shifted his weight uncomfortably. 'They've been going out since last spring,' he said.

'And by "going out", what do you mean? What does that entail?'

Another round of snickers.

'They dated. You know, went out partying together and such.'

'Okay. And where did they party?'

Kip shrugged. 'People's houses mostly, until they found that vacant place.'

'What vacant place?'

It was obvious that Coach and Kip had had this conversation before, because Coach was asking all the right questions, and Kip saw them coming. Still, he looked like he wanted to die.

'An old house on Monroe Street. It was a pretty nice place, you know, but it was empty for a long time. Chuck discovered it at the beginning of the summer and he figured out how to get the back door open. He used to take Tanya there to drink and smoke . . . You know, all that stuff.'

Coach was nodding pensively. The library was like a tomb.

'So what you're saying, Kip, is that Tanya was an accessory to trespassing, even breaking and entering.'

'Yes, sir. She — they — almost got caught once. Somebody moved into the house about in July when Chuck was away on vacation. The first time he tried to take Tanya over there when he got back, the place was all dark, but he still couldn't get in. When he tried the back door, the people called the cops on him.'

'But they got away — Chuck and Tanya?'

'Yes, sir. They were pretty mad about it, too. Chuck used to drive by there at night to try to see who lived there, and one time he dumped a bunch of garbage on their porch, just to get back at them for movin' in, I guess.'

'And how do you know all this?' Coach said as he felt the guidance counsellor starting to get to her feet.

'I went there once — to party — when he first found it. And then, I was with him once when he drove by and — when he dumped the garbage. The rest was just stuff he told me. He — and Tanya.'

Coach reached over and squeezed Kip's shoulder. 'Thanks for being honest, son,' he said.

As Kip stepped down, Tanya's counsellor stood up. Some kind of verbal volley started between her and Coach, but I missed it. I was in shock.

So it *had* been Chuck — and Tanya too. The thought of the two of them together in my Dad's house started the nausea coming right up my throat. Nobody in the room knew it was my place, except maybe Tanya herself by now. I buried my face in my hands. If I told that, the case was easily ours. But then Tanya could be in even deeper trouble than she was already. Kip's testimony had been hearsay. Mine wouldn't be.

She deserves it, Janice, one side of me said.

Maybe so, retorted the other side, but if she weren't so starved for somebody to love her, she'd never have gone along with something that stupid.

I looked at Tanya, who had slid down as far as she could in her chair and was pushing the cuticles back on her finger-nails. Her body language read, 'I really couldn't care less about this entire affair', but her face read, 'I'm terrified.'

'I'm just trying to show that Miss Early is not entirely above reproach,' Coach was saying. 'I think we've proven here that she is capable of the kinds of things Miss Kennedy has accused her of.'

'I'm going to keep that testimony in, Mrs Rankin,' the judge said to the counsellor. His face was as white as Kip's, Tanya's, and, I was certain, mine. Things were turning out to be a little heavier than he'd expected, I was sure.

'Do either of you have any other witnesses?' he said. Without looking at me, Coach put his big hand on my shoulder. 'I want to call Janice Kennedy.'

I'd known he was going to do that, of course. We'd discussed it several times. But I was still like a bowl of jelly as

201

I went towards the chair. If I could just keep my eyes on Coach, if I didn't look at that huge crowd of people, I'd be okay.

Perching on the edge of our table, Coach Spike led me through everything that had happened with Tanya since I'd first come to Madison High. There were parts of it I'd wanted to skip. They made me sound like a real crybaby. But Coach had said we couldn't afford to leave anything out, so I tried to tell it all without whining. When I'd finally got through the last attempted fight, he said. 'Thank you, Miss Kennedy,' and winked softly. Oozing relief, I started to get up.

'I have some questions.' Mrs Rankin stopped me with her voice, and with a sickening sense of dread I sank back into the chair. I could feel my pulse in my tongue, for Pete's sake.

'We've heard a lot about the things Tanya has done to you, Janice,' she said, not unkindly. 'But let's talk a little about some rather ugly things you might have done to her.'

Stupidly I said, 'Okay.'

'What about her boyfriend, Chuck Slade?'

'Ma'am?' I could hardly hear her for the pounding in my ears.

'Did you ever try to "steal" her boyfriend away from her?'

I shook my head.

'Pardon me?'

'No, ma'am.'

'Last Friday, did Tanya catch you kissing Chuck Slade in the hall outside the girls' locker room.'

'No, ma'am,' I said faintly.

I could hear the kids in the room stirring to attention, but I didn't dare look at them.

Mrs Rankin had her eyebrow raised in true surprise. 'Oh? But Tanya says she saw you.'

'She thought that's what she saw. What she saw was *him* kissing me. He'd been doing it for about two weeks, trying to get me to — kiss him. I was trying to get away when she saw us — and she assumed, I guess, that I was — kissing — him — back.'

My voice trailed off, and all I could think of was how Tanya must be feeling. I didn't glance towards her table. I was afraid I'd find her dead. What else in heaven's name could end for her today?

'Why would she assume that?' Mrs Rankin was saying.

'Ma'am?'

'If you were entirely innocent and she had no reason to believe you were after her boyfriend, why would she assume that?'

I looked sadly at my hands, and then I looked back up at her. 'I guess you want to trust the person you love,' I said.

The room was completely quiet as I left the chair and went towards our table. Coach was leaning over the back of his chair, whispering to someone. When I got there, I saw it was Lincoln.

'Do you have any more witnesses, Coach Petruso?' the judge said. His eyes were practically pleading. He knew as well as I did that although we'd basically ended Tanya's life in an afternoon, there was still no proof that she'd tried to wipe me off the track.

'I do,' Coach said. 'Lincoln Lewis is going to take the stand.'

All the banging in the world couldn't bring the crowd to a hush. There was a combination of guffaws, moans and general jeering as Coach ushered the little guy to the witness chair. Poor kid. His face was as brown as ever, but I reckoned he felt plenty pale inside. I hoped *he* knew what he was doing, because I sure didn't.

Mrs Rankin was tapping her pencil when the place finally got quiet.

'Spike, are you sure this is a reliable witness? If you'll recall, he's been on trial once this year himself.'

'For excessive tardiness, Mrs Rankin. I don't think that makes him an enemy of the court.'

To my horror, everybody on the jury panel was cracking

up. Whatever it was Lincoln was going to say, they were never going to believe him.

And then Mrs Fruff stood up.

You could've heard a fly blink.

'I have no idea what Mr Petruso's purpose is in calling Mr Lewis to the stand,' she said, 'but I can assure you that the boy is honest.'

Mrs Fruff had been right. When she made her opinion known, they listened. The jury sat back in their seats.

'Go ahead, Coach,' the judge said.

With the rest of the room, I took a breath and held it.

'Now, Lincoln,' Coach said, leaning casually against his shoulder, 'I think you ought to tell us first why you didn't come forward before.'

Lincoln opened his mouth, and then closed it again. His eyes were like smoke rings, getting wider by the second.

'Take your time, Lincoln.'

Panic-stricken, Lincoln shot his eyes all over the room. I don't think he could even remember where he was except in a sea of faces, until he happened on me. I was nodding like a palsied person. He started nodding too, and then he started to talk.

' 'Cause I was scared,' he said.

'Of what, Lincoln?'

'I didn't want nobody comin' 'round scratchin' my eyes out,' he said. He was looking right at Tanya, and the crowd broke up.

'You thought somebody would want to get back at you if you talked?' Coach said.

'You got it.'

'So why are you coming forward now?'

Lincoln looked at me. ' 'Cause don't nobody else know what I know, I guess.'

'Okay. What is it you know?' Coach said.

Please, I thought. Do tell.

'I seen her trip Janice,' Lincoln said clearly, pointing a finger at Tanya. 'I was runnin' behind the trees by the road where they was runnin' and I was watchin' her.' This time he pointed at me. 'Janice come around a corner and there was this chick — her — runnin' real slow like she was waitin' for her. I was like up on the cliff, kind of up above 'em, so I seen.'

He put his big brown eyes right on Coach. 'Coach, that Tanya girl just step her foot over there so slick, and Janice's knee go all sideways, and she was on the ground.'

On the ground. My mind rewound to the scene. I'd gone over it a hundred times since Saturday, but for the first time that detail was there: that voice saying, 'Get up. Come *on*, girl. You ain't no quitter. Get up and run!'

He'd been there. He *had* seen.

I stopped the mental tape and flipped back to the witness chair. Lincoln had really got into it by that time. I think he was kind of sorry there wasn't more to tell. I don't like talking in front of a bunch of people, he'd told me once. Ha. He was loving every minute of it.

'I swear, that girl, that Tanya, she tripped Janice — and I seen it.' Lincoln gave it a final nod and sat back in the chair.

There was a you've-got-to-be-kidding-me hush in the room, followed immediately by an excited buzz. The jury left. Coach was squeezing Lincoln's shoulders so hard he was practically giving him a massage, and I could hear the gang calling me from the fourth row.

But I was too stunned to even turn around. Feeling every emotion you could name, I watched Tanya and Mrs Rankin take refuge in the librarian's office. If I could've found an excuse to get out of there, I'd have done the same thing — even though it looked now like I was going to be the winner after all.

In less than ten minutes the jury was back, and so was Tanya. I heard Mrs Fruff say, 'The panel has found the defendant guilty and is recommending expulsion from the track team for the remainder of the school year and suspension from school for ten days.'

Relief and sadness poured into me at the same time. Helplessly, I looked at Coach.

Thank heaven for that man's uncanny knack for reading

minds. 'The panel's always a lot tougher than the vice principal,' he said. 'She probably won't get the suspension.'

I was in tears. 'I'm sorry, Coach,' I said.

He put a big arm around me. 'For what, hon? We won.'

'But she won't be on the team anymore. We'll lose the regionals.'

He gave me a squeeze. 'It takes a lot more than running to make a winner,' he said. 'And you, Miss Kennedy, are a winner.'

19

The track team was on me before I could even stand up — Corie gurgling in one ear, Dixie tugging on one arm, and the Wookie trying to lift me up on his shoulders. Funny, though. All I could think of was that I wanted Tanya to know I was sorry that so many things had sneaked their way to the surface in the trial and hurt her.

But by the time I could even get a glimpse from under Lance's arm, I saw only her back as she elbowed through the crowd and out of the library door.

'We had a victory today, ya'll! What does that mean?' Tony was standing on a chair and ignoring the evil eye of one of the Brown Brogue Twins.

'A party at Poe's!' was the unanimous reply.

'What time?'

'Right now!'

'Until when?'

'Until whenever!'

Even Coach Spike didn't protest.

It was almost dark, and a fine, cold drizzle was falling when we got to the truck. Virginia winter had arrived while we'd been inside sweating it out.

'I'll get soaked back here!' Tess whined from the tailgate.

'Enjoy it while you can, gang,' Tony said. 'We have to give this vehicle back to Eddie today.'

I froze in mid-step.

'Why?' I said.

'He loves Lance, but he doesn't love him that much,' Tony said. 'He wouldn't *give* this truck away — although it's no prize, I admit —'

'Hush up, Tony,' Corie said. She looked at me as she pulled the hood of her coat on. 'Eddie came home from the hospital this morning. He's meeting us at Poe's.'

Lance put a big paw on my shoulder. 'You can sit up front if you want,' he said.

I looked at him through the freezing rain. My brain was racing. 'I think I better go home first,' I managed to say.

A little too casually, he shrugged. 'All right. I'll drop you.'

But I shook my head. 'I'll walk, okay? I need a few minutes to collect my thoughts.'

'You sure?' he said, scowling.

'Yeah.' I faked a smile and pulled on the cords to my jacket hood. 'You don't have to worry about me now.'

'What's going on?' Corie called. 'Aren't you coming to your own party, Janice?'

'I'll be along later,' I lied.

The laughter in the back of the truck went down several notches, and Lance manoeuvred it unnecessarily slowly out of the parking lot. I dug my hands into my pockets and walked in its wake.

They were great, and I knew now that they were my friends. But I'd been through enough for one day. I couldn't face seeing Eddie too.

Hunching my shoulders against the cold, I passed in and out of the twilight puddles of amber which the old-fashioned street lights formed on the sidewalk along Main. On either side of me, colonial curtains and oil-lamp globes looked out cheerfully from their cosy windows, and the smell of wood from the first of the season's fireplace fires surrounded me,

207

even in the dismal cold. I wasn't sure, because I'd never really experienced it before, but I thought I felt at home. Home must be a place where you were secure even when half your world had fallen away in a big chunk.

Secure or not, however, I lurched forward in instant panic when a voice said, 'Say, baby — what are you doin' out here in the rain?'

'Lincoln!' I pulled my fist out of my mouth. 'You scared me half to death!'

'What are you doin'?'

'Walking home. Same as you. I needed to think.'

'I knew you was strange.'

I'd started walking again and, as I hoped he would — *knew* he would, he fell into step beside me.

'What happened to that kid who was afraid to talk in front of a bunch of people?' I said.

I was watching the puddles, but I could feel him grinning beside me.

'I was all *right*, wasn't I, girl?'

'You were — okay.'

'I was awesome!'

Glancing at him sideways, I said softly, 'Thanks for what you did today. I know it was hard.'

'It wasn't that hard.'

'Right.'

We exchanged looks.

'Well — once I got up there, you know, *then* it wasn't that hard. I knew we was gon' win then.'

'We?' I yanked his hat down over his eyebrows.

'Hey! Don't be touchin'!'

We'd got to the corner of Monroe, and I stopped.

'I've got to go this way,' I said. 'Want to come over? Have some hot chocolate?'

Lincoln shook his head, but he wouldn't look at me. He busied himself blowing air out of his cheeks.

'Tell me something, Lincoln, really. Why *do* you hang out with me — and get mixed up in my problems — and come to my rescue even?'

'Go on!'

'Why?'

For a second his creamy brown eyes looked serious, but just as quickly they started to snap again. 'I don't know, girl. Soon as I find out, I'll let you know.'

He started to go, but I grabbed his sleeve.

'Love you, Lincoln,' I said to the side of his head.

He broke into a run, but even as I watched him disappear he turned around and started to run backwards. 'You the strangest!' he called through the rain. 'The *strangest*, girl!'

Dad and Suzanne must not have expected the trial to last as long as it had, because neither of them had left a light on for me. But the house was still friendly around me, and I kept smiling at its leathery den furniture and its Suzanne-planted cuttings in tiny flower-pots on the kitchen window-sill. I could have been consuming a major meatball sandwich at Poe's, but the left-over meatloaf and mayonnaise I put together and carried up to my room was Home, and just then, that was what I wanted.

I snapped on only my desk lamp and curled up on my bed, under the duvet. From there I could watch the rain form icy sparkles on my window and wait for my family to come home. Yes. Family.

Life, I decided as I sat there chewing and watching, wasn't the cardboard box with the flaps I'd once thought it was after all. It was more like the rope climb Coach Spike had made us do in PE one day.

I'd found out right away that you didn't just grab the end and smoothly ease your way to the top. You got there by letting go and grabbing higher, then taking a second to gather momentum, and then letting go and grabbing higher again.

The times when you were moving upward on the rope — those were like the times in life when it all came together. Like taking first place in a cross-country race. Having Mrs Fruff ask me to be her lab assistant. Sitting in a tree with Eddie.

The times when you were just hanging there, gathering momentum for the next grab — those were like the times in life you thought were bad, when all they really were the things that taught you lessons. Like putting up with Tanya. Finding out Dad was in love with Suzanne. Losing Eddie.

And the times when you let go to make another grab — those were like the times in life when you were scared right down to your earwax. Like sitting in a courtroom and ratting on Tanya. Walking into Madison High knowing absolutely no one. Walking into University Hospital to see Eddie.

Several people in the rope climb had fallen, but Coach had made them get back on and try again, and again, and again, until they made it to the top. Some of us had got rope burns. Everybody had had a different technique. But sooner or later everybody had got the hang of it and reached that big old hanging hook at the ceiling.

I surveyed the remains of my sandwich thoughtfully. The only way you wouldn't make it in life, I knew now, would be if you got off the rope, and quit trying. Of course, there was no one like Coach standing at the bottom of the Life Rope, making you get back on until you made it.

I looked up at the sparkly window again and smiled. Or was there? I thought. Or was there?

The back door rattled, and I glanced at my watch. Dad and Suzanne had said they'd be home at 6.30, but it wasn't even 6.00. Even while I crawled to the end of my bed to see if the Golf was out front, the fear etched right up my spine like an engraving needle. Staring out at the empty driveway, I froze.

The screen door slammed against the outside of the house. I could hear it even through the storm windows. And then the back door grunted — rhythmic, familiar grunts — as someone threw his weight against it. Once. Twice. A third time.

Ears pounding, I tore across my room in a blind frenzy. The wardrobe. I had to get to the wardrobe.

I hurled myself behind the clothes and shoved my body into the corner formed by the attic stairs above me. I clapped both hands over my mouth so Whoever It Was couldn't hear my terrified gasps downstairs.

Whoever It Was.

My eyes came open. Kip on the witness stand. Chuck in Coach's office. Chuck attacking me in the hall.

It was definitely one of the letting-go times on this rope climb. I wasn't any less scared when I threw open the wardrobe door and took the steps down two at a time, but I was ready for the next grab.

Fumbling fiercely with the dead bolt, I yanked the back door open. Chuck's head jerked up from where he was squatted on the step, black hair shiny with sleet, eyes clouded with unmistakable hate.

He had a can in his hand, the can that had sprayed on to the cement the red 'S' and the red 'L' that were already draining their way off the side of the step like a surrealistic painting.

He stood up slowly, arms curved out from his body like two steel bands, chin jutted towards me.

He tried to fool me. He jerked his head to the side and spat, angrily, over the side of the porch. But I knew it anyway. He was scared.

'Get out,' I said. 'Get away from my house.'

He didn't move. 'Why aren't you out celebrating with the rest of them?' he said.

'Get out.'

He took a step towards me and inside the back door, but I didn't move.

'Why did you tell all those lies?' he said. 'Big-city tramp. All hot on the witness stand. What was it they told me you said, "you want to trust the boy you love" — or some bull — '

I slapped my hands on to either side of my head. 'Shut up! And get away from my house or I'll call the police!'

'You do that. Make up some more lies. Tell them I offered you a beer at mile two. Tell them I burned your Bible in the bottom of your locker. Tell them I tried to rape your little tail right here in your living room.'

He came towards me again, this time with his head lowered, his eyes bulging at me from under his eyebrows.

'Tell them all the things I would have done sooner if I'd known this was your house. A ripped-off door and a load of garbage wouldn't have been the half of it.'

Then, suddenly, with the heels of both hands he knocked me backwards. I flailed to keep myself off the floor, but I hit it hip first. Clawing at the rug to get upright, I tore after him — but he'd already been stopped six feet from the back porch — where Eddie had him pinned.

I didn't get further than the bottom step before they rolled a few times and Chuck wriggled away, racing across the lawn through the rain after some nebulous finish line.

Eddie stood up and watched him go. 'Are you okay?' he said to me from very far away.

'Yeah,' I said. 'I'm okay.'

But okay or not, darn it, I started to cry. And for a long time I cried, in the freezing rain, in the dark, in Eddie's arms.

Suzanne and Dad arrived about five minutes after Eddie and I finally had sense enough to come in out of the rain. We told the story while Dad paced in a panic and Suzanne dabbed at my runny nose with a Kleenex and said, 'Sugar!' about thirty times. But with the facts sorted out — everything from the trial to Chuck's interrupted artwork on the back porch — they both went into action. Dad took care of the phone call to the police, and Suzanne took care of 'spiked tea' and warm blankets for Eddie and me.

And then, bless them, they left.

I'm sure Suzanne was responsible for that move, because even at the door Dad looked at his watch and said, 'We'll see you at Poe's in *one hour*.'

'He's not going to freak out and come back, Dad,' I said. 'You should have seen how scared he was.'

'One hour — or I send a posse.'

212

'You'll do no such thing, Loren Kennedy,' Suzanne said as she pushed him out the door. She was still talking long after it had shut behind them.

A funny silence settled over Eddie and me, and we sat in opposite corners of the couch, wrapped in blankets, examining the palms of our hands. It was an instance of *déjà vu* if there ever was one.

Suddenly I looked up at him.

'Eddie,' I said, 'what were you doing here, anyway?'

He threw up his hands and grinned — the big ol' hangin' grin I hadn't seen for so long. The one I loved so much.

'I'm innocent!' he said. The bubbles sparkled at the corners of his mouth. 'I came to see why you weren't at your own party. They were all pounding their fists on the tables and yelling, "*Jan-ice, Jan-ice*". Somebody had to break it up.'

'You're lying.'

'I'm not . . . And besides —' He pulled his mouth into an uneasy knot. 'I needed to find out if — you were gonna forgive me.'

It was the second time in less than an hour that I'd seen a tough guy look scared. It was beginning to get really easy to recognize.

'I think I've hurt you pretty bad. No, I know I have, because I hurt myself pretty bad at the same time.' He swallowed — painfully, I could tell. 'I don't know if you'll remember, but I told you one time that I didn't believe in one-girl/one-guy and all that going-together stuff.'

'You told me several times.'

He grinned sheepishly. 'No doubt. But see, the reason I had to say it all the time was because I was trying to convince myself. I mean, I think I used to believe it. Having a girlfriend cramped my style. A commitment to one person gets in the way of things. Am I making *any* sense?'

My head was spinning, but I nodded.

'It just seemed like I couldn't give all I had to running

213

— and to God, like I wanted to, if I tied myself down. And besides —' He leaned out of his blanket. 'It scared the heck out of me.'

A laugh I couldn't stifle bubbled in my throat.

'Don't you laugh at me, Janice Kennedy!' he said.

I put both hands over my mouth and muffled out, 'I'm sorry.'

'You should be, because *you* came along, and yeah, at first you were like this challenge —'

I opened my fingers. 'A project,' I said.

A slow smile spread across his face. 'A project. But then I found out who you really were and I just wanted to be around you all the time. So I started making up excuses to be over here — and I even started believing them. But then that night we went out and climbed the tree . . . You remember that night?'

I gave him a look.

'It just hit me up the side of the head that night that I was hooked, and even showed you I was. But when I got home, I got the shakes so bad I couldn't stop. Maybe if I hadn't felt so rotten anyway — am I making excuses?'

'I think so.'

'Okay, okay. Big rationalization. But, Jan — I just laid there in that bed for three days feelin' lousy and thinkin' about you and telling myself I'd made a big mistake by saying all those things to you and kissing you and everything. I really messed up bad, Jan.'

I put my hands on the back of my neck and looked at my knees. 'It's okay,' I said in a voice I wasn't sure he could hear.

'No, it isn't.' Eddie threw the blanket off and came across the couch at me. 'That day you came to see me in the hospital — do you know you were the only friend I have who actually *came*? Everybody called and sent cards and balloons. Dixie had a pizza delivered! But they were too scared to come and see the freak with the disease — and I didn't blame them. I felt like a freak. But you —' he grabbed my hand and pulled it between his two pieces of ice. 'You came and you didn't try to make it all better or pretend nothing happened. You came in there, knowin' I was probably gon' pull this big rejection thing. It isn't just that I entertain you or make you feel good about yourself. You really care about *me* — don't you?'

I tried to pull my hand away, but he wouldn't let go. Still staring at my knees, I nodded.

'Then I don't care if it scares me to *death*.' Eddie put a trembly finger under my chin and tilted it up. 'I care about you too, Jan. I don't want Slade or any other guy *touching* you. Because I even think I love you.'

Sighing a sigh that came from somewhere outside both of us, he touched his forehead against mine. Then with an abrupt bounce, he was off the couch, tearing off his sweatshirt.

'What are you doing!' I said.

He dropped his shirt on the floor. 'I found this in the bag after you left the hospital.'

I splattered a laugh and stood up.

He was wearing the T-shirt I'd had made for him — the bright blue one that said in big white letters THE EDDIE PROJECT.

'Now just wait a minute,' he said. He went for the jacket he'd hung on the fireplace screen and reached inside it. Something blue flew across the room and into my hands.

'Put it on!' he said, the ends of the grin meeting at the back of his head.

I held it up in front of me, but I already knew it said THE JANICE PROJECT.

'Come on, put it on!' Eddie snatched it from me and, chattering the entire time, pushed the neck hole over my head and grabbed an arm.

'I can dress myself!'

'Hurry up, then! Yeah.'

He gazed at me like I was wearing a strapless prom dress, and all the jitters went out of his face. That soft, wonderful, confused look was back. I knew my face had that look too.

'Come here, Jan,' he said softly — and he pulled me into a hug, and he kissed me.

'Poe's?' he said down into my hair.

'Oh, yes,' I said. And then I nuzzled my face into his warm neck, and I smiled.

20

About the middle of December, a record snowfall turned our part of Virginia into a colonial Christmas card. Every red-bowed street lamp sparkled down on to a sugary lawn of snow that crunched under our feet when we walked home with packages in our arms.

Dad, of course, was in his glory. This was why he'd come back to Virginia, he said. This was what made it seem like home.

I had to agree, and I was — almost — as excited as he was when he said he thought he and Suzanne and Eddie and I ought to drive to Williamsburg for dinner and spend the night at the Williamsburg Inn, to celebrate his and Suzanne's engagement.

I was ready an hour ahead of time — in a pale-blue, drop-waisted dress that shimmered when I walked and reminded me of the Roaring Twenties. Suzanne had talked me into it, of course, telling me it went with my hairstyle, which was even shorter by then — in an A-line, she called it.

I'd planned to give myself some extra time that night because I wanted to write to Jack. I'd scratched a few lines to him right after the trial and everything, but this was a different kind of letter, and I needed some alone time to put it together.

Scooting myself into my desk — which I'd moved under the window so I wouldn't have to miss any of the show

God was putting on out there for Christmas — I started to write.

> *Dear Jack,*
>
> *I know, I know — I just wrote to you a couple of weeks ago and you haven't had a chance to answer back yet — but I'm okay. I just needed to talk to you.*
>
> *Since my last letter, I've hardly had to let go of the rope at all. It's just been one smooth climb. You don't know what I'm talking about, of course, but that's okay.*
>
> *Even seeing Tanya doesn't put me into a stupor any more. She doesn't speak to me, naturally, but she doesn't curl her lip when I get within a hundred yards either. For some reason I'll probably never figure out, I wish we could be friends, because we have more in common than just a history with Eddie. But too much has gone down between us. I guess we'll be thirty-five before we can put it all in the past.*
>
> *Dad and I decided to press charges against Chuck. You wouldn't believe it, but we actually discussed it, and we decided it was time Chuck took the consequences for something he did. And, of course, with Coach, the guidance counsellor, and the principal all putting their heads together down at the school, it was about unanimously decided that Chuck ought to come off the track team too.*
>
> *That doesn't leave us much of a team for next season, but we're working on it. Lincoln's going to be our water boy — so that ought to keep everybody's adrenalin pumping. Tess and Corie run with me twice a week. When we aren't messing around, slowing down to check out the shop windows, or waiting for Corie to tie her shoes, we get some good training in. Suzanne's working with Dixie on a diet, and if it were anybody else supervising I'd say it was amazing to see a waist emerging on Dix.*
>
> *Besides that, Eddie, Coach and I are running*

three times a week together to stay on top of things. Coach says he refuses to pressure me about college — but every chance he gets, he drops these hints about what a wonderful women's athletic programme they have at Old Dominion University in Norfolk. Mrs Fruff says she isn't pushing me either, but every time I go to my desk in her office — yes, be impressed, I have a desk now — I find these college catalogues with the corners of pages turned down to schools that offer pre-med. I have my own ideas about what I want to do, though. There's going to be a cure for diabetes one of these days — and I'm going to be in on it. I find myself day-dreaming about working in a lab, poring over a pancreas . . . Well, anyway, in the meantime, Eddie believes there will be a cure too, and he's trying to take good care of himself so when it comes, he'll be ready for it. You know, Jack, diabetes isn't an okay disease the way everybody thinks it is. You don't just take your insulin and cut down on the cookies and feel great. Eddie has to control his body all the time. But he says it's a bummer he can handle. (Or as we say here — a 'bummah'.) Isn't he the neatest guy?

Now, don't get the wrong idea. Eddie still wants to go to Furman University next fall, and I know he's going to get that scholarship because he has important plans for his life. We aren't into giving each other bracelets and rings and thinking we'll be together for ever. Well, okay — so I think it sometimes. But can you blame me? When a guy is cute, funny, smart and loves me, what do you expect?

I admit, it's not always easy. That means — well, you're a smart guy, you can figure that out. Eddie sees the big picture, and I see the little details, so sometimes it's hard for us to agree on what we should get on the submarine sandwich we're going to share or how we should view stuff like God letting suffering happen.

*But — you aren't going to believe this, Jack — I
mostly tell him how I feel, even when it doesn't make
him grin that big ol' hangin' grin of his. We even
have* real *arguments.*

*I told him one day that he was copping out by
not admitting that he didn't like Chuck. He got real
mad at me and gave me dirty looks for about ten
minutes and then went home. But he called me up two
hours later and told me I was really cruel for making
him face up to stuff like that. He said he basically
can't stand the guy because he messes up Eddie's
I-love-everybody-and-everybody-loves-me philosophy!*

*By the way, why didn't you ever tell me how
nice making up could be? I'd have got into this stuff
sooner!*

*Which brings me to the point of this letter. After
some of my arguments with Eddie, where I haven't
frozen up or backed down or wished I was dead, I've
realized something about me. I'm a normal person.*

*Now, don't be sighing and rolling your eyes and
saying 'I told you so'. I know you did. Without
you I'd probably have spent this whole year here in
my room with the boxes still not unpacked. You gave
me a push before I left Chicago, and that got me
rolling. I'm no Student Body President mind you. I'll
probably always be kind of shy. I don't jump right in
there and introduce myself to new people, and I really
like to be alone or with just a couple of friends.
I don't want to be the life of the party like Eddie. But
I know I'm just as good as anyone. God loves me
as much as he does Eddie or Tess or anybody. I know
how much I owe to him. I'm getting a real family
now — Dad and Suzanne and me. I have friends —
Dixie and Lincoln and Lance — a bizarre collection,
I admit, but the first real friends I ever had.*

*Bad things do happen — to people who believe
in God just as they do to everyone else. Eddie and I
still argue that one out. But maybe what seems bad*

now isn't. There's always that guarantee for parts and labour, right?

The point is, because of that, Jack, I guess you and I — we don't need each other like we used to. You're off the hook! I don't need to be your 'project' any more. Or Dad's or Suzanne's or Coach's or Mrs Fruff's — or even Eddie's for that matter. I'm not finished, of course. I'm still in progress. But I guess what's really important is that I know now, I'm God's 'project'.

Sweet Mother of Jefferson Davis, Jack. Ain't it great?

Much love — always,
Janice Kennedy

Also from Lion Publishing

A RING OF ENDLESS LIGHT

Madeleine L'Engle

'. . . this was the first time I'd been involved
in this part of death, this strange, terrible saying
goodbye to someone you've loved.'
   The death of a family friend isn't the only
tragedy of the summer, and Vicky Austin
sometimes wonders if she'll ever be happy again.
But that's before she is befriended by Adam
Eddington, a young scientist, and his remarkable
dolphins.

A Ring of Endless Light is a Lion Modern Classic.

ISBN 0 7459 1383 0

NOTHING EVER STAYS THE SAME

Peggy Burns

Why, why, did everything have to change?
   For Sandie it meant a whole new life – with
the mother she'd hardly seen since she was
a small child. It wasn't just that they didn't get
on: Sandie's mother hated music – the one thing
Sandie loved most in the world, the talent she had
inherited from her father. It looked like the
end of all her ambitions, but she wasn't going to
give them up without a fight . . .

ISBN 0 7459 1249 4

TOUGH CHOICES

Shirlee Evans

'Gail felt numbed. Empty. Her fantasy – of Steve encircling her in his arms, taking care of her – was not to be. She turned away, tears edging her dark eyes. She had felt alone many times during her fifteen years, but never quite so alone as at this moment.'

Rejected by her own parents, Gail finds herself unmarried and pregnant at fifteen. Steve's reaction to the news shatters her dreams of marriage and hopes for a happy family life – now she has to decide what to do with the baby.

Gail's whole future is in the balance. Everyone is ready with advice about what to do, but it's Gail alone who must make the final, difficult decision.

ISBN 0 7459 1513 2

More stories from LION PUBLISHING for you to enjoy:

TEENAGE FICTION

SWEET 'N' SOUR SUMMER Janice Brown .... £1.75 ☐
NOTHING EVER STAYS THE SAME Peggy Burns .... £1.75 ☐
THE SPLITTING IMAGE OF ROSIE BROWN Peggy Burns . £1.99 ☐
IN SEARCH OF LOVE Audrey Constant .... £1.50 ☐
SHADOWS IN THE VALLEY Audrey Constant .... £1.95 ☐
TOUGH CHOICES Shirlee Evans .... £2.25 ☐
A RING OF ENDLESS LIGHT Madeleine L'Engle .... £2.50 ☐
SUMMER DREAMS Dorothy Oxley .... £1.99 ☐
WINTER SONG Dorothy Oxley .... £1.25 ☐
THE TRAP, AND OTHER STORIES Pat Wynnejones (ed) .. £1.25 ☐

All Lion paperbacks are available from your local bookshop or
newsagent, or can be ordered direct from the address below. Just
tick the titles you want and fill in the form.

Name (Block Letters) ....

Address ....

....

Write to Lion Publishing, Cash Sales Department, PO Box 11,
Falmouth, Cornwall TR10 9EN, England.

Please enclose a cheque or postal order to the value of the cover
price plus:

UK: 60p for the first book, 25p for the second book and 15p for
each additional book ordered to a maximum charge of £1.90.

OVERSEAS: £1.25 for the first book, 75p for the second book plus
28p per copy for each additional book.

BFPO: 60p for the first book, 25p for the second book plus 15p
per copy for the next seven books, thereafter 9p per book.

Lion Publishing reserves the right to show on covers and charge
new retail prices which may differ from those previously advertised
in the text or elsewhere, and to increase postal rates in accordance
with the Post Office.